THE DRAGON'S GAME

EDEN CHRONICLES IV

JAMES ERITH

COPYRIGHT

For Robert and Sara

It started out as a story for my Godchildren:
Isabella, Daisy, Archie, Iso and Ernest

Special thanks:
Tom and Marsha Moore, Nicola Traynor, Ed and Philip Erith.
Also to my Eden Team for all their help and support.

CONTENTS

The Riddles

'The first you hid in the heart of the house
'That warms you night and day
'Get it out by poking me,
'And singing your favourite song along
    the way!

'For the second one you have to find
'You burp it from the family belly.
'To do this, you have to eat
'Blabisterberry jelly!

'The third you search for is underneath your
    nose.
'It's clear, pure and cold.
'In order to draw it out
'You need to send a rose.

'Put them all together,
'Then get out of the way
'What you find will prove a guide
'For all the other worlds.

'You have but seven days and seven nights
'As Earth moves in its cycle
'From first lightning strike and thunderclap
'The world awaits your arrival.'

ONE
STONE READIES HIS MEN

Commissioner Stone, the commander of the flood disaster faced his young officer. 'Dickinson, this time, I want results so don't screw up,' he said, his icy blue eyes fixing him with a stare most people flinched away from.

'Yes, sir,' Dickinson replied.

'We've been played for fools, and events are moving fast. Too damn fast for my liking. We've got one day to bring in Archie de Lowe and one day to extract the information he holds.'

The strange thing about Stone, Dickinson thought, was that he became entirely fixated on one thing to such an extent that other targets, options and opinions were wholly overlooked. But Stone had the knack of getting the right man. He'd almost single-handedly brought down mafia bosses, drugs barons and illegal arms dealers. And now in his sights was a boy, Archie de Lowe, and his siblings, who had developed a habit of slipping through his fingers.

'The problem we have, sir, is the fog.'

Stone's fist crashed down on the table. 'I don't care about the weather,' he roared. 'Get that boy and his sisters out of that cottage and bring them to me. You are professional soldiers.'

'With respect, Sir,' Dickinson stammered, 'the pilots will not fly the helicopters—'

'NOT fly! Bleedin' heck, Dickinson. Extort them! Make them do it.'

'I've expressed that it will be a dereliction of duty—'

'Not enough! Bribe them.'

'I've tried that too. They say it's suicidal.'

'Then use blackmail. Surely you have information on these men that you can use.'

Dickinson shook his head. 'The weathermen say it is the worst case of fog ever recorded.'

Stone stood up and glared at the young man. 'Then use the damn boats.'

Dickinson breathed deeply. He'd been dreading this conversation. 'Masham was ransacked overnight, sir. I'm not sure if you're fully up to speed, but it's bedlam out there. Several attempted break-ins to the compound resulted in at least twenty-five people being shot dead.' Dickinson paused. 'It'll be hard enough to get to the boats—if they haven't already been stolen by the mob.'

Stone ground his teeth and stared frostily at Dickinson and then at the wall, thinking. 'Recruit ten of the best men out there, Dickinson; special forces,' he ordered. 'We need to find these stupid kids. You won't know it, but intelligence reports coming in hint that other nationalities are threatening to send in crack squads. They're under the deluded belief that this is the work of some insurgent group, a bunch of lunatic religious terrorists.'

'What do they intend to do?'

'Find the bleedin' de Lowes, of course.' He sighed. 'Apparently, two scientists here at Swinton Park let slip to US intelligence that these kids had found the Ark of the bleeding Covenant with powers to destroy everything on the planet and powers to rule.' Stone removed his glasses and stroked his moustache. 'Madness, the lot of it. Of course, now the news has spread like wildfire; the Americans and the rest of the world are saying it's a religious phenomenon. Mass prayers twenty-four-seven, followed by mass rioting. People are cruci-fying their neighbours and all the while the Islamic extremist fantasists are baying with a kind of 'I told you so,' attitude. Believe you me; they too are very keen to get their hands on this supposed "Ark". And all the while, Dickinson, people are randomly dying from the disease—even those with no reli-gious affiliation whatsoever.'

'What if the de Lowes really have found something mystical and other-worldly,' Dickinson asked.

Stone picked up a mug and launched it at Dickinson's head.

The officer swayed out of the way as the crockery exploded on the wall. 'They haven't!' he roared. 'Don't be bloody stupid! They probably know something ... something about a biological weapon or a chemical leak in Upsall and have run into hiding.'

'They might even be dead,' Dickinson volunteered.

'Yes, indeed,' Stone said, the corners of his mouth turning up at the thought. 'But we do know they survived the flood and that boy Kemp keeps showing up on the surveillance cameras at Eden Cottage. We also know there's a link between him and Archie because Kemp told us and, oddly, I'm inclined to believe him,' Stone said as he checked his watch. 'In the marrow of my bones,' he continued, slowly, 'I believe there's something very, very fishy going on. I've had strong feelings like this before, Dickinson and, as you know, I'm always right.'

'Your ten men, Sir,' Dickinson said. 'Do you want to brief them, or should I?'

'Tell them to be ready in one hour. Gives me time to make arrangements.'

Dickinson frowned. 'Arrangements?'

'I'm going to lead this squad.' He peered over his glasses. 'Got a problem with that?'

'No, sir. It's just that you're in overall control here—'

'Look, we've got two days, Dickinson. What does it matter if I'm absent? The world is crashing and burning, and this is the single most important issue by a country mile. There are plenty of decent officers who can run the show here.' Stone sat down heavily, reapplied his bifocals and stared at a list on his desk. He looked up. 'Oh, and Dickinson, let me brief you on some other facts— "need to know" stuff.'

'Sir.'

'We're not going to be evacuated...' He left the words hanging.

'I'm sorry, sir. What did you say—'

Stone raised his eyebrows. 'When the Americans drop the bomb, no one—me, you, everyone here—is going anywhere. It's all a big, fat lie. There aren't the resources and besides,' he said with a sly smile, 'we can't go anywhere in this fog anyway, can we?'

Dickinson's face drained. 'So, we've had it?

'In a nutshell, yes. This hotel is possibly the safest place on the planet right now and if we can't find out what the source of this damn situation is, well then...'

'We're toast.'

'Precisely. In the meantime,' Stone continued, 'if there's even a sprinkling of truth about this Ark of the Covenant bullshit then I think we have a duty to find out before anyone else, especially those extremist terror groups. Don't you think?'

Dickinson began gathering his things. 'What's your plan, sir?'

'We take two boats and cross the flooded Vale of York as near to Eden Cottage as possible. We'll wire the perimeter with explosives, alerting and slowing down any unnecessary intruders, then march on the target.'

'But what if the de Lowes run into the devices?'

'They won't. They're in there, Dickinson, tucked away in that ramshackle old cottage. They have to be. We'll lie in wait. If I'm wrong and the bomb goes off, then tough. Nothing much more we can do, is there? My hunch is that they'll crawl from under some rock and when they do, we'll pounce and inform the Americans to hold off. Then, by God, I'll interrogate the little bastards.'

Dickinson saluted. 'One hour—twenty-one-hundred-hours—in the main hallway?'

'Yes. Wait for me there. Bring heavy armour and,' an idea popped into his head, 'flamethrowers, grenades—if there are any. Might be able to eat into this fog. Remember adequate provisions, fuel and all the necessary equipment. Understand? Make sure the satellite systems are functional. I imagine it will take at least four hours to navigate across and then we'll start on the climb after wiring the perimeter. With any luck we'll be surrounding that farmhouse by five tomorrow morning with everything in place.'

'Yes, sir,' Dickinson said, closing the door behind him.

For the first time that day, Stone smiled. What if this really was a wild goose chase after a lost, fabled relic? Of course, the whole idea was preposterous. But what if there was even a tiny element of truth in it? Stone clapped his hands. Then it would only be right, he thought, if I was the one to control it, to prevent others getting their hands on it, from exploiting it.

Stone twisted the ends of his silvery moustache and nodded to himself sagely at this remote possibility. Curiously, a feeling of warmth fizzled through him as he sensed that possessing ultimate power might be within his grasp.

He shook his head, but no matter what, the thought kept re-emerging. And when it did, his skin began to tingle and a curious buzz tickled the nerve-receptors in his brain.

TWO

DAISY RETURNS

Daisy thumped the mud repeatedly, brown flecks spraying her jeans. Her cries reverberated back in the empty void. A fight between two people she cared deeply about, in different ways, had taken place. One lay dead. The other had vanished.

As the light around her brightened with the dawn of a new day, Daisy knew that she'd witnessed something extraordinary. It was between Gus, her old school friend, a boy who had single-handedly saved Isabella's best friend, Sue, in a tiny boat when the storm had crashed and destroyed much of the northern half of the country, and Kemp, Archie's best friend, Mrs Pye their housekeeper's long-lost son and Isabella's enemy no. 1. He was also the first boy who had tugged at her heartstrings.

What was he to her? A boyfriend? A friend? A foe? An enigma?

He'd expressed his affection, his love for her. And, when they'd talked for hours, her heart had soared as she realised that the thug he portrayed was merely a shell masking his real self, like the rough, spiky husk of a chestnut protecting the soft fruit inside.

In a moment of madness, thinking that Kemp was defeated, she'd rolled a rock from under her foot. Her heart sank thinking about it. And with the same stone, Kemp had broken Gus. Poor, dear Gus whose body now lay at the mercy of some strange multi-changing beast at the other end of the ruin.

Kemp had offered to save her, to take her away. He'd offered her the chance to start again. However, the monstrous beating the boys had given one another did not obscure their enormous overall task, that of finding the three tablets that led to the Garden of Eden. Daisy knew full well that she couldn't give up. Not yet. They had come so far, and as far as she knew, everything on planet Earth depended on their success.

Oh, the muddle.

She had to return rapidly over the almost impenetrable chaos of the Yorkshire Moors hills to their curious farmhouse, Eden Cottage. She needed to be with her brother and sister and their caretaker, Old Man Wood and Mrs Pye. More than anything else, she knew that together they needed to find the third tablet, even if it killed them.

She picked herself up, her body feeling like lead. Should she tell the others what she'd seen, or keep it to herself? She mulled this thought over as she trudged forward. If she told them about Gus, then what would Sue's reaction be? Would Sue blame her for taking Kemp's side rather than helping Gus out?

Isabella's reaction—well, that was hardly worth even thinking about. And the headmaster, Solomon, who was trying to help, would he give them up? Would Solomon be so lenient if he knew she was party to a murder? After all, he'd been sent by Commissioner Stone—the man in charge of making sense and getting to the bottom of the terrible disaster. He would try and find their whereabouts, and, quite possibly, intern them all.

Daisy wiped her eyes and tucked a loose strand of her blond hair behind an ear and headed on. Carefully, she picked her way over the mud and debris-filled, barely visible track, using every ounce of concentration to enable her magical eyes, a power she'd discovered after being struck by lightning in the storm. Now, her eyes glowed like flaming torches, burning a hole through the fog. The sound of the silence accompanied her, occasionally interrupted by the distant booming of explosives way off in the distance.

The noise made her think of her friends—most of whom she knew were dead or missing. It made her remember the global pandemic in the world around her. She wondered who was blowing things up. Was it the military quashing the unrest that Sue had told her about, or people, rising in a state of panic?

Before long, familiar shapes became clearer—rocks she recognised, stumps of ancient trees, the ruts in the track now filled with water. Picking up her pace, she soon found herself back in the flag-stoned courtyard of Eden Cottage.

She removed her muddy jeans and hoodie, folding them and sliding them out of sight before lighting several candles. She listened hard—another curious power she'd discovered that enabled her to hear minute sounds when she really concentrated.

Confident no-one was up and about, she added paper, kindling and a couple of logs to the embers of a fire inside the belly of the metal range cooker, which quickly sparked into bright, orange flames. She filled the kettle and put it on the stove to make it look as if she'd arrived downstairs for an early morning cup of tea before collapsing heavily into a wooden chair next to the thick, old table.

She scolded herself. Why hadn't she checked the cattle tucked in the corral by the ruin? She remembered that the last time they'd been up there, a helicopter whizzed by, searching for them. Then, they'd noticed a few cattle missing. Had more animals been lost to that strange creature she'd seen lurking on the old stone walls while the boys fought? In any case, they always checked the animals. It was just something they did.

Presently Daisy caught the distinctive squeaking noises of floorboards at the top of the house. Archie stirring, his boyish stomping down the stairs to the bathroom was a dead giveaway.

She grabbed an apple and bit into it, savouring the sweet juice that washed over her mouth. Why did Old Man Wood's apples always make her feel better? She recalled how he'd produced the apples at the dawn of a new day in the cave they'd found themselves trapped inside. Was that two days ago already?

She put her legs up and onto the dark, thick planks of the oak tabletop, and closed her eyes as a brief moment of sleep overcame her.

Her eyes opened as she sensed someone entering the room.

'Morning, Daisy,' Archie said. 'Can't believe you're up before me. Any idea where Gus is? He's not on the sofa.'

Daisy looked away.

'I'd almost forgotten he was here,' he continued. 'What's the betting he's with Sue?' he smiled boyishly.

Daisy chomped on the apple and muffled a deliberately unintelligible reply.

Archie shook his head. 'I mean, Gus with a bird, like Sue. Bit weird isn't it? Those two being all lovey-dovey slightly freaks me out.' He nudged her shoulder and lowered his voice. 'And, if I'm not mistaken, I think there was someone else who had a bit of crush on somebody last night.'

Daisy felt her heart sink. 'Yeah, yeah. Dream on superman-boy.' She was referring to Archie's extraordinary feats of strength, a power that had grown within him since the beginning of the storm.

'I've never seen Kemp as animated, or as positive, or as friendly with anyone in my whole life. He couldn't stop staring at your eyes—'

'Well, they do glow.'

'Yeah, I know that, but he was smitten, my dear twin. Smitten.'

Daisy swung her feet off the table. 'Check the kettle will you. It's taking ages to boil—'

'Kemp's in seventh heaven now that he's found his mum—'

'I know,' she said, trying to sound enthusiastic. 'Mrs Pye, and after all this time. Amazing, isn't it?'

Archie rubbed one of his hard hair spikes, which had become a little floppy. The spikes were another consequence of his being struck by lightning. 'He went over there to sleep in her flat, I suppose.'

'Yeah,' Daisy said, quickly. 'Let's leave them, right? They've got a lot of catching up to do.'

Archie agreed and pulled two mugs from the cupboard placing them on the thick worktop. Old Man Wood's heavy tread made them turn.

'Morning, you look as if you slept well,' Archie said.

The tall, almost entirely bald headed frame of their adored friend and confidante, who claimed to be their Grandfather many times over, yawned and stretched out his large, thick arms. 'I most certainly did, littlun,' he smiled. 'No dream for me—first time in a long while. I feel apple-tastic. Any sign of Isabella?'

'Here,' came a sleepy voice from behind him. Isabella stood, staring out of the window that looked over the valley. On a bright day, the peaks of the Yorkshire Dales in the far distance were easy to see. Now a curtain of white space filled it. 'It's foggy out there,' Isabella said, waving an arm at the window. 'Gives me the creeps.'

'No matter,' Old Man Wood said, 'we'll need to get moving soon, after a bite to eat, fog or not. Is anyone hungry? I'm still rather full from eating all that Banoffee Pie,' he said, chuckling and thinking how they'd had to eat their way into finding the second tablet.

'Me, same,' Isabella said.

'Well, I'm starving,' Archie said.

'Only cos you puked yours up,' Daisy said.

Archie grinned at the thought of having swallowed the eyeballs whole. 'Those eyeballs tickled my gut,' he said. 'They're in a jar of water if you want to see them. I think they're rather remarkable. Two pairs, one brown and one icy blue—'

'That's disgusting,' Isabella retorted.

Archie looked a little put out. 'Actually, they're amazing—full of tendrils and nerve endings and stuff. Any chance of a Mrs Pye Special?'

'A Mrs Pye special for one,' Old Man Wood said, referring to the large breakfast sandwich Mrs Pye had made famous in the household. 'Any other takers?'

Daisy put a hand up. 'Go on. One for me, please.'

Isabella sighed. 'Sure, me too,' she said reluctantly. 'Big day ahead so might as well fill up before we get eaten alive. Do we really have to go up to the ruin?'

'Yes, we do, Isabella,' Archie said. 'Please don't tell me you're going to get the jitters again. It's all or nothing. And that, big sis, is the bottom line.'

Isabella groaned and placed her head in her hands.

With breakfast in full swing, Sue appeared. She looked around and sat down, a confused look on her face. 'Um,' she said tentatively, 'has anyone seen Gus this morning?'

Archie winked at Daisy. 'I thought he was, you know, with you?'

Sue shook her head. 'With me? No. Gus slept on the sofa.'

'Last night?'

'Yeah. He left just after midnight.'

While Archie looked confused, Daisy stared at Sue momentarily wondering what to do. Her eyes slipped down to her less-than-inviting breakfast as she forced the food in, her cutlery clanging clumsily on her earthenware plate.

A slightly awkward silence passed over the room as they tried to think where Gus might be.

'Perhaps he sleep-walked over to Mrs Pye's flat or ran off into the fog. He can't have gone far,' Isabella volunteered. 'Maybe he found another room, or you never know,' she said, smirking, 'he might have slipped in with Mr Solomon.'

The idea that Gus might have ended up with the portly headmaster made everyone laugh.

Archie couldn't help himself. 'Classic. Gus and the head-master. Always knew he was the teacher's pet.'

Isabella glared at him. 'My bet, Archie, is that he found the warmth of the Cupboard above us. He's either listening to every word or fast asleep. We'll check before we go.'

For the time being this appeared to be a reasonable answer.

With their stomachs full, Old Man Wood stood up with a groan followed by a smile. 'Time won't wait for us,' he said. 'We need to be getting a move on. Ready to locate this third tablet? Isabella, Daisy and Archie, meet me back here in ten minutes.'

While the de Lowes rushed upstairs to their bedroom in the attic of Eden Cottage, Sue explored the house, looking under every bed and inspecting every room and hidey-hole, including the airing cupboard, known as "The Cupboard". She even woke Mr Solomon.

When they reconvened, a tense nervousness filled the air.

'He's absolutely nowhere to be found,' Sue said. 'I've checked everywhere—'

'But that's impossible—'

'Twice,' she said. 'What if Gus headed out into the fog?'

'Why would Gus do that?' Isabella asked.

Sue looked blank. 'I don't know. He's not the sort of person to do that kind of thing: Gus is sensible and practical. Going out there would be completely out of character.'

Sue noticed that Isabella's hands had begun shaking.

'Are you all right, Bells?' Sue asked. 'You look peaky. Have you eaten something?'

'It's nothing to do with food,' Isabella said. 'What if...' her voice trailed off.

'What if ... what?' Sue asked, her voice betraying her increasing sense of panic.

Isabella sat down. 'Sue, I've had a terrible feeling about some sort of monster up at the ruin. Every time I think of it, I come over feeling sick and weak and terrified. Deep down, I can sense its power, its terribleness.

'What's this got to do with Gus?'

Isabella turned her eyes up. 'What if…'

'The beast came here and got him,' Archie finished off.

Isabella nodded.

Sue laughed. 'Here? It's not possible—'

Archie flicked his eyes at Isabella. 'That's the thing. If there's one thing we've found out, it's that anything is possible' he continued. Then, realising he'd unsettled her, he added, 'of course we don't know, maybe he went for a walk and got lost—'

'But he wouldn't have walked off without saying something—

'…or maybe the monster, you know, lured him out?' Isabella said.

Sue squealed and buried her head in Old Man Wood's chest.

For some time, the entire gathering remained in the living room lost for words.

Finally, Daisy, sitting quietly by the fire spoke up, 'I know what happened,' she said, her voice barely above a whisper.

Collectively, they turned to face her.

'You know? How?'

'I saw it all. Last night…'

Old Man Wood straightened. 'What happened, Daisy?'

Daisy wiped her eyes. 'I was there…'

The old man bent down to her. 'What did you see, Daisy?' he said, kindness in his tone.

Daisy's eyes had turned a sorrowful purple-red colour. 'I heard noises, just before dawn,' she said. 'I followed the sounds out of the door and then on, into the fog.'

Sue gasped. 'Why would Gus do that? Where did these sounds take you?'

'Up towards the ruin—'

Sue cried out again.

The headmaster, Solomon, had joined them. 'But how?' he said. 'With respect, if I've got my facts right, nobody apart from you, dear Daisy, can see through that fog.'

Daisy wiped her nose with the back of her hand. 'He wasn't alone. Someone took him up there.' Daisy stared at the floor.

'Who?' Archie said. 'No one on earth could have made their way up here through the fog. How could anyone have abducted him?'

'There's one person nobody's mentioned this morning who is also missing.'

The others collectively racked their brains.

'There's one person who is more mysterious than anyone else right now.'

Archie looked puzzled. 'Who?'

Isabella twigged. 'Why, Sherlock, it's the same person who escaped a high-security hospital and who managed, single-handedly to row across the flood to find his mother,' she said, 'It's that bloody oaf, Kemp, of course.'

Daisy met her eyes. 'Correct. It was Kemp, and Kemp's foul accomplice.'

THREE
A RULE IS BROKEN

G enesis, the large, old dreamspinner, a spider-like creature forged from the gases and minerals at the beginning of time, listened to the wind gusting down the distant valleys and the barren landscape of a planet deep in the outer rim of space. The creature thought about her encounter with Abel's spirit and extended a long, delicate black and silvery leg towards the dreamspinner who hovered nearby. In a claw at the end of this thin leg was a glint of shiny metal.

Gaia, the other dreamspinner who had found her mother hiding in the far reaches of space, couldn't tell if this was something she held or if the light had briefly touched upon a shiny rock beneath her.

'Gorialla Yingarna, the beast who guards the third tablet, is in breach of the rules of the universe,' Genesis said. 'A human who is not an Heir of Eden has entered the labyrinth. We must go to Gorialla Yingarna this instant and warn her of the laws, and, more importantly, of the consequences.

Both dreamspinners inverted into the electric-blue holes in the middle of their abdomens called magholes and instantly reappeared in the entrance chamber of the labyrinth on Earth, in the ruin near Eden Cottage.

In front of them lay a boy, his face and body smeared with

blood, his countenance still and his complexion pale. To the side, a small viper-looking snake hovered over him, its tongue flickering in and out of its mouth.

Both dreamspinners reverted from an invisible status into their visible form.

'Gorialla Yingarna,' Genesis called out. 'There is no place here for this human.'

'Ah,' the snake hissed. 'Dreamspinners. I wondered when you demons of the night would come sprinkling your dreaming powders. It has been a long time, and you are never welcome. Pray tell, why should I not enjoy this one before my battle ahead.'

'The human-child is not an Heir of Eden. It is not time.'

'Then pray tell, witches of the dark, what is this corpse doing in my lair?'

'I believe you know the reason,' Genesis said, by way of vibrating her legs into speech. 'A ploy, perhaps, to upset the balance. Do I need to repeat the rules of your trial at the Great Closing of the Garden of Eden? No humans aside from the Heirs of Eden are permitted inside the labyrinth until the tablet is held by an Heir of Eden—'

'Or until one of the Heirs lies dead,' Gorialla Yingarna completed. 'Does it really matter?' the snake continued as it morphed into a small dinosaur-like beast, sniffing the body beneath it. 'This child would not know, no one else would be wise to my repast—'

'Failure to adhere to the rules and you will remain trapped here forever, Gorialla Yingarna. And your chance of freedom will have gone.'

The beast, now a small, alert-eyed raptor creature, shuffled and barked in defiance. 'Then what would you have me do? Toss it out? Bury it?'

'We will hide the body, Gorialla Yingarna,' Genesis replied, 'so that no man nor beast may see, feel or fall upon it.'

Genesis stepped directly over Gus' body and, using her six

legs she began to wrap him in spider silks. Soon her threads covered Gus from head to foot.

Gorialla Yingarna sniffed the body again. 'I am weary of entrapment and I am desirous to leave. I will return for the flesh of this human child when I have destroyed the Heirs of Eden.' Gorialla Yingarna curled up into a snake and its tongue flashed in and out of its mouth. 'I hear they are small children of less than twenty seasons,' he hissed. 'The universe has sent juveniles to defeat me? What cruel fate it brings upon a world to do such a thing. I will tempt the sweet-smelling children of humankind to come and play games with me in my labyrinth. What fun it will be.'

Then its voice grew dark. 'And I will play with these Heirs until they beg me for mercy. After they have pleaded for their lives, and starting with the eldest, I will remove each arm from its socket and then each leg, and suck out their eyes and tear off their heads. And I will suck blood from their necks, and feast on their young flesh and the old man will watch, and he will scream and pound the earth. I have foreseen it. It will be a lesson the universe may wish to remember.'

Genesis finished off disguising the body of Gus, sliding a slender leg inside his covering, making sure all parts of him were contained.

For a millisecond, the old dreamspinner froze, noting a pulse.

She checked again. A murmur. In a flash she injected the child, a tiny prick from the end of a claw that was now a needle, with a substance she knew might sustain his heartbeat. If the child chose to survive, he would be safe.

'We are done here. Play your games, but this child here will not be detected. When the "Lyre of Awakening" calls, your time has come, Gorialla Yingarna. You will die, or you will be free.'

FOUR
GUS AND KEMP GO MISSING

'It can't be true,' Archie said. 'Kemp's been with Mrs Pye all the time. I'll go and check it out.'

Archie opened the front door and headed into the thick fog, feeling as though he'd walked into a vast, high-gloss, woolly blanket the moment he stepped outside. The head-master and Sue joined him, linking arms, as they made the short but now perilous journey around the courtyard, using the stonework as a guide.

When they arrived at the steps they breathed a sigh of relief.

Inside, Mrs Pye sat in her rocking chair, knitting.

'Morning all,' she said, chirpily.

Archie and Sue came forward and gave her a peck on the cheek. 'You looking for something, are you?' she said. Her strange smile, which to the unknowing looked more like a grimace, filled her face.

'Well … yes,' he stuttered. 'Not exactly "something", more "someone".'

'What are you babbling on about, eh? You lot have turned awful queer.'

Archie reddened. 'We're looking for Kemp. Is he over here with you? The thing is, we don't know where he is—'

Mrs Pye's face contorted with alarm, her forehead scar

suddenly looking more pronounced. 'No, my little angel. He went early as far as I could tell—had to meet someone, so he said. He did promise he'd be back.'

The others exchanged nervous glances.

'He didn't by any chance tell you where he'd gone and when he'd be back?' Solomon asked.

Mrs Pye rubbed her chin. 'Now you mentions it, he didn't. I think he said he'd return "soon".'

Mr Solomon smiled his headmasterly smile. 'And might you have any idea whom he might be seeing?'

Mrs Pye shook her head a couple of times and regarded the man. 'He's not in trouble, is he?'

Archie laughed. 'Your lad's always in trouble, Mrs P—and landing me in it half the time.'

As Archie started telling Mrs Pye about their long hours together in detention, Mr Solomon turned his attention to the table and the selection of photographs sitting randomly on it.

When Archie had finished, his story, Solomon sat down on the bed and addressed Mrs Pye. 'Your boy, my dear, has had a remarkably difficult upbringing. Considering what he's been through, his demeanour, which I have to admit hasn't always been of the highest standard, has been nothing short of stoic.'

Solomon smiled at her. 'Had you found each other several years ago, I'm sure some of his behavioural issues would be non-existent. But this is all hearsay. Kemp has talent in abundance, though regrettably,' he said, flicking his eyes at Archie, 'it has often been misplaced.'

Mrs Pye beamed back at him. The words "talent" and "abundance" close to one another filled her with joy.

Solomon stood up and returned to the table again where he had previously inspected some of the framed photographs. The others watched as he stopped, stone-still, staring at one in particular. He picked up the silver frame, turned it towards the window and quickly replaced it back down on the glass top.

'You must go,' he snapped to Archie and Sue. 'Come on. Chop, chop.'

'What is it?' Archie said, confused by the headmaster's sudden brusque manner.

'Trust me, Archie. You chaps need to get going this instant.'

The headmaster swivelled to Mrs Pye. 'With any luck, my dear, we'll catch up later with more news.'

'BUT IF THOSE TWO, Gus and Kemp, went off together,' Sue pondered, now that they had reconvened in the sitting room, 'what were they doing?'

Archie shrugged. 'Beats me. Not as if they would have slipped off to have a kickabout. Gus hates footy.'

'Perhaps, there's some comfort in the thought,' Solomon added, 'that at least both boys were together. I'm inclined to agree that Isabella's theory about being snatched by a wild beast might be a little far-fetched.'

'But they absolutely hate each other,' Isabella said. 'The question is, why would friendly, nice-guy Gus want to go off with jerk-features Kemp. Kemp is trouble. The only reason I can see that they would go anywhere is to beat each other up. I think Kemp challenged him and Gus couldn't resist.'

Archie rubbed his chin. 'Or the other way around. Sparks were flying between them just before the storm. You remember, Daisy?'

Daisy squirmed. She just wanted to do something—anything—rather than sit in the living room discussing Gus and Kemp's mysterious disappearance.

'Kemp is still a jerk,' Isabella said.

'He's not a jerk,' Archie fired back. 'He's had a shocking childhood, something you wouldn't recognise, and, he's Mrs Pye's long-lost son—'

'Archie, I don't care. He is a brute who goes out of his way to intimidate and bully—'

'Watch your tongue, Isabella.'

'No, I won't. He's a good-for-nothing moron, Archie. If I were Gus, I'd have beaten him up long ago.'

Archie's hair was beginning to harden. 'And you're saying you don't beat him up with words, Isabella?'

'If you can't see what a loser he is,' Isabella stormed, 'you're a bigger idiot than I thought. How you choose to hang out with him makes me sick—'

'You think you're so superior,' Archie seethed, 'but you're a selfish bully in your own right—'

'Stop it! Stop it, both of you!' Daisy cried.

She stood up, tears rolling down her cheeks. 'I … I was there. I saw it all.'

'Really?'

'Yes!' Daisy stood up, stared out of the window and turned. 'You're right, Bells. They went to fight each other.'

'Ha! I told you!'

'Be silent, Isabella,' Solomon boomed. 'We need to hear this. Daisy…'

The room fell quiet.

Daisy summoned her strength. 'It was a set-up. A set-up to see who goes with this weird buddy of Kemp … this ghost. He promised to save one of them.'

The others stared at her.

'I'm sorry,' Solomon asked, kindly, 'but who is going to save who?'

Daisy rubbed her brow. 'Kemp's mysterious friend is going to save either Gus or Kemp. Do you know why? Because this companion, or ghost, or whatever it is, knows every detail about our task and it told them that we haven't got a chance in hell of succeeding.'

Old Man Wood leaned in. 'Who is this "companion" you talk of?'

'I don't know,' Daisy said. 'It's a spirit that somehow blends into Kemp and then, when they're together, they kind-of disappear.'

Old Man Wood shook his head trying to make some sense out of it.

'According to this ghost, the third tablet is somewhere under the ruin. It is guarded—'

'You saw the tablet?' Isabella asked.

'No. I told you, I just followed them up there.'

Isabella rubbed her hands together. 'But you saw the beast?'

'Yes, I did, Isabella,' she replied, curtly.

'What's it like?'

'As far as I could tell,' Daisy said, not holding back. 'It is the bollocks—'

'The what?!' Solomon exclaimed.

Daisy reddened. 'Oops! Sorry. From what I heard, it can do amazing things—' she said, fanning her face.

'What kind of things,' Isabella said, her voice wavering.

'It can morph—'

'What is morph?' the headmaster queried.

'Morph—you know, change—into different things,' she began, 'It alters its shape, from one type of reptile to another, at will—'

'How on earth can it do that?'

'I don't know!' Daisy replied, her voice exasperated. 'I heard them talking about it. The ghost told them this creature couldn't lose,' her voice went quiet. 'Said it had beaten armies on its own.'

Silence filled the room.

'That's it! I'm not going!' Isabella spat, stamping the floor. 'I can't—it's going to rip us apart, tear us limb from limb.'

Daisy rolled her eyes and sighed heavily. 'You have to, Bells' she said. 'Look, we've been through this over and over, every single time. None of us particularly fancy the prospect, but, for some weird reason, saving the planet—as we know it —appears to be up to us. We have to try.'

Isabella shook. 'I AM NOT GOING!' she roared.

Daisy stood and faced her. 'YES, YOU ARE, Isabella!'

The girls stared at one another until Archie pushed his way between them. 'Calm down, both of you. Arguing will not help us find the third tablet or Gus.' He turned to his elder sister. 'Isabella, you know we have to do this and I, for one, am not giving up without a fight.'

FIVE

CROSSING THE FLOODWATERS

For several minutes the throb of the engine, pulling the other rib behind it, was all the troops could hear.

Occasionally a scrape on the frame of the rubber husk of the rib made the men turn anxiously towards one another and peer nervously overboard. Due to the thick, dense fog and the black night, there was little choice but to follow the dots on the bright screen of the satellite communication device.

Checking the readings, they were nearly halfway across. Having started on the side of the Dales, they were heading towards the hills of the Yorkshire Moors on the other. Depth-metre monitors flickered from one reading to the next, blipping to alert them when the water became shallow and potentially unnavigable.

Going was slow, the chugging, buzzing engine working at quarter throttle. While the soldiers sat alert to every sound and jar, the gentle vibration of the motors made Stone feel drowsy. After long hours of trying to make head or tail of the sudden, catastrophic events, which was now a global problem, the commissioner shut his eyes.

An hour later a jolt set him awake.

Soldiers prodded sticks into the water around.

'What is it now?' he croaked.

'An obstruction, sir. Something under the boat mucking up the propellers.'

'The depth reading?'

'We're in deep water, sir. Just trying to find out what it is—a net or something that hasn't been picked up by the sensors.'

The crew sat nervously in the boats as two men from the lead vessel, levered up the propeller and others fished under the ribs with sticks.

'Can't seem to find anything, Sir.'

'What's the noise?' Stone said, peering overboard. 'Quiet!' he ordered.

Around them, the water jumped, like a boiling kettle.

'We noticed the blobbing noise about ten minutes ago, sir,' a rough, stockily built, semi-bearded trooper called Jenkins said. 'Comes back every so often, like the sound of pebbles hitting the water—all around us.'

They listened.

'I reckon it's fish,' Lambert, a squat, shaven-haired soldier from the leading boat, yelled out. 'Reminds me of the shoals we used to see off the coast of Belize, sir.'

'Fish? What the hell, Lambert?' Stone said before calling out to the other boat, 'what's your reading?'

'Just over fifteen metres, sir. Might be over a river. Could be the River Wiske.'

Stone played with the ends of his moustache. 'The depth-meters share the same reading. They're correct. What do you suggest, Lambert—what would fish be doing under the boat?'

'Swimming?'

'Yes, very funny. Any more wisecracks and you'll be joining them. Is that clear, soldier?'

Lambert coughed, realising that now wasn't the time or place. 'Maybe something's wedged up under the boat. We could try accelerating—see if we can ride through it?'

Stone scratched his chin. 'OK, let's give it a try. But steady —you've got a lot of kit in here that I don't want to lose. For heaven's sake, do not let the boats separate.'

As the navigator pulled the throttle, the engine roared,

and petrol exhaust filled their nostrils. The boat lurched forward jagging the men back and forth. Under the vessel, a chopping, slicing noise rang out as the metal propeller grated and strained and thrashed. Then, it juddered to a halt altogether, bubbles rising to the surface of the water close to the outboard motor.

Stone cursed. 'Jesus. What is going on?'

'The propeller's stuffed, sir,' Geddis said, peering over the edge.

'Another clever one, aren't you,' Stone replied, sarcastically.

Jenkins stretched out a hand, dangled it in the water and then drew it back in. In his cupped hand sat a small amount of flood-water. 'It bloody stinks,' he said. An acrid smell swept over both crews.

'Oi, Lambert, shine a torch over here a minute, mate.'

The soldier moved along the side of the other rib and swung the beam of a powerful white LED lantern from the water's surface to Jenkins.

'Not at me, you idiot. At my bleedin' hands,' Jenkins exclaimed, holding them up.

The torch rested on his cupped hands, which trailed red stains.

'Christ, mate,' Lambert shouted over, in disgust. 'That's not water. It's…'

'Blood,' Jenkins said, as he sniffed his hands. 'Fish blood, I reckon. We've been mincing fish under there.'

'Why would fish do this,' Stone yelled. 'And why are there so many?'

'They've clogged up the propeller, I reckon,' Lambert said, as he turned to the other crew members. They leaned in. 'What if it's … you know, NOT fish but… human…'

As the boats sat in the silent envelope of fog, the flood water rippling meekly under their bows, the soldiers exchanged worried glances.

Stone's irritated tone cut through the fog. 'For God's sake, get on with it, you lot. You're supposed to be professionals.

Switch the boats around; we'll pull you. Lucky both weren't in operation, or you lot would be rowing to the moors.

'Lambert and Dickinson—pick up the rear. And everyone,' he shouted, 'please don't waste any more time. We've been splashing around here for twenty minutes, and, as you're all fully aware, time is the one thing we don't have.'

They hastily unfastened the ropes but, at the exact moment the painter was thrown from one boat to the other, a sudden ripple, a wave, divided the boats instantly pushing them apart. A beat later and the fog had eaten them up, surrounding each like thick, white paste.

Stone, like all the others, didn't notice until it was too late. 'I don't believe it. Why wasn't the other boat secured?' he roared, now that he couldn't even see the other rib. 'What the heck is going on? Dickinson, Lambert, get your rib back over here.'

'We're being pulled away, sir. And fast,' a voice replied from the blank wall.

'Row. Use the bleeding oars, man. Now!'

As the soldiers called out to one another, a more significant wave shuttled between the gap, followed by a lurching movement through the waters.

Silence descended over them.

'It's like there's a sodding great whale under us,' Lambert, in boat two, said, his voice loud enough for the crew to hear.

All along, Dickinson had been deathly silent, hating every moment. 'Something really doesn't want us to get any further,' he said. 'We'll inspect the propeller later. As Stone said, get those oars out, gentlemen, we're going to have to row.'

Lambert sidled up to Dickinson. 'Don't know about you, but I don't fancy swimming for our lives in this fish-pit if we can help it. What we're doing here don't seem right. Something's wrong. All wrong.'

SIX

TENSIONS RISE

S olomon and Sue excused themselves and went to the kitchen.

Old Man Wood coughed. 'Bells, Archie's right,' he said, smiling at her. 'I'm afraid there's nothing more I know, other than the next task will take us into a great labyrinth under the ruins. The memory trees at the Bubbling Brook that I found had no more information. You see, I never told them the secrets of the third tablet,' he said, pausing for a beat, choosing his words thought-fully. 'When ... when I originally put these spells into place...'

'WHAT!' Isabella exploded. 'You mean, you, Old Man Wood, are responsible for this incredible mess?!'

Old Man Wood's huge wrinkles scrunched together. 'I, er, I,' he stuttered, trying to find the right words. 'A long time ago I told the trees at the Bubbling Brook about the first two tablets, but the third, and the labyrinth, I never discussed with anybody,' he blurted out. I'm afraid I have no idea what's in store for us. But my gut tells me this beast might not be very friendly.'

'Great!' Isabella fumed. 'I can't believe it, and frankly, I'm too frightened to care. I don't want to be a part of US anymore. You know, maybe this ghost has a point. How can we beat a beast that can get inside your head and then change into different creatures!'

'Hang on a minute,' Archie said. 'Who said anything about it getting inside your head?'

'Oh, let's take a wild guess,' Daisy began. 'She probably dreamed about it, but forgot to tell us!'

'Is that right?' Archie asked.

Isabella bowed her head and nodded.

'Hey, thanks!' Archie said, 'thanks so much for sharing. You know, Bells, we're in this together—don't think the last few days have happened just to entertain us while Mum and Dad are away. This is real,' he said, calmly. 'We're in it up to our necks because we've been chosen—I have no idea why— but it's probably because we're related to Old Man Wood who's an old wizard of some sort. Aren't you?'

Old Man Wood was slightly embarrassed. No one had called him a wizard for many hundreds of years. He was a little overcome. 'I think I used to be pretty good—'

'Good? Seriously?' Isabella said, incredulously. 'I don't know about that,' she poked a finger through the penny-sized hole in her palms, the result of resisting a lightning strike.

'Are you suggesting Old Man Wood isn't a good wizard?' Daisy said, taking over from Archie.

'Well, he hasn't exactly showered himself in glory—'

Daisy's red eyes bored into Isabella. 'You know what, I'm not interested in what you think Bells,' Daisy snapped. 'And I'm fed up trying to explain.'

'I'm not tough like you,' Isabella countered, her arms flailing. 'I can't do it. Leave me out of it.'

The heat in the room was increasing once again.

'Please, Bells!' Archie remonstrated. 'Haven't you learnt anything from the dreams, the trials, the water, the cave, the riddles, the first two tablets? It took ALL of us to do it. Not one, or two of us, but all three of us. We wouldn't be here without you and vice-versa.'

'I just don't care anymore!' Isabella answered, her eyes full of tears.

'Don't care? You HAVE to care,' Archie fired back. 'This only stops when we find the tablets. Sue's life, Gus' life, Mum and Dad's – everyone's lives depend on you—ON US—'

The tension in the room had reached a breaking point. Sue and the headmaster reappeared with a tray crammed with mugs of tea and an assortment of biscuits and set them down quietly in the corner.

Old Man Wood calmly spoke. 'Now, littluns, before you tear yourselves apart, there's something I think we should do.'

From his coat pocket, he produced the first stone tablet, which was no bigger than an ordinary paperback book. On the front it had a tree of life emblem etched in gold. He set it down on the table. From his other pocket he pulled out the second, identical in every way.

'I've been thinking,' the old man said. 'It would make sense to put these two tablets together and see what happens.'

Old Man Wood carefully placed the second tablet on top of the first. As he did, sparks splayed out from the sides like metal on a sharpening wheel, and a hissing sound, like air escaping from a balloon, filled the room.

Automatically, everyone stepped back.

Now, a sticky, steaming, melting reaction took place as the tablets joined together. When this had finished, a burst of multi-coloured glitter fizzed into the air like a sparkly fountain. A roll of thunder shook the building, rattling the windows.

The tablets were now locked and sealed together as one, with no signs of any joins or glue.

The children, the headmaster and Sue looked at one another, the colour draining from their faces.

'Blimey,' Daisy gasped. 'If that's what happens with two, what's going to happen if all three come together?'

SEVEN

ANOTHER WORLD REVEALED

'Look!' Daisy said. 'The top part! It's changing.'

Everyone collectively hesitated, neither moving forward nor backing off, to inspect the new, larger tablet.

As they examined the top of the tablet, which bore a simple, almost geometrical golden pattern, a moving image that started to leach out of the sides and top like a gas.

Soon, growing out of the tablet were the stalks and leaves of unfurling plants, followed by trees and beasts and sky and light. The image was spewing into the room in three dimensions, surrounding the onlookers.

'It's a massive hologram,' Archie cried, laughing. 'A landscape...'

Daisy dropped to her knees and held her hands out. 'Hey, Archie! Fields, woods, lakes, animals.' She looked down. 'Weird rabbity things. It's beautiful—'

'Where is this, Old Man Wood?' Archie asked, twisting to the old man whose face was cracked with emotion, his lips quivering.

THE IMAGE EXPANDED QUICKLY and quietly, as the countryside they were going through surrounded them and stretched ahead so that soon all they could see was a whole new world in every direction. Before long, they were standing in a prairie-like landscape on one side amidst unfamiliar coloured grasses with all sorts of trees on the other.

'We're … in a picture' Sue said, running over to Isabella. 'I can feel the heat of the sun,' she splayed her hands to the sky. 'Lovely and warm.'

'And listen!' Solomon said, removing his glasses and rubbing his eyes. 'If I'm not mistaken, the wind is playing a tune with the leaves on the trees … like tree-music!'

Isabella sniffed. 'Sue, can you smell that?'

'Scent?'

'Roses and eucalyptus and pine and lavender and, oooh, a kind of sweet mint,' she closed her eyes, drinking it in.

'Pink grass!' Daisy said, inspecting the blades beneath her feet. 'Moving in time as though it's grooving … singing … can you hear it, Arch?'

Archie's jaw was almost on the floor. 'Oh yes,' he said. 'Hey, look! Over there! The trees! They're moving! Walking, or waltzing; exactly as Old Man Wood used to tell us in his stories!'

They watched the scene unfurl around them, discovering new creatures, plants and life-forms with every passing moment.

'It's like "Tree-Strictly-Come Dancing",' Daisy whispered.

'There's a family of oak-trees, I think, over there,' Isabella said, squinting. 'They're playing in the water!'

As they watched, the group found themselves moving through the changing landscape as though on an invisible, silent, non-existent hovercraft.

Old Man Wood watched, intrigued, especially when they floated towards a huge apple tree laden with fruit.

'Have you ever seen such juicy apples?' he said. 'They're the size of your footballs, eh, Daisy!'

Soon, they came to a large pool where an assortment of birds dive-bombed with timed precision and, re-emerged, squirting water over one another.

Without warning a sharp ear-splitting noise smashed into the scene.

The children froze. As one, they instinctively ducked and covered their ears.

In the picture, a scene of panic emerged.

Strange animals, some single, others in packs, ran wildly, their eyes wide in fright. More charged past, roaring and tooting wildly.

Huge trees and even small grasses darted here and there, trying to get out of each other's way, stampeding further into the image.

The onlookers crouched down, covering their heads, muffling their ears as evil roars and cries of death filled the room.

Above, the sky filled with black clouds and the stench of fear and death permeated their nostrils.

Wherever they looked, screams and howls of pain surrounded every one and every thing.

A blast of heat—not fire, but a furnace-like white-heat shot through the picture, withering leaves, shrivelling everything in sight.

In moments all that remained were the burned-out skeleton of the big apple tree and a vast, smoking expanse of grey, smooth ash. Then the branches crashed to the ground, followed by the bough breaking in two as it disintegrated as dust upon the earth.

Seconds later, the scene was sucked back into the tablet as if by a giant, unseen vacuum.

The living room was back as it always had been. Floral curtains covered the window, Old Man Wood's old leather armchair sat, as it always did, by the fire, the sofa remained covered in the blanket from the night before, and the assortment of pictures the children had pulled off the walls the previous day, surrounded them.

The three de Lowes, Sue, Solomon and Old Man Wood slowly unfurled themselves, stood up, and dusted off imaginary specks and mopped their sweaty brows.

On the tablet, the neat image of a tree had been replaced by a rose, carved into its upturned face.

And, resting neatly on top, lay a tiny musical instrument.

Daisy was the first to react. 'The tablet!' she gasped, stepping closer. 'A mini harp—or something.'

The others followed her lead. Tentatively, they edged towards it.

She picked up the instrument, which was no longer than the palm of her hand and carved from silvery wood in the shape of a tall 'C'. Several taut strings stretched from top to bottom.

Solomon wiped his hands, rubbed his glasses and joined her. Nestling his specs back on the end of his nose, he said, 'I do believe it is a kind of mini lyre.'

'A liar?' Daisy said, thickly. 'What makes you think it's lying?'

'My dear,' Solomon said, containing himself. 'A lyre is an ancient musical instrument, often depicted in Greek mythology.'

'What's it for?'

'Music, dur brain,' Archie quipped. 'Obviously.'

Daisy turned to him, her eyes blazing. 'Maybe it's for calling someone, Archie.'

'But if so, who?' Isabella said.

Daisy looked at her. 'How should I know?'

The lyre passed from one hand to another.

'My guess is,' Daisy said, 'that we have to play it.'

Archie reached for it again.

'No, Archie. Please. You'll break it,' Isabella snapped, whisking the tiny instrument away from him. 'What happened in the picture, Old Man Wood?' she said. 'Everything died and vanished to dust. Why? Why did it all suddenly change? Where did it all go?'

'It didn't go anywhere,' he coughed, his voice croaky with emotion. Tear marks stained his weathered cheeks.

'You alright, Old Man Wood?'

The old man smiled. 'Yes. It's just…' the others leaned in.

'What we saw, I believe, was a piece of the Great Closing of the Garden of Eden.' He sat down heavily in his armchair. 'It's the place I come from,' he continued. 'Once, it was so beautiful, so plentiful, a world full of joy and invention. The Garden of Eden bore the hope and inspiration for all of nature.'

'But what happened?' Isabella asked, placing the lyre back on the tablets.

'The Garden of Eden burned itself to the ground, littlun,' he said, quietly. 'Burned itself to prevent its secrets passing into the wrong hands, into the wrong worlds.' He wiped his eyes, pulled a handkerchief out of his pocket and blew his nose rather too loudly.

Before anyone had a chance to ask him more, the lyre began to play all by itself, melodic sounds reverberating through the house. They listened to the notes, which danced and sang, warbling like a nightingale one moment, then hollow and haunting the next. The melody reached into the core of each and everyone in the room, massaging the souls of those who heard it with a profound sense of energy and love.

When it ceased, a strange contented silence hung in the room.

Old Man Wood stretched his arms out, his wrinkled face coming alive. 'I am apple-sure the Willows told me about this,' he said. 'I believe it is known as the "Song of Awakening". Legend has it that its notes reach all those who may help.' He turned to the children. 'It is time for you to face your task.'

He clapped Isabella on the shoulders and searched her eyes. 'The Garden of Eden is waiting to be re-born, my dear, lovely child. You cannot ignore Mother Nature's wishes. Together, Isabella, and as one, we must gain the third tablet.'

EIGHT

SOLOMON UPDATES THE HEIRS

Solomon stood in the corner nursing a brain ache as if he'd eaten an entire tub of ice-cream in one mouthful.

His body shook uncontrollably, and his heart thumped so loudly, he thought he might suffer a heart-attack. He took off his glasses and grabbed several deep breaths to calm himself down.

Never in his wildest dreams had he expected this. His investigations had led him to believe that something strange and alien was going on. But nothing quite so earth-shattering, nothing that might challenge every belief system known to humankind.

He had no doubts about what he had to do next.

He moved into the middle of the room and coughed. 'That, my dear friends,' he began, 'was quite immense—more a word you'd use, perhaps, Daisy. There is something you must know before you go, and go you must, in haste.' Solomon patted his belly, selecting his words.

'While in Mrs Pye's room, I detected a surveillance device which, I suspect, links directly to Commissioner Stone. While I now understand the deep gravity of your situation,' he said, as earnestly as he could, 'it pains me to tell you that Stone has every intention of finding you and interrogating you so that he might get to the bottom of the mystery. Believe me when I tell you that our world is toppling, like dominos, towards a cataclysmic disaster. It must not happen.' He smiled his knowing, headmasterly smile.

'Stone has significant means at his disposal to find you and to harm you. He will hinder you in his quest for what I can only describe as his own "truth" whatever that may be.'

Solomon fiddled with his glasses momentarily. 'He will have studied the camera images, and the moment he has noticed something at odds with what we have told him, he will come here with everything he can muster. And knowing the man, I can tell you this. He will not give an inch until he has you in his grasp.

'Sue and I have so far done what we can to divert suspicion away, but typically, they will have set off at dawn and, even though it is like pea soup out there, his force will be plentiful, highly skilled and motivated.' He nodded sagely to himself, pausing for dramatic effect, his eyes flicking from one face to the next.

'I wasn't going to tell you, but I have no choice. Your problem is now a world problem. The damage of the Ebora virus now reaches into every corner of the globe,' he paused again as all eyes stared at him. 'The Americans are due to annihilate the region of Upsall.'

The children looked upon their headmaster in shock. 'Bomb Yorkshire?!' Archie said.

'Yes. In two days' time, with a very large device,' Solomon continued.

'They're going to nuke us?' Daisy spluttered.

Solomon nodded. 'The idea, dear Daisy, is that if the source of the outbreak is nullified, it will cease—'

'That's insane,' Isabella said.

'Indeed, it is. But can you really blame them?' Solomon asked. 'After all, with the world slipping into meltdown at such lightning speed, they must be seen to be doing something.'

Archie did a small calculation. 'Two days is the end of our seven days,' he said quietly. 'So, if we haven't got the tablets, we're history anyway. Unless, of course, they jump the gun, or you've got the dates wrong.'

'How can you be certain he's seen us?' Isabella asked. 'We've hardly been up to Mrs Pye's flat. Only Sue's spent time over there, and Stone knows about her anyway.'

Solomon shook his head. 'I noticed a hidden camera on one of the picture frames. Even though the camera was facing away from where you three stood when you visited Mrs Pye, there is one person who will not have escaped his notice. Yet again, he has escaped ours.'

The de Lowes regarded each other quizzically. 'Who's that?' Archie asked.

'It seems that everywhere we go, the boy wreaks havoc, whether he means it or not. Why, Kemp, my dear friends. Stone will have seen Kemp.'

NINE

BRANCHWAND

'A gift has been given,' Gaia, the curious spider-looking dreamspinner, said, speaking by way of rapid vibrations in her legs. 'Abel's spirit has requested that it should be returned to his father, Adam.'

She reached into the hole in her abdomen where a churning mass of blue electrical currents flashed randomly and pulled out a gold nugget—like a small stud. She held it in the air with a long pincer on the end of a thin, wiry leg. With a flash, the golden stud transformed into a long silvery-golden sparkling twig.

Genesis, the mother dreamspinner, who had spun the Tripodean dream containing the prophecy to the three Heirs of Eden, Isabella, Archie and Daisy, reached over and tapped the glowing twig with the end of a long bony claw. Through three deep black eyes, she stared at it, momentarily mesmerised.

'This, Gaia,' she began, 'is what humans called a "Branchwand".'

Gaia laid the stick across two of her six long, slender, black and grey-stripped thinly haired legs and admired how it glimmered, rotating it with one of her other limbs, studying the pleasing engravings of an ancient script that flowed down the slender stem. As she did this, the branchwand flashed from gold to green to silver and from blue to red and back to gold. With another tap of her claw and a tiny flash, the twig returned to a small pinhead again.

Gaia was enthralled. 'Is this a magic branchwand given by the Tree of Knowledge from the Garden of Eden?'

'Yes,' Genesis said. 'The Tree sleeps in the Atrium of the Garden of Eden, waiting for life to return, waiting for the powers of creation to resume.'

Genesis tapped the stud again making the glowing sprig reappear. 'Like the Ancient Woman, Eve, the tree bides its time until the Heirs from Earth, or from Havilah, unlock the key to its rebirth,' Genesis said, referring to the planet on which the ghost, Cain, lived. 'Four branchwands were cut. Only three given: one for Adam and one for Eve so that they might protect themselves in their new environments after the great closing of Eden. Another was given to the dragon beast, Gorialla Yingarna, to use if it ever gained its freedom from the labyrinth. Do you know the story?'

Gaia vibrated a negative response.

'After the creation planet of Eden had been closed, Adam went to Earth. There, he introduced fish and plants to the sea, animals and organisms to the land and birds and wind and rain to the air. After Adam had enabled the roots of the trees and plants to push into the soil and established organisms to clean up the seasonal litter, he gave the planet order and balance. After this, a labyrinth was built to contain Gorialla Yingarna for the time when the prophecy would come around so that the Garden of Eden might be reborn.

'Earth settled. Time slipped by. Adam realised he didn't need his branchwand anymore, so he requested its removal, lest this powerful tool of magic was discovered and used in the wrong way. The spirit of Abel, the brother of Cain, was entrusted to its safekeeping.'

Genesis, the ancient dreamspinner tapped the branchwand, and it reverted to its smaller pin state. 'Now it must be returned to its rightful owner.'

Suddenly, all around them, a strange, beautiful, melodious, yet haunting sound filled the air, vibrations reaching out into every corner of the ether.

Genesis shifted. 'The lyre sings the Song of Awakening. The trial for the third book is about to commence. It is a battle to the death—the Heirs win, or they lose. There is no middle way. Take the branchwand to Adam this moment. Hurry. The Heirs do not know what lies in wait and the old man needs his tools. There is nothing to lose but all to gain, Gaia. I do not wish to see Gorialla Yingarna devouring the Heirs of Eden in such a way as it described.'

Although haggard by time and grave in her demeanour, Genesis raised herself up on her back legs so that her maghole fizzled impressively like a lightning-streaked orb in her middle.

'It is your duty now, Gaia, to make sure dreams come true. Use dream-powders that will make him remember how to use his branchwand. Do this before they meet Gorialla Yingarna. Give the branchwand back to the old man in any way you can. Cain and Gorialla Yingarna may be up to their old tricks, but we have a few ourselves.'

TEN

FAREWELLS ARE SAID

'Archie, Daisy,' Solomon said. 'I have an idea that might help—before the curtain rises.'

The twins shifted closer.

'Do you have any sound amplification appliances?'

Daisy and Archie looked at each other.

'A gramophone with batteries, perhaps, or, a wireless set?'

Archie stuttered. 'I don't know what you're talking about, sir.'

Solomon smiled badly. 'I'm after an electronically-based musical sound-system device that might deter Stone and his cronies.'

'Oh, I see,' Archie said. 'A radio! Mum and Dad might have one in their room. I'll go and check.'

He rushed upstairs and emerged shortly with an old, blue Roberts radio. 'Is this what you mean? I'm not sure if it works.'

He turned it on, and a low fizzing and whistling sound came out. He twisted one of the nobs and, after hearing crackles, a noise emerged of a couple in a discussion, their low tones broadcast out of the small speaker.

'Excellent,' Solomon said, patting it lightly. 'I hope the batteries are reasonably fresh. It might just help, who knows.

Any unusual sounds out there in the fog might give our foe the willies. Now, time for you two to get on.'

Archie slipped his tight black jeans inside his leather walking boots and tied the laces. He placed his beanie on top of his head spikes and pulled the zip up on his sleeveless, dark green leather-padded hunting jacket.

Daisy tied her blond hair in a bun, donned her pink-lensed glasses then slipped into a neat, tight, light brown leather coat with a wool collar and matching leather trousers. She knocked her lace-up boots together, spraying mud over the floor.

'Where the hell did you get that?' Isabella asked, stroking the jacket.

'Found it in Mums cupboard. You'd be amazed at the amount of awesome stuff in there. Jackets, boots, trousers, hats—you name it.'

Without hesitating, Isabella and Sue ran upstairs, and, as Archie and Daisy waited, twiddling their thumbs, Isabella soon appeared and waltzed down the stairs wearing a black leather jacket with silver studs around her cuffs and collar, and tight black leather trousers with silver studs above each pocket.

Archie burst out laughing. 'If Daisy looks as if she's about to fly a first world war bi-plane,' he said, 'you, Bells, well, I ... wow. It's like you're the lead singer in a heavy-metal rock band.' He examined her again. 'What have you done to your hair?'

'Sue put it in a plait so it wouldn't get in the way.'

Archie nodded. 'Nice idea, Sue. Isabella boffin, meet Isabella wild-rock-chick.' He threw her the fingerless leather gloves, which Daisy and Mrs Pye had altered. 'It even matches your gloves.'

Daisy punched him playfully. 'What about those knives you used to throw around?'

'He's not bringing those,' Isabella said.

'Why not? We're hardly going in heavily armed. They might come in handy. Better off with, right?'

This time, it was Archie's turn to dash up the stairs. He returned with his throwing knives wrapped in a leather holster that he wore around his torso under his hunting jacket.

'Is the fashion show over?' Daisy said. 'Can we please get going!'

Sue and Mr Solomon stood in the doorway of the cottage and embraced each one in turn.

Sue's eyes leaked tears as she hugged Isabella. 'Good luck and please—'

'Yes, yes. Don't worry, we'll find him, I promise.' Isabella said. 'And Sue, look after Mrs Pye and Solomon, OK.'

Sue smiled. 'I meant you, Bells. You come back. Please.' She dived in for another hug. 'I know you can do it, Bells. None of this would have happened if you couldn't. Just concentrate, or whatever it is you guys do, extremely hard.'

From somewhere inside the fog, a strange holler started to emerge, which, as they listened, turned out to be Mrs Pye tiptoeing around the courtyard, and, by the sounds of it, bumping into things as she went.

'Ere, where're you lot off to now?' she said as she joined them, slightly out of breath. She studied the children and tutted. 'You lot getting stranger by the minute. I daren't ask what's going on; all dressed up like television celebration people.'

'We've got to go. It's something we have to do, Mrs P,' Archie said.

'Have you eaten anything?' she asked. 'You look starving, you do.'

He smiled. 'We have, and I'm not—'

'And are you warm enough?'

'Yes!'

'How about a bit of starlight apple crumble—for the journey?'

'NO! Thank you,' Archie said, and he reached in and gave her a giant hug.

'Well then, be off with you,' she said, her voice wavering.

'And go and do this daft thing. And, while you're at it, see if you can find my boy and bring him back, right?'

'Mrs Pye,' Isabella said, in her bossiest voice. 'You've got to stay here and look after everyone, like you always do, perfectly. Mr Solomon and Sue might have to go out, but, if anyone turns up, it's important you don't say anything about us. Do you understand? Some big men with guns and helmets and radios might show up, but you mustn't let them know we're about because it might upset things.' She leaned in and hugged her. 'Promise?'

Mrs Pye burst out crying, her red, piggy eyes streaming with tears. 'I'll do whatever you say, my darling littluns. And you promise me you'll come back safe and sound.' She pulled herself together. 'Now, get off before you upset me waters further.'

ELEVEN

STONE'S FISHING IDEA

A s the soldiers stuck their oars in the rowlocks, Stone's boat pitched in the stillness,

'Boat two, Dickinson, Lambert—can you hear me?'

A voice echoed back through the veil.

'I'll radio him, sir.'

'Make sure he holds his position,' Stone demanded. 'We've got to get these boats together again.'

He turned to the others. 'Come on, lads. Get that engine working and make sure the propeller is extremely high in the water. If the fish keep coming back, shut off the engines and row, with one oar each. Then we'll switch over after half an hour taking it in turns. If we don't hook up with them, and soon, getting stuck out here will mean it's curtains, for all of us.'

Stone rubbed his eyes. Their four-hour trip across the water would easily double. While he'd planned to arrive in the early hours, even if they rowed at double speed they wouldn't be at the farmhouse until ten o'clock, perhaps even later. And by then, who knows who else might have turned up.

He turned to the crew as an idea popped into his head.

'You lot are a bunch of miserable amateurs. I thought you were our finest. Jenkins, how many hand-grenades have we got?'

'A whole box, sir. They're here. Each boat has one.'

'Then get one out and let's blow these slippery bastards out of the water.'

'With respect,' the soldier replied, nervously, 'are you serious, sir?'

'Of course, I'm serious,' Stone roared. 'Come on!'

'These are powerful explosives, Commissioner. We'll blow ourselves up.'

'It's worth a try,' Stone said. 'If we survive, then we might get to the other side.'

Stone reached into the box, grabbed a grenade and, in one movement, took out the pin.

Instinctively, the veteran troopers dived to the floor of the boat.

Moments later they heard a splash.

They waited.

With a whoosh, a bellow and an infernal roar, water, fish and debris showered them, the boat lurching one way, then the other.

They picked themselves up, throwing dead fish back in the water.

Stone looked at them, a triumphant expression on his face, a large dead salmon sitting on his lap.

'Now, we know what to do,' he said, calmly. 'We blow the shit out of them.' He glanced down. 'I've even caught your breakfast.'

TWELVE
INTO THE FOG

After only a couple of paces, the unforgiving fog surrounded them. When they turned back, a wall of white obscured the cottage.

By the time they reached the boulder with 'Eden Cottage' inscribed on it, Old Man Wood, Isabella, Daisy and Archie couldn't tell which way they had come from, or indeed which way they had to go. And for a journey that would usually take no more than a minute, it felt as if half an hour had passed.

'Listen Arch, stop kicking my heels, or I'm going to belt you,' Daisy said, as he stumbled into her for the fourth time.

'I'm not doing it on purpose!' he cried. 'It's just that you keep stopping and I can't see you,' he replied. 'And for some reason, you won't turn on your eyes.'

'Well, I can't,' she snapped. 'I can't concentrate, other things on my mind.' She took a couple of deep breaths trying to eradicate the haunting image of Gus and Kemp from her head. 'Give me a minute will you, I need a little more time to compose myself.'

'Well, in that case, I'm going to keep walking into you, whether you like it or not. At this rate, we'll never get to the ruin.'

Isabella stopped and braced herself as everyone crashed into her.

Collectively, they groaned.

'Let's hook up,' Isabella said. 'I'll guide you with my hands, but whatever you do, don't let go. Daisy, are you ready yet?'

'Yeah, I think so. Sure. Sorry.' Her eyes suddenly blazed like headlights on a car.

'At last,' Archie said. 'And brighter than before—nice one, sis.'

Isabella had an idea. 'Somewhere in Tibet, I think, blind monks, walk for miles with a bell jangling at the front to warn people they're coming and then line up behind one another with a hand on the shoulders of the person in front. Let's try it. Means we won't keep crashing. If anyone takes their hand off, remove yours and stop.'

Daisy led from the front burning the fog out of the way followed by Isabella, a hand on her shoulder, her brow set in concentration as she gently manoeuvred her sister lightly left or right as necessary. Behind her, and with his hand on her shoulder was Archie and taking up the rear was Old Man Wood.

Moving faster, they passed familiar landmarks; craggy boulders, dips in the track, trees they identified now stripped bare by the rain. As Daisy cleared a path before her, the dense fog soon folded around them like a sheet.

On and on they went, their rhythm steady, listening, alert to any sound.

'OUCH!' Old Man Wood suddenly yelled, his cries echoing back at them eerily. He raised his hand to his ear. 'Something bleeding bit me!'

They stopped.

Old Man Wood rubbed his lobe, finding a hard lump. 'Be on your guard my littler folk,' he whispered. 'I reckon an almighty bug or such like has just attacked me. Stick tight now.'

They huddled closer together, keeping silent. Now and then, Daisy turned sharply to avoid puddles or rocks, or fallen branches and, when necessary, informed them of upcoming obstacles and holes in the ground.

As they wound their way ever closer to the ruin on the edge of the Yorkshire Moors, every footstep was magnified in the watery void. Every breath they took reverberated inside their heads.

THIRTEEN
A SHOCKING REVEAL

Old Man Wood groaned. 'Now then, Daisy, do you mind if we take a break. Feeling apple-tired; all come over.'

They paused by a rock which Old Man Wood lent into, yawning.

'This fog,' Isabella said quietly, 'I suppose it's not all bad. I mean, at least the serpent won't be able to look into our eyes, will he?'

'What do you mean "look into our eyes"?' Archie whispered. 'Like hypnosis?'

'Bells dreamt of being hypnotised by a serpent,' Daisy remarked casually. 'It suffocates us before pulling us apart, limb from limb. Then, it rips out our eyes and sucks our bodies dry.'

'Thank you for that, Daisy.' Isabella said flatly. 'I'm freaked enough just being here…'

A foul, cackling, evil, hyena-like bark filled the air, and several animal noises echoed back. Shivers ran down their bodies.

'Crickeymoses!' Isabella said. 'Was that it?'

'Sounds like our friend is on the move,' Daisy whispered. 'It's the same as we heard earlier. Still a little way off, I think.'

But Daisy couldn't figure out from where a low, chattering noise was coming. 'Do you hear that?' she whispered. 'Listen.'

The noise increased, especially when Daisy moved nearer to Isabella.

'Hang on!' She sidled next to Isabella's head. 'It's your teeth, Bells.'

'Very funny,' Isabella said. 'I'm just cold.'

'She's terrified, more like,' Archie said, almost gleefully.

'Of course, I bloody am,' she shivered. 'I have some idea what this thing can do. It's lethal.' Then she added, 'aren't you?'

'Nah,' he replied. 'For some reason, I'm feeling incredibly calm and happy. Odd, isn't it.' Archie draped an arm around her. 'Don't worry, sis, if we play our cards right, everything will be just fine.'

They continued until at last they reached the outer boulders of the ruin passing several well-known, bulkier stones and the skeletal frame of a doorway.

'By the way, anyone got any idea what we're looking for?' Daisy whispered. 'A hole, a gate … a trapdoor?'

The strange bark rang out.

'OW!' Daisy cried, as she thrust her fingers in her ears losing her concentration. Her eye-lights extinguished.

Isabella swore.

All of a sudden, they were stranded, as blind as bats in the thick foggy soup.

They felt their way to a larger rock and cowered down. Immediately, stampeding noises, hooves thudding on the harder stony ground came directly at them and then moved swiftly away.

'Cattle? Sounds like a lot of them,' Archie said, quietly. 'It's like something is chasing them.'

Blinded by the fog, it was impossible to tell.

'Curl up in a ball—all of you—don't move a muscle,' Old Man Wood whispered, 'No sudden movements. Something strange out there—I can feel it in my bones.'

Now the sounds grew as though more animals joined the

stampede. Then, a flapping noise, like the giant beating of wings whomped and flip-flapped over their heads, turbulence stirring the fog, the odour of rotting flesh momentarily drifting over them. Just as they were about to stand up, the giant wingspan whooshed over them, faster this time, a sense of urgency about it, long claws brushing the rock above them.

'It flies!' Isabella squeaked. 'It's a…'

'It's a massive dragon,' Daisy said, coolly turning her head skywards. 'I've always wanted to see a dragon.'

'Me too,' Archie whispered. 'At least it won't be a surprise later.'

Daisy flinched, looking up.

'What is it, Daisy?'

'A noise,' she said. 'A sound that reminds me of those lightning bolts.'

Above them, the dragon released a huge stream of fire which ripped into the cloud, melting it, illuminating the area like daylight. Then it roared.

Daisy plugged her ears. 'It's coming around,' she squealed, as they huddled tight under the stone. The beast circled and, with another ear-splitting sound, the mix between a bark and a trumpet, it ejected another long burst of flame, continuing until the area around them had no fog remaining.

Then the creature simply vanished.

Isabella stood up smartly, her face like snow.

'Bells?' Archie cried. 'What the—'

Without hesitating or looking back, Isabella turned and sprinted into the fog.

FOURTEEN

SOLOMON AND SUE MAKE A PLAN

'Well, quite frankly, I've never seen anything like it,' Solomon exclaimed as he rushed around packing a rucksack. 'I knew something was up—from the books in the library mainly and from the stained-glass window, but in all honesty, that hologram show was quite remarkable.'

Sue smiled. 'Crazy isn't it? I mean, who would believe that the de Lowes were chosen to save everyone, and just because they live with Old Man Wood. Doesn't seem particularly fair to them. In fact, it's not especially fair on the planet, is it?'

She filled a couple of water bottles and gave him one. 'What's the plan?'

'My dear,' Solomon began rubbing his head. 'I suggest we head out into the fog and do whatever we can to mislead anyone who happens to be sniffing around. I'll try and set up the transistor radio to confuse them, but otherwise, I think we might just have to make it up as we go.'

'What if they catch us?'

Solomon slipped his glasses up his nose. 'I suggest we do whatever we can to feign our innocence in the whole matter. For example, if they ask what we're doing out in the fog, tell them we heard noises and came to investigate. If they don't believe us, tell them you got lost. They're hardly going to argue with that because I imagine, out there, we will almost certainly have no idea where we're heading. How does that sound?'

'Simple plans are often the best,' she replied. 'And if we get separated?'

'I suggest you go on your own. We've both got food and water for a day or so, and I can't believe this fog will hang around permanently. You may as well head towards the ruin, that's the likeliest spot these events are going to develop. And besides, according to Daisy, that was the last known position of Gus. You may wish to see if you can find him.'

She knew Solomon didn't mean to hurt her feelings by mentioning Gus. But all the same, it took considerable effort to fight off tears.

'Are you ready?' she said, donning her coat.

'Yes, indeed. I'll quickly radio HQ and give them an update. I'll let them know that we've been looking through the pictures—but with no joy, thus far.' He smiled at her thinly. 'That can't really rouse Stone's suspicions—if he's there.'

A short while later, holding a rucksack each, which they'd discovered in the boot room, they ducked through the soupy fog towards Mrs Pye's apartment.

'Sue,' Solomon whispered, 'there's a camera that looks like one of those small, pill-like round batteries nestled on a frame around a portrait picture of the family. Understand? So, make sure you're seen—it'll have the effect of making sure they know we're doing what we said we would be doing. A nice touch.'

Soon, Sue trundled slowly down the staircase to Solomon.

'Everything all right, dear girl?'

'Mrs Pye's very upset,' she said. 'She sits there silently, rocking backwards and forwards as if she's trapped in a kind of meditational enchantment. Probably shock.'

'Oh dear,' Solomon said.

'It's as if she knows that the people she loves most in the world are about to be taken away from her for evermore.'

Solomon draped a friendly arm around her. 'Dear Mrs

Pye has had an awfully rum time of it, hasn't she? The thing is,' he continued, staring into the fog, 'If they don't come back, then I suppose she's right. But then it's the same with all of us, I suppose. Come on. Let's see what we can do to help, however futile our distraction-methods prove to be.'

They stepped out of the courtyard in the general direction of the track.

'This is ridiculous,' she said. 'I can't see a thing.'

'Great deeds have often been forged from such reckless endeavours,' he replied. 'I'm afraid we may get a little bashed as we go. Be prepared for a rough ride.'

Sue felt comforted by his words, knowing that the headmaster found the going as tricky and as fool-hardy as she did.

FIFTEEN

ISABELLA RUNS

A rchie and Daisy looked at each other and burst out laughing.

Very shortly they heard a "doff" followed by a yowl.

Archie exploded into hysterics.

'She's run straight into a tree,' Daisy chuckled, staring intently into the fog. 'I will never, ever let her live this one down. Come on, Archie. We'd better go and sort her out.'

Isabella lay on the ground but when she heard the twins, she shifted, sat up and rubbed her head.

'Don't you dare say a thing,' she said, massaging her scalp. 'I don't know what came over me but ... anyway. Woo. Groggy.'

'Are you all right?'

'Spinning. Phew, a bit of a headache.' She took a couple of deep breaths. 'Think it's OK now. Truly, I feel as fresh as a daisy. Like you,' she exclaimed, pointing at Archie, 'Where am I? Are you a good one, or a bad one?'

Archie and Daisy exchanged a confused glance.

'Um. A good one, I think—'

And then she sang a scale like an opera singer. 'La, la, la, LAAA!'

'Sshh, Bells, ssh. Shut up,' Daisy whispered.

But Isabella merely looked past her as if she didn't exist. 'Tra-la-la-LAAA!'

'Bells, Please, for goodness' sake, quieten down, or we've had it.'

'La-la-la-Liii.'

Archie put a finger to his forehead and twirled it around, 'She's away with the fairies.'

'That's all very well, but she's going to get us killed.' Daisy held two fingers out. 'Bells! How many fingers?'

'Ten,' Isabella answered. 'Okay, eight.'

Daisy frowned. 'What's your name?'

'Prime Minister de Lowe at your service,' she said. 'And I have eight children whose names all begin with "K". Keith, Kelvin, Kev, Karl, Kathy, Kate, Kitty and Kat.'

Archie started tittering. Daisy punched his arm.

'And where do you live?'

'Buckingham Palace,' Isabella said abruptly, before roaring with laughter and slapping the tree in front of her. 'Oh, aren't you gorgeous,' she said, as she wrapped her arms around it and moved in for a hug.

Daisy's face said it all. 'Unexpectedly big problem, Arch,' she said. 'She's got a massive concussion.'

'Old Man Wood's Resplendix Mix! That'll sort her out.' The strange medicine Old Man Wood had found in his cellar had already cured them of multiple injuries after the storm.

'Sure. Definitely worth a try,' Daisy said. 'Only, I don't know if it works on brains. I hope he remembered to bring it … bit of a classic if he hasn't.' She looked over towards the rock where they'd left the old man. 'Archie, you stay here and make sure she doesn't do anything too stupid—try and calm her down, talk to her about something she's familiar with— meteorology or science or anatomy or something nerdy—I'll get Old Man Wood. Back in a tick.'

She dashed off.

A short while passed. Isabella sang a couple of chart hits, followed by, Archie thought, the Song of the Trees from when they'd found the first tablet with swishing, whirring, gurgling and whooshing noises spilling from her mouth.

Daisy's lighted eyes and slurping footsteps made him turn. 'How's she doing—any better?'

Archie shook his head. 'No. Worse, if anything. Any luck with the Resplendix Mix?'

Daisy sighed. 'Right, a couple of things. Good news or bad news?'

'Good news, first,' he replied.

'There isn't any. In fact, Arch, this entire thing is turning into a complete disaster. The first thing is that, just beyond the rock, sitting quietly in the courtyard are literally all the animals from the hills and zoos—'

'Zoos? Animals?' he replied incredulously. 'Animals?'

'Yes, four-legged things,' she chided. 'All kinds. They appear to be waiting for us. God knows why, but I'm not sure it's good. You'll see them in a minute.'

'What's the other thing?'

'Old Man Wood's out like a light. I slapped him and pinched him, and then I kicked him and … well, nothing. He's sound asleep. I searched his pockets but only found the jam jar where he'd put the Havilarian Toadstool powder poison.

'The toadstool poison that nearly killed him?'

'Yup, that same vile stuff.'

'What about the Resplendix Mix?'

'Ah. There isn't any. Unless he's hidden it in his pants.' She kicked a loose stone which flew into the fog. 'Typical. Just when we really, really, really need him, he's gone and done it again.'

SIXTEEN
AN UNEXPECTED ARRIVAL

J anana, a small dreamspinner, squeezed her invisible
spider-like form underneath Old Man Wood's knees and
began to administer the dream made by Genesis and
given to her by Gaia.

With every breath of the old man, the dreamspinner
moved her many legs and claws to blend the powders and
then sprinkled them at precisely the right time and rate so
that the dream was just right.

And when it was done, without anyone knowing, or
caring, or having the slightest inkling of what was happening,
she inverted through her maghole and away into the universe.

ARCHIE AND DAISY sat behind the rock, trying to figure out
what to do next.

'If we leave him here,' Archie said, 'he'll get eaten—either
by the beast or by that lot over there.'

'But we have to leave him here,' Daisy reasoned. 'How
can we possibly move him? And anyway, what about Isabella?
We can't go without her.'

'Agreed,' Archie said. 'Look, I'll carry him on my back,
while you escort Isabella.'

'That's ridiculous…' Then she thought about it. 'You're going to do your superman-boy bit, aren't you?'

Archie grinned.

Noises approached—hooves in the mud. Daisy and Archie froze. 'I think it's the old deer I saw earlier,' she whispered.

'An old dear?'

'No, not one of those, a real one, you dumb…'

'Heirs of Eden,' said a deep, powerful voice, 'we await your instructions. The Song of Awakening called us. Time draws on. You must open the labyrinth. We must all face our future.'

Daisy squeezed the little lyre she'd put in her pocket.

Archie stood up, feeling his heart thumping in his chest. A colossal reindeer, an impressive crown of antlers nestled above its his head, stood in front of him, flanked by a grey wolf, a black bull, a fox with a bushy tail and an eagle.

'Who are you?' Archie said, nervously.

'We offer our services to you,' the wolf said, bowing its head.

'Offer your services?' Archie said, noting the size and sharpness of its teeth.

'We come to help the Heirs of Eden,' the booming voice of the reindeer said. 'If you do not find the tablet, we perish too.'

Archie looked confused.

The bull, Burger, blew out of his nose 'Ancient lore says that other humans may not enter the labyrinth. However, those with hooves and claws and fur and flight are free to pass.'

Archie and Daisy hadn't even registered this consequence, and the idea that their status made them responsible for the entire animal kingdom temporarily rendered them speechless.

'How many,' Daisy squeaked, 'are you?'

'We come as one body in every shape and size from every part of this land and from over the waters where possible. We are your shield; we are your protectors.'

'Holy-smoke,' Daisy said out-loud. 'Er, your deeriness,' she began, 'would you mind if I speak to my er… colleague alone for a few moments.'

'My name is Thunderfoot. Do as you wish.'

Daisy marched off to the side dragging Archie with her. 'Blimey! Firstly, have you noticed that we're both speaking fluent "animal"! Awesome—I don't even know how! Secondly, what the hell are we supposed to do?'

Archie shrugged. 'Dunno. I suppose we've got to find this labyrinth entrance. We could ask them if they've got any ideas? What do you think?'

'Yeah. I've got a bit of a brain-freeze,' Daisy said, running a hand through her hair. 'I'm guessing that in the animal kingdom, this "legend" you know, us, has been passed down from year to year, whereas we, the human race, have had to rely on Old Man Wood. That's pretty crappy, right?'

Archie nodded and took her hand. 'Then remember, Daisy, that we're these special Heirs of Eden or whatever, so I think they're expecting us to be, like, super-amazing.' He winked. 'Statesman-like-ish, yeah?'

'Yeah, I think I get it,' she tapped him gently on his arm. 'We can definitely crush this, bro.'

'Crush it,' he repeated, trying to think what on earth he was going to say. 'I wish Old Man Wood would wake up.'

They returned to the animals. Daisy looked from one animal to the next. 'So, what next. Pray tell?' She said, immediately reddening. She sounded so amateur.

Thunderfoot tossed his head. 'We will protect you, to give you time, though it be bloody and at great cost. Gorialla Yingarna is, in one moment a huge meat-eating dragon with fire in its belly and the next a small, venomous slithering snake. However, in all known time, the Council of the Great Kingdom of Animals has identified one possible weakness.'

'Only one?' Archie whispered. 'In all of time…'

'That sounds like a pretty long time,' Daisy added, cringing. 'And, this one weakness is…?'

Thunderfoot pawed the ground. 'Gorialla Yingarna is

cold-blooded. She changes only into cold-blooded animals. Therefore, the beast will tire if it does not feed regularly. The more energy Gorialla Yingarna expends, the greater your chances.'

'That's the weakness?' Daisy said.

Thunderfoot raised his head up and down which, to all intents and purposes signalled to Daisy that it was.

'And, do you have a plan?'

The animals confirmed that they did.

'Well, that's great,' Archie said, enthusiastically.

Daisy coughed. 'You may tell us what it is.'

The huge grey wolf with a black stripe that extended in a single line from the tip of his nose all the way to the end of his tail stepped forward. 'I am Icefang, Slayer of cold northern lands where the sky dances. When the entrance seal breaks, magic is released. From that moment, the beast is free to kill not just for food but for pleasure. You will need our help.'

'And where is the entrance?' Archie said.

'That is for you to find.'

'Great,' Daisy whispered to Archie. 'What a belter: Isabella knocked out, Old Man Wood asleep, another bleeding riddle to figure out.' She addressed the animals. 'How do we do that?'

'You are the Heirs of Eden?' the fox piped up, a tone of disappointment in his reedy voice. 'We are led to believe that you have been shown these things. Did you not understand?'

The animals grunted and groaned.

Archie needed to buy some time. 'We are waiting for the old man to wake and for Isabella to come to her senses. Please, if you don't mind holding on for a bit, I'm sure it's only a temporary thing. He is quite old you know.' He flicked a glance over his shoulder.

Daisy understood. 'We'll check on him and be back in just a mo.'

The fox snarled as the two young humans slipped out of sight. 'Friends,' he said, stepping forward and then turning to the congregation. 'With respect, these Heirs of Eden are but children. They are cubs. Look at them,' he said dryly. 'They will fail, miserably.' He turned. 'I will order my band to leave so they may spend their last hours foraging in the wreckage of the storm. It will be better that way.'

'You will do no such thing, Red,' Thunderfoot said. 'They have been chosen for a reason. You must trust the energies of the universe.'

'A universe which sends children to save us deserves everything it gets.'

The bull pawed the earth. 'We are too far gone to leave now, Red. Let us go to our ends with an honourable fight.'

'Aye,' the great eagle said flapping its wings. 'Death is inevitable. Let us go with dignity. We birds will stay.'

The fox backed away and turned its pointed nose up at them. 'I will ask my band of animals what their will is.'

He trotted off, just as Archie returned.

'Friends. Do you know exactly what lies under here? Does anyone know how the labyrinth is laid out?'

Icefang stepped forward. 'That is for the old man to tell. Legend has it that it starts with a big cavern. Paths wind and turn until the belly is reached. Discomfort, anxiety and worry grow in the marrow of those who journey to the middle.'

'And, all the while,' Archie asked, 'the monster can change into any reptile?'.

'Indeed. The stories say that it is cunning and merciless, and must never be bargained with. It will never do anything for another that does not accelerate its own purpose.'

'And it fears nothing,' the eagle said, bowing her head. 'The beast is cruel. Ancient birds recorded that the beast would toy with its prey, like a cat.'

Archie rubbed a hair spike. 'Who is best to spot when the beast changes.'

The eagle flapped her wings. 'Creatures of the skies have sharp eyes. We see all that is below. We watch, and we warn as it roams within these walls,' the eagle added.

'And it cannot get away from here?' Daisy said.

'Until Gorialla Yingarna defeats the Heirs of Eden, it is held within these ancient walls.'

'Good,' Archie said, as a plan started forming. 'How many birds have we, eagle?' he asked.

The magnificent golden bird shook her head. 'Many, of all types.'

'And how many of the groundlings—badgers, rabbits, weasels, squirrels, stoats those creatures?'

'They too are numerous.'

'Good,' Archie said as he clapped his hands. 'Let me recap. This monster, being cold-blooded must keep feeding to sustain its energy, right? And you will do whatever it takes to protect us?'

'That is the lore,' Thunderfoot replied.

Archie puffed out his chest. 'Then we have an advantage it cannot have imagined,' he said addressing them one by one. 'Creatures big or small, have but one set of eyes. If it is a tiny snake or even a wriggling newt, those creatures nearer the ground must attack the eyes of the beast. Make sure the ground animals go in groups deep into these passages. Eagle, your birds must do likewise; divide into patrols, some far into the labyrinth and some close at hand. If the beast becomes a flying dragon, target its eyes with your claws and beaks. They must charge without regard and with all the bravery they can muster. By relentlessly attacking its eyes in small numbers, we will keep the beast moving. You must not give it time to feed. If this is successful, it may retreat or make a mistake or do something that assists us in our quest to find the tablet.'

A murmur of approval broke out among the gathering.

The eagle flapped its wings. 'I will tell fox that the Heirs of Eden are not merely cubs, after all. There is hope, still.' The eagle launched itself into the air.

Thunderfoot nestled closer to Archie. 'Why does the old man sleep?'

Archie shrugged. 'I don't know. Look, don't you worry, he kind of does this a lot—he's super-old. He'll be up soon though. I'm sure he'll be alright.' Archie hoped like mad he'd done enough to win them over.

He nudged Daisy who, he noticed, was staring at him with her mouth open.

'Creatures,' Archie continued. 'Generous, valued animals and birds of this planet that we share, it's time we got a move on—'

'Yeah,' Daisy said, punching the air. 'Gather your tribes, dudes. Let's find the entrance to this thing and go and kick some butt.' She winked at her brother.

Archie marched over to where the old man was snoring. In one go he picked him up and, without straining a muscle, hauled him up until he was draped entirely over his shoulder like a large rug.

The bull followed him. 'Do you wish to lay him over me, young Heir of Eden?'

Archie smiled. 'Thanks for the offer. But in all honesty, it's really no big deal.'

SEVENTEEN
KEMP TELLS SUE WHY

Sue picked her way over the tree stumps and rocks bashing her shins on the jagged surfaces and grazing her limbs on fallen branches for what felt like the millionth time. She rubbed her bruises and traced her fingers over a multitude of small cuts.

She had lost Solomon shortly after they thought they had found the track. A fallen tree had blocked their path and, while Solomon clambered over it, Sue decided to go around it. There she slipped and fell careering head over heels out of control before landing in a pool of mud.

She'd replied to Solomon's concerned calls, yelling up to him she was OK. They decided that to communicate, they'd make owl-hooting noises; twit-twos, with the knuckle of their hands.

She didn't mind being separated from him, lovely though he was. Eating at her heart was Gus. His toothy grin wouldn't leave her alone.

Gus and Kemp had fought on the ruin, Daisy said, under the gaze of a strange monster, who kept changing into different creatures—a massive python one minute or a dragon the next followed by a cobra with a hood over its eyes.

Daisy told them that the boys had given each other a terrible hammering until Gus fell hard. She remembered how tears had rolled down Daisy's cheeks, how Daisy couldn't look anyone in the eye. Then, she told them, he'd collapsed and disappeared.

The thought of this made Sue determined to go to the ruin for herself. But of course, in the blinding fog, she had no way of knowing where she was. And, wallowing in despair, she'd tripped on a dangling root and fallen again, tumbling further downhill, colliding with branches, collecting mud and bruises, unable to get a foothold or a hand-hold as she fell, desperate to cling on, to hold onto something that would break her fall.

When her battered body finally came to a shuddering halt in a pool of muddy water, she found, much to her surprise, after checking herself over, that she hadn't sustained any lasting or, she hoped, permanent injuries.

She stumbled on, finding that moving on her hands and knees was her safest mode of transport even if the going was slow and uphill. She knew she had to find the track at the top. Then, with any luck, a left turn would lead her straight to the ruin.

She scrambled up a small hillock, her calf muscles straining as they pushed down to lever her up. The higher she went, the more she noted that the fog had lightened. Visibility, she guessed, was now a metre or two.

She sat down to catch her breath when suddenly a hand clamped tight around her mouth.

'Shhhh,' a familiar voice said. 'Lie down, behind the rock.'

She struggled, trying to scream.

'Don't move a muscle, Sue. I swear, if you don't shut up and remain completely silent, you're going to be caught.'

Kemp?

At that moment, the stomping of boots broke into the small space directly in front of her on the other side of a large rock.

'Look, very carefully over there, Sue,' the voice whispered in her ear again. 'It's Commissioner Stone. If he finds you here, you know what he'll do to you. And believe me, his method of interrogation is liable to be painful.'

The hand was removed, and she found herself turning to see the bald head of Kemp eyeing the troops as they collected in front of them, the far side of the boulder.

His expression implored her, a finger to his lips, to keep silent. She did.

The three troops murmured amongst themselves when the distinct tone of Stone's slight Yorkshire lilt rose above them. 'Team two. Team two, do you read me?' the commissioner said, talking into his radio.

The radio hissed and crackled. 'Come in, team-leader.'

'Are the traps laid? Trip wires rolled out?'

'Affirmative.'

'Good. Anything else to report?'

'A couple of the crew reported seeing light through the fog, sir.'

'Exactly what kind of light? Over.'

'A glow, sir. Faintly—pink to orange in colour. Mills thought it might be a flamethrower, sir.'

Stone flicked a lump of mud off his boot. 'Interesting, where did it come from?'

'Our coordinates point to the ruined castle on top of the hill, sir, over.'

The radio remained quiet as Stone pondered the news.

'What are your coordinates right now, Talbot?'

Stone signalled for the man next to him to record where it was.

'Right, I'll tell you what we'll do,' he said. 'I'll get the boys to engage our flamethrower and give it a blast into the air. From your position, can you see if the light looks similar and then report in. We might have company, so full alert from now on in. Over.'

EIGHTEEN

FINDING THE ENTRANCE

A lthough he was almost entirely swamped by the old man, whose head and feet dangled only a few inches from the ground, Archie casually tilted his head towards the band of animals. 'Tell the fox and his kin and pass on our plan to all the groundlings. Eagle, do the same with yours.'

The animals made affirmative noises as Isabella rounded the corner.

Isabella clapped her hands playfully and burst into song, 'Oh! We're going to Ibiza ... we're going to the morning sun, oh! We're going to Ibiza ... whoa.' She studied the scene, rubbing the bull and wolf on their coats.

'Wow, the zoo just turned up,' she said, before dancing off out behind a stone.

Archie faced them, his face beetroot. 'Sorry. She's had a bit of a bash on the head.'

'I'm not sure I can take much more of her,' Daisy said. 'Arch, I hope you know what you're doing.'

Isabella reappeared shaking her head. 'Where's the hotel? I can't remember where it went.'

An idea shot into Archie's head. 'Yes, you can,' he said, gently. He wondered if she might be referring to the entrance. 'Why don't you take us all there?'

Daisy cottoned on remembering Isabella's extraordinary

guiding skills when she'd navigated the sports field in the torrential rain. 'Yeah! We could have a bit of a party in your hotel room, right?'

Archie frowned and turned back to the animals. 'My sister will lead us. Go now, back to your brethren, tell them what is about to happen. You will know when we have found the entrance. When the time comes, don't hesitate or flounder. Be filled with courage and greatness. We will be waiting for you.'

'WHERE DID I PUT IT?' Isabella said holding her hand out at right angles. 'Somewhere over here, I'm sure.'

'Go for it, Bells,' Archie said. 'I'm sure you know where it is.'

Daisy prodded Archie in the back. 'You're suddenly all confident,' she said. 'What makes you so certain we'll succeed?'

'Because we dreamt about meeting and talking with the Ancient Woman,' Archie said, jogging the old man on his shoulder casually. 'All our dreams are based on truth—they're real. So finding this tablet must be possible. I suddenly realised that as long as we believe in ourselves, no matter what, above everything else, we can succeed.'

Daisy raised her eyebrows. 'OK. But what makes you think Bells can find this entrance now that she's gone totally crackers?'

'Dunno,' he said. 'Just do. It's around here, somewhere, I'm sure.'

A commotion to their left stopped them dead in their tracks, like statues. Up until now, they had sensed that a body of assorted animals had been following them; their hooves occasionally clacking and clipping on rock or stone. But now, the animals began running in circles as if trying to avoid being snared.

'Quick, under here!' Archie said, lowering the old man. The children nestled under the overhang of rock and listened.

They held their breath as the commotion around them increased. Something was going to happen. They could feel it.

A part of a snake's body slithered out of the fog past their hiding place. Instinctively, Daisy lent over and muffled Isabella's mouth before she had a chance to scream. 'Oh my God!' she squeaked. It's the width of a slide.'

'More like an oil drum,' Archie whispered back, as he sat on top of Isabella. 'Why are they running?'

'If I were them, I'd run too!' Daisy whispered. 'It's probably hungry?'

A strange noise filled the air, like an old tractor spluttering into life. The noise grew louder and louder until it reached a frenzied pitch and stayed there. The sheep were darting in and out, bleating and snorting like crazy. Daisy covered her ears as the noise reached a climax.

The children weren't expecting to see the serpent's head. But when it burst out of the fog a couple of feet from them, Daisy and Archie smacked their heads together trying to recede even further under the hard incline.

Its head looked like a red dragon or a Tyrannosaurus Rex, Daisy thought, with jaws stuffed full of sharp white teeth. Its marbled green eyes were the size of cricket balls, and two small arms with clawed talons protruded out of its thick body.

The dragon swooped high above them silently, only the beating of its wings making any sound. It was as though the engine had been turned off, and then with a whoosh followed by a sickening crunch it pounced.

Only the desperate bleating of the sheep could be heard until this too faded away.

The children, crammed under the rock, breathed hard. For a while, none of them dared to make a move or speak.

Eventually, Archie, fed up with having a slither of rock digging into his side and Old Man Wood snoring on the other moved out into the open and broke the silence, 'OK. Sure, it's pretty big, but we can do this. I mean, it wasn't that big.'

'Not that big?' Daisy responded incredulously.

Isabella stared at him. 'The hotel is over there,' she said, 'by the cafe.'

With Old Man Wood once again balanced over his shoulder, Archie grabbed her hand. 'Excellent, Bells. Lead the way. Let's check in.'

They moved off, Isabella singing as she went until she stopped by a large, semi-domed grey boulder.

Archie looked at the rock. 'Daisy, quick update. What's the beast doing?'

Daisy poked her head around the corner. 'Urrghh!' Daisy replied. 'It's now a huge snake, pulling the entire sheep into its mouth as though on a conveyor belt.'

'Gross,' Archie said. 'It's our chance to find the entrance.'

'You're kidding me.'

'No, I'm not. Come on, hurry!'

'Seriously, Arch? We don't have the faintest idea where it is,' Daisy said. 'And anyway Bells is a wreck. She couldn't guide us to a science lab even if the words were written on the door.'

'What do you suggest then?' Archie countered, his voice barely above a whisper. 'Stay here in the fog? Offer ourselves up as a dessert? If we can discover the end of the snake—it might lead us to somewhere near to the entrance. Come on.' He smiled at Isabella. 'Lead on, Miss Einstein.'

Archie, with the old man draped over him, followed Isabella who danced and skipped and sang all the way to a position some distance behind the head of the beast.

'Over here,' Archie whispered. 'Look!' He pointed to the outline of the main body of the serpent that stretched and wove around several rocks dotted nearby.

Archie put a finger to his lips. 'Not ... a ... sound!'

Very quietly the children tiptoed around the rocks following the thick black scales until they came to an obelisk-shaped rock the size of a small pickup truck.

The children stared at it in dismay.

'It stops,' Daisy whispered. 'It doesn't make sense.'

'The entrance must be around here somewhere,' Archie

said. He disappeared into the gloom as far as he dared before feeling his way back.

The tail moved, and the children backed away, behind a rock.

When they looked again, there was no sign of the tail at all.

Daisy crept nearer to the rock and peered around it, trying to see if there was another way. 'Why are these things always so damn complicated?' she said. 'All these silly tricks and weird magic.'

Archie attempted a shrug.

Daisy walked around the boulder one more time. Returning, she raged. 'This is stupid. I don't understand and, I don't know about you, but I'm getting pretty fed up.' Annoyed, she kicked out at the stone.

But instead of impacting on the hard surface, her foot continued on its arc, and Daisy found herself connecting with thin air. The next thing she knew, she had landed firmly and somewhat painfully on her bottom.

Archie, watching, burst out laughing, trying hard to contain himself. But when Daisy walloped his leg to shut him up, it only made matters worse. He found himself chuckling so hard that his shoulders began to gallop up and down.

And now Isabella was roaring with laughter too.

'You're going to get us killed,' Daisy said. 'Shut up, both of you.'

Archie tried to bring his coat to his face to smother the noise but, in the process, he lost his hold on Old Man Wood. He swayed, but couldn't re-balance and, as he pushed a hand out to steady himself against the hard surface, the two of them toppled through, disappearing.

'I don't believe it!' Daisy huffed suddenly feeling incredibly vulnerable.

'Wasn't that utterly hysterical,' Isabella said, slapping her leather trousers. 'I wonder if there's a taxi?'

Daisy's face was thunderous. 'Hysterical?' I'll give you—'

An ear-splitting cough echoed around them.

Daisy instinctively crouched and turned. Marble-like, luminous-green eyes stared directly into theirs.

'Don't look at it!' Daisy shrieked. But already Isabella was staring back, transfixed, her eyes large and watery, unblinking. Hypnotised.

Daisy shielded her eyes and shuffled in front of her sister. 'Bells,' she said, slapping her sister hard on the bum. No reaction. 'Only one thing for it, sis,' she said. She hugged her. 'Let's hope this works...'

And with a big shove, she pushed her sister, at the same time launching herself. Moments later both had disappeared into thin air straight through the obelisk.

NINETEEN
ISABELLA'S MEETING

As she grappled with the feeling of airlessness, of sailing through the hole, a dark voice had entered Isabella's mind.

The huge reptile with the dragon's head had spoken to her intimately, right inside her brain, full of intent, menace, pain and destruction.

'Daughter of Adam,' it had said. 'You have arrived at long last. Welcome to my labyrinth. You come in here with nothing, and you will never leave. There will be no trace of your passing through these walls. Soon, I will be free.'

Isabella shuddered as the ground hit her. Her legs folded on the rocky surface and her head smacked on the rock below.

She lay still, seeing stars. A curious swimming sensation washed over her as if her head had, momentarily, been injected with jelly.

Isabella groaned and pulled herself into a sitting position. She dabbed at the impact mark on her skull wondering if she could feel the stickiness of blood running through her fingers.

Blinking, she examined her hands. Clear. As reality set in, and her mind returned to normal, Isabella tried to recall what had happened. The one thing she truly understood was that the beast was far, far worse than anything she had ever dreamed.

TWENTY

KEMP EXPLAINS

With clinks and metallic snaps of the thrower coming together and the general stomping of the soldiers' boots, Kemp and Sue shrank down out of sight.

'What the hell are you doing here?' she seethed. 'You're the last person I want to see.'

'I needed to find you,' Kemp whispered, matter-of-factly.

Sue looked confused. 'Find me? In this? Why?'

'Because I need to tell you what happened,' he whispered. 'And I need to tell you *why* it happened.' Kemp twisted his head first one way and then the other making sure the soldiers were out of earshot.

'I'm all ears, Kemp,' she spat back.

'First things first. I'm not responsible, Sue—'

'Don't give me that—'

Kemp opened his eyes wide as imploring her to keep her voice down. 'It's this ghost, this spirit who calls himself Cain. He put both of us up to it—he made us fight each other to the death.'

'You expect me to believe that,' Sue said.

'He's the one I travelled through to get here. It's complicated, neither of us wanted it—'

'Why should I believe anything you tell me—?'

'Because you have to,' he replied. 'How else do you

account for me popping up here and there? Do you seriously believe I rowed across the flooding—without sat nav? Look, I promise you. Gus came at me as hard as anything—he had me, but...'

'But what?'

'He'd won. Here.' Kemp lifted his shirt showing a swathe of blue and black bruises.

She sucked in a breath. 'That was from Gus?'

'Yes. Then something happened—'

'What, Kemp?'

Kemp hesitated. 'I ... I was lying on the ground, finished, defeated, when I saw—out of the corner of my eye— someone hiding in a crevice, nearby.'

Sue's eyes bulged. 'Do you know who it was?'

Kemp stared at the floor.

'Who was it, Kemp?'

'It was...'

'Yes.'

'It was Daisy,' Kemp croaked. 'I could tell by the red glow of her weird eyes.'

Sue reeled. 'I don't understand. So, so what? She told us she'd seen you fight. That's how we knew he was missing—'

'But you don't know the whole story,' he cut in.

'Then tell me. I want to know everything.'

Kemp looked at his knees and took a deep breath. 'Daisy kicked a grey round stone the size of a tennis ball to me. Instinctively, I grabbed it.'

Sue's heartbeat thumped in her chest. 'Daisy gave you a weapon?'

He nodded.

'And...'

'And when Gus came over, to finish me off, I ... I swivelled and cracked him on the shin with it. He went down and...'

'And what, Kemp?' Sue said, tears rolling down her cheeks. 'What...?'

'Well, I struck him a couple of times.'

Sue shrieked into her jumper.

'I had to—'

Sue held her head and sobbed. 'You beat Gus to death with it?'

'Honestly. You've got to believe me; I didn't want to. Gus was about to do the same to me.'

'Why?' she cried. 'Why didn't you just leave him? You didn't have to.'

Kemp squeezed his eyes together, tears running over his cheeks. 'I tried. You don't understand.'

Her body convulsed. 'Don't understand? What, exactly don't I understand?'

For several moments they sat in the kind of silence you can almost touch.

Kemp knew he had nothing to lose. 'The thing is, Sue,' he said, his voice full of remorse, 'this Cain-ghost-person, believes—no, he's convinced—that the de Lowes won't make it out of this labyrinth alive.' Kemp turned on his knees to see what the soldiers were doing.

'How does this ghost-thing know?'

'Because, before this ghost-thing called Cain was burned alive, the beast belonged to him. Cain told us that until the dragon's capture nothing had ever defeated it.'

Sue's brain reeled. It was hard enough to contemplate Old Man Wood coming from a very distant past. But a ghost?

Kemp sensed her unease. 'And, even if they do get out alive, there's one other thing the de Lowes have to do,' he said, pausing and letting the hook hang.

'What's that?'

'They have to do something … unspeakable. It's so awful that, to all intents and purposes, they've already failed.'

'Are you sure? Sounds a little far-fetched to me.'

'Yes, Sue I'm positive. It's what this whole thing is about. Their failure means that disease will spread, the rain will continue, and the world will swiftly fall apart. If you could see it, you'd realise it's happening already. Why do you think the soldiers are here?'

Sue leaned her head back against the cold stone. 'Why are you telling me this, Kemp,' she said. 'There's something else, isn't there.'

Kemp's face fell. He looked away. 'I know it's pretty hard to fathom, but in return for helping him, this ghost promised me that he would save my mother and me. You see, I've never known her, and … and well, having a mother—a family—is all I've ever really wanted. It's why I'm such a mess.'

Nearby, a radio fizzed into life. Footsteps approached. They ducked down and pulled in their knees.

'You're right, though,' he whispered. 'There is one other reason.'

'Team two, come in,' Stone's distinctive voice shouted from the other side of their boulder.

'Catch that, sir. Are you ready to fire? We think we've got your position. Let's go to ignition in ten-seconds.'

Kemp whispered. 'Thing is, the ghost can save you too.'

TWENTY-ONE
OLD MAN WOOD RETURNS

Old Man Wood woke up with a start and instantly felt as if he'd been through one of Mrs Pye's spin cycles in the washing machine. His head swam with unusual shapes and images bouncing in his mind. He opened his eyes to darkness.

Someone, he sensed, was beside him. 'Eh, who's that?!' he demanded.

'Old Man Wood—you're back!' Archie cried.

'Back? Where am I?'

'The entrance to the labyrinth under the ruin! We found it —that's where we are now.'

'But how did I get here?'

Archie chuckled. 'Actually, I dropped you in it—after Daisy had made a bit of an ass of herself with an outstanding air-kick. Are you OK?'

'What happened?' Old Man Wood said, groggily. 'What's been going on?'

'One minute you were walking along complaining you'd been bitten in the ear, the next you were slumped against a rock fast asleep, snoring like a champion while we trembled for our very lives in front of a dragon. At the same time,' he continued, 'Isabella bashed her head and went mad while hundreds of animals looked on expecting us to know all the answers.'

'Answers? Animals?' he queried.

'Yep. Tons of them. Big, small, flying, quacking, bleating, barking. They're out there, and they claim they want to help us. Other than that, nothing much.'

Old Man Wood stretched out a leg, followed by the other. 'Who carried me here if I was asleep?'

'I did,' Archie said, 'until we fell through the boulder.'

'Impossible—'

'Aaaaaahh!' Daisy and Isabella tumbled and slid down the chute crash-landing next to them.

Daisy rolled, righted herself and looked around. Her sister lay still for a moment.

'Hey, Bells, you all right?' she asked, as her eyes adjusted to the light.

'Uh-huh,' Isabella eventually replied, sitting up and rubbing her head, her voice thick with confusion.

'Bells?'

'Ow,' she groaned. 'Bruised. Head … sore.'

'Archie!' Daisy said. 'Where are you?'

'Over here,' he replied, the sound of his voice echoing back. 'I think we're in a chamber of some sort.' He started chuckling again. 'Daisy, that was the funniest thing I've seen in ages. The look on your face…'

'Yeah, really hilarious.'

'By the way, Old Man Wood's woken up!'

'Does he know about the animals?'

'Ask him yourself.'

'Old Man Wood, what do you know about the animals?'

'I wish I were still asleep,' the old man moaned. 'I was having a GREAT dream—'

'Yes, but what do you know about the animals out there?'

'I wish I was still asleep too,' Isabella interrupted. 'That thing spoke to me WITHIN my head. It's going to kill us to get its freedom.'

'Bells, you're back too!' Archie said.

'Back from where?'

'A hotel, I think,' Archie said. 'We were about to have a party.'

'Really?'

'Well, yeah,' Archie said. 'To be honest, you guys have been pretty freaky. We haven't got much time—Old Man Wood, what do you know about this beast?'

'What do I know?' Old Man Wood said, thinking. 'If I recall, the beast was thrown out of the Garden for being too disruptive and dangerous. It is powerful and untrustworthy—'

'Don't tell me: it's the same snake that tempted Adam and Eve in that Creation story?'

Old Man Wood sighed. 'Well, that, littlun depends on what you believe. Now, if I recall correctly, shortly before the Great Closing of the Garden of Eden, the Beast of Havilah, also known, I believe, as Gorialla Yingarna, was tracked down, snared and summoned for execution.'

'What's it doing here?'

'I believe I offered it as an alternative.'

'You did what?!' Isabella stormed.

'I reasoned that it would be better to use the beast as the guardian of the labyrinth. Everyone agreed, and the beast was given to me.'

'How' Isabella muttered in disbelief, 'could you do something so incredibly dumb?'

'Because I needed the keeper of the third tablet here in the labyrinth to be the very best—so that everyone involved in the Great Closing would be satisfied that the Garden of Eden couldn't be found by accident or by some foolhardy adventurers. Only the real Heirs to the secrets of the Garden would succeed—still with me? You see, the beast has never lost.'

Isabella exploded. 'Have you seen this thing?' she roared. 'It's like the perfect reptilian killing machine.'

'Hmmm,' he pondered, 'I suppose that's true.' He rubbed his chin thoughtfully. 'Isn't it amazing what one can remember after a good sleep!'

'Now I wish you hadn't told us,' Isabella said. 'That information is entirely unhelpful. Will someone fill me in on what's been going on, and please, can someone find out how to get some light in here.'

TWENTY-TWO

THE BRANCHWAND

A part from the hole above, darkness hung around them like a heavy curtain.

'What's the beast doing right now?' Old Man Wood asked.

'Just before we fell in, it was eating a sheep,' Archie replied. 'Whole!'

Old Man Wood groaned as he began to stand up. 'Excellent. That'll give us time, how do you say, "*a window of opportunity*"? We must get going.'

'Where to?' Isabella asked. 'I can hardly see my hand in front of my face. Daisy, do your eye thing.'

Daisy sighed audibly, her voice quavering. 'Nice to have you back your usual cheery self, Bells. How's the head?'

'Bit sore. How about some illumination?'

Daisy didn't reply. 'I just can't – I can't concentrate on anything right now.'

'Ah-ha,' Old Man Wood cried, 'I thought I might find it somewhere. My earlobe! Of course! Here, look. Excellent!'

A glow appeared from his earlobe lighting the lined features of the side of his face. 'Ha! It's a branchwand from the Tree of Knowledge,' he said. 'Just as I dreamed a moment ago. This is wonderful news.'

'What wonderful news?' Isabella asked, her voice wobbling. 'What is that thing?'

'It's a branchwand, Isabella, that's what it is,' he said, pulling the stud out of his ear. 'You've seen them in those books of yours with wizards and witches and so forth.'

'A branch-wand?' Daisy said. 'Bit of a roundabout way of saying a "wand" isn't it?

'I suppose,' Old Man Wood said. 'But branchwands came long before there were wands,' he said, his eyes boring down onto the small stud that sat in the palm of his hand.

Daisy stood up and inspected it. 'It doesn't look like a wand; it looks like a small ear stud with a tacky light in it. Do you have any idea how it works?'

'Now then, let me see.' He held the stud out and closed his eyes.

'GAGOG, GAGOG—BARK!' the strange roar of the beast echoed down the chute and echoed through the room they were sitting in.

As one, they looked up. Scraping sounds, and growls and grunts—noises of a scuffle sounded above them.

'Hurry! Old Man Wood.'

Old Man Wood flinched and the stud fell to the floor. Light was replaced by dark. More noises spewed in from above.

'Quick! Help me find it.'

Furiously they scratched around on the floor. Archie touched what felt like a stone, and a glint of orange light radiated out. He passed it to Old Man Wood.

In silence, they watched the old man.

'I need to remember,' the old man said.

'Remember faster,' Isabella said.

He held the stud cupped in the palm of his hands.

The children held their breath as the old man scrunched up his face, deep in thought.

Old Man Wood began, his voice quiet but clear. 'Spirit of Nature, awaken, for I am a child of the universe and you are its deepest secret.'

From the tiny ear stud, there emerged a thin, gnarled twig not much longer than Old Man Wood's forearm, glowing brilliantly white and then mixing through a spectrum of colours.

Daisy squeaked, 'so your stories about turning frogs into haystacks are … TRUE!'

'Oh yes,' Old Man Wood said, using the radiating light to usher them deeper into the chamber. 'And there's more; so much more. The wizardry of old is all but lost, thanks to cars, and kettles, and life support machines, and those mobile phones of yours and all that stuff. But a long time ago, there were great wizards with great powers.'

'Where did it go?' she said. 'The magic, I mean.'

'Problems started,' he continued, 'when it became hard to tell what was real magic—that is to say, proper—magic, and what were illusions and slights-of-hand by tricksters, fraud-sters—you know the sort. You see, some magic wasn't magic at all, and then, sooner or later, confidence in the real magic deteriorated. Fear and misunderstanding took its place—'

'Excuse me,' Isabella said, her teeth chattering. 'I'm sure the legitimacy of the history of supposed magic is important, but right now we could do with some light.'

Old Man Wood flicked up the branchwand and swirled it up and then to the left in an arc. 'Illuminate the labyrinth!' he commanded. Instantly several braziers hanging on the walls burst into flames, their shadows dancing on the walls.

Daisy shielded her eyes, 'Ow! Too bright! Order your twig-thing to turn it down!'

Old Man Wood beamed with delight and barked another couple of orders, with varying results. After a couple of tries and much to everyone's astonishment, Old Man Wood managed to get the braziers to burn at a brightness that suited everyone.

TWENTY-THREE
THE HEIRS HAVE COMPANY

Now they could see, they found themselves in a cavernous shiny, damp stone chamber, its walls patterned by water that had seeped through the rock over time. Some areas were smeared with green slime, others bore the streaks of white calcium-deposit. Above them, a domed stone ceiling connected the chamber to the entrance and, on the walls, at long intervals, big, burning metal sconces, high-lighted the way to the passage into the labyrinth at the far end.

'What is a labyrinth?' Archie asked as they inspected the room. 'I mean everyone's heard of one, but what's the point of it?'

'It's a route,' Isabella rattled out, 'or a journey, that allows the person to traverse from passageway to passageway to a mid-point or central space or chamber. The path is often long and complicated by twists and turns,' she paused, catching her breath. 'A good labyrinth is said to test the spirit, the mental endurance and belief-system of the journey-taker; it is also a physical test of mind, heart and soul. After that, the route out follows an almost identical pattern to the one in—'

'So, it's different to a maze?'

'A maze is there to trick you; it's a route with false turns—

more of a puzzle, whereas a labyrinth is a path to challenge one's nerve and endurance.'

'Then, this is like a race to the middle—'

'That would depend on where the tablet is. Logically, the most secure place for the tablet would be the centre because it is only halfway. In the event that we find it there we still have to wind our way out. And that means the beast still has, in theory, a fifty percent chance of getting us.'

Archie rubbed a hair spike. 'You built it Old Man Wood —what do you know?'

The old man thought a while. 'Isabella's right, I suppose,' he replied. 'But the path is made harder because the beast can turn up at any point along the way—'

'The beast can cheat!' Isabella thundered.

'Cheat? No. I wouldn't say that. Well, not exactly,' the old man countered. 'The serpent is the guardian of the tablet, and it knows every nook and cranny. Why wouldn't it travel through the ventilation system or the water ducts? It can go where it likes within these tunnels and in whatever form it chooses.'

'This isn't getting any better.'

The commotion at the entrance of the cave increased dramatically.

'There's no time to lose,' Archie said.

'Now before you get too hasty,' Old Man Wood said, 'what was it, Daisy, that you were saying about some animals—?'

Without warning a stampede of hooves and animal groans and baas and crows and yaps grew at the chute as if a battle raged directly above them.

The four retreated, backs to the wall, listening nervously.

There was suddenly a cacophony of flapping, squeaks, squawks and squeals followed by a blizzard of feathers that flashed through the air in front of their disbelieving eyes. Then, descending the chute, was a furry conveyor belt of smaller animals; rabbits, weasels, rats and mice, to name but a few, which scurried, tumbled and slid, and then dashed out of the way.

The four humans fled to the far wall.

'Look! The eagles,' Archie cried. The birds flapped, shook out their feathers and landed in front of him.

'At your service, young Heirs of Eden. You have recovered?' the bird asked Old Man Wood.

'Welcome, eagles of the moors,' he said. 'Yes, thank you.'

As the multitude filled the chamber, the eagle they had met earlier bounced from foot to foot as if waiting for a sign.

Archie noticed. He looked from one sister to the other and then spoke to the large bird. 'Set up in groups along the passages,' he ordered. 'Take some as far as you can, to the middle if you have the numbers. Remember to tell your winged friends that they must attack the eyes, and to keep the beast moving at all times.'

A young rat cartwheeled over before careering into a rabbit, landing at Daisy's feet. Daisy eyed it curiously for a while and then bent down righting both. 'Thanks for coming, brave creatures of the moors,' she said sweetly.

'My name is Speck,' the rat gushed.

'And I'm Springer,' said the rabbit.

'Well now, Speck and Springer,' she said, copying Archie's lead. 'Take off along the passages and wait in small groups all the way until you reach the middle. Leave the strongest and the bravest till last. They will need to be patient. When the beast appears in whatever form, attack its eyes in pairs. Keep it busy for as long as you can—and make sure it does not eat. Is that clear? We're gonna wear it out, big time. Go now. Tell your comrades.'

Speck and Springer scuttled off gathering others on the way including rabbits, rats, mice and other vermin, creating a stream of fur as they hurried off down the passageway.

'Remember, go for the eyes,' she called out after them. 'Always the eyes, understand?'

'The eyes, the eyes,' they sang.

'Are there any mongooses, snakes, hedgehogs or honey-badgers in our group?' Archie said, addressing the animals.

A hawk fluttered above the body of animals searching the floor with its sharp eyes. 'There are adders, and a couple of big lazy home-snakes, many hedgehogs and other such types.

'Hawk,' Archie said, 'Make sure that the snakes, hedgehogs and mongooses patrol the vents and the smaller holes where the beast may try and crawl or wriggle through if he takes the form of, say, a lizard. Find them and get them to wait in every cavity, and every little nook. Speak to them now.'

'I understand,' the hawk said, raising himself up and dusting himself down, before taking off towards a muddled-up, knotted-looking nest of snakes.

During this time, the children had been forced back against the wall, as the flow of animals of all shapes and sizes continued to tumble down or fly in.

'I'm sure I've seen a massive cat,' Daisy said, as she joined her siblings. She inspected the crowd again, her eyes shining bright red. 'And a bear? Archie, what about you?'

But Archie was too busy thanking animals and trying to organise the smaller ones to notice.

Suddenly, the remaining sheep from Old Man Wood's flock tumbled in. Hot on their heels, Old Man Wood's cattle followed, succeeded by a curious mix of horses, foxes, badgers, roe deer and muntjac. Many bore wound marks. Then, several dogs and cats jumped neatly in and, in the cats' case, they bristled and slunk off down the passageway. After the confusion, where hooves, paws and claws muddled together with a cacophony of bleating, barking and mooing, the animals fell silent.

The children looked on amazed.

The cavernous space felt tiny.

Thunderfoot, the reindeer, addressed them. 'Today is the day that our forefathers talked about in stories passed down for generations. We will take humankind to the place of reckoning. Together, as a body of animals, we will protect the

Heirs of Eden. Let us go, for the beast will not linger long now that the spell is broken.'

The ensuing movement of animals heading towards the Heirs of Eden was nothing short of chaos. Creatures crashed into one another to create a sense of overwhelming disorganisation.

'If the dragon pops its mouth in the hole and delivers a long stream of fire,' Daisy began, 'this is going to be the world's biggest barbecue.'

"GAGOG GAGOG—BARK!"

This was followed by a huge roar. Everyone froze.

The sound made the hairs on the children's necks bristle as, only a few paces away, a lion leapt onto the back of a huge bull.

'Good Lord,' Archie said, his jaw hanging. 'I didn't think it could get any weirder.'

The bull stood firm, unflinching under the weight of the cat.

'LISTEN TO ME!' it roared.

Isabella slipped to the floor as Archie pinned himself to the cavern wall, his eyes out on stalks.

'I am Leo Magna,' the cat purred. 'Larger animals! Do your duty and form a phalanx around the Heirs. Smaller creatures claim the sides. **NOW!**'

Instantly, the mood changed. Animals shuffled around the children, who soon found themselves squashed in between bulls and cows and sheep. Cats and dogs ran beneath, bats and various birds hovered above.

'There is one thing you must do,' Leo Magna said, patrolling. 'Know thy neighbour! Make a bond with all the big and all the tiny animals next to you. The beast will attempt to trick us, but do not be found out. Know all creatures, big and small, surrounding you,' he repeated, snarling at those who had the tenacity to turn towards him with a confused look on their faces. 'And remember, together we are strong. Do it now!' he roared.

An extraordinary noise rose up in the chamber as the animals turned to one another.

The largest of the sheep, a ram, with small, but perfectly formed, horns addressed Archie.

'We know of your noble mission, Master. Bethedi the Willow told the birds about your trials.' The ram stopped talking even though its mouth continued to grind around in circles. 'My name is Himsworth. I will not let you down.'

Suddenly there was a further commotion as a bundle of animals tumbled down the chute. Geese, ducks, more rabbits, stoats, deer and countless birds flooded the room.

'We'll help too!' the birds cried, swooping and cawing as they went.

Archie looked around and found Old Man Wood in conversation with Leo Magna, who looked up and caught his eye.

Seconds later, the lion, with a couple of bounds jumped over three sheep and landed on top of a black and white cow that stood directly in front of them. The bovine wobbled in surprise, her legs buckling somewhat before straightening out again.

'Greetings, Heirs of Eden,' the lion said, looking down at their astonished faces. 'We will escort you as far into the tunnels as we can. Show no fear. Worry not about the waste of life. Only the outcome is important. That is all you must remember.'

The lion's head examined each one. 'You will ride to your fate. Those whom you ride will know your needs. They will charge where necessary; they will travel at great speed. Show no fear.'

Archie, Daisy and especially Isabella nearly collapsed in shock when another ear-splitting noise blasted around the chamber.

'GAGOG GAGOG GAGOG—BARK!'

A deathly silence filled the room.

As one, the assembled mass turned towards the chute.

One by one, four magnificent horses, their coats glistening

in the firelight, jumped gracefully through the hole, and the creatures in their path scrambled out of the way.

'Ride what? Those horses?' Daisy said.

'Horses?' said the lion. 'You will not be riding horses.'

From near the chute, four white equine creatures flashed through the assembled throng halting near to the Heirs.

'You have got to be kidding me!' Isabella scoffed. She looked increasingly flustered. 'But they're ... that's ... it's impossible.'

'They've got horns!' Archie blurted out. 'And sparkly bits on their manes.'

'They're those unicycle-horse things, aren't they,' Daisy said, clumsily. 'Aren't they ... they're made up—'

'They're beautiful,' Isabella gushed.

'Stunning,' Archie agreed.

The lion motioned towards them with a fat paw. 'The unicorns have travelled far. They are a gift. They will protect you from your greatest danger at any one time. They will always go to wherever they are needed the most. They are swift, fearless and cannot be poisoned. Fire bounces off their coats and rarely are they injured. Furthermore, Heirs of Eden, they will know you and understand you, even though you will never hear one speak.'

The unicorns nuzzled up to each heir and individually snorted into the face of each one, including Old Man Wood, who laughed.

'Mount your steeds.'

'Seriously? You want me to ride one of those?' Isabella complained. 'I was hopeless at riding, always falling off—'

'You're going to ride a unicorn, whether you like it or not, Isabella,' Archie said, a smile spreading across his face.

Isabella trembled. 'Ride a unicorn—goodness. Didn't see that coming.'

'Be not afraid,' Leo Magna growled. 'Each one will take good care of you to the point where you have either succeeded or you have failed within these walls.'

Old Man Wood enveloped Isabella with a reassuring hug before turning towards the body of animals.

When the old man spoke, his kindly face and bright eyes darted over the animals that stared back at him. Speaking in a wispy, blowy sound, in a way that reminded each one of the children of the Song of the Trees, he began. 'Brave and noble animals of Earth, your sacrifice will be remembered for all time. Let us go forward now together, as one, and face our destiny.'

Leo Magna turned to the Heirs. 'Heirs of Eden. There are things I must attend to. I will delay the beast for as long as I can. For all our sakes, I hope that we see each other again. Go, NOW!'

With that, he turned towards the chute and, with a huge growl and a single bound, the lion sprang through and into the rocky confines of the ruin roaring his defiance at the beast.

Each white unicorn, as though intuitively knowing what needed to be done, knelt down in front of the Heir of Eden. Moments later, the procession along the crumbling passages lit by the flickering firelight of the old braziers, had begun.

Sandwiched on all sides, birds circling above, cats and smaller creatures darting in and around the legs and hooves of the larger animals, they headed deeper and deeper into the labyrinth.

The pace settled into a steady rhythm. The further the horde went, the quieter they became until there was only the clacking, scuffing of hooves, the fluttering of wings and the occasional snort, whinny and grunt.

There was little doubt in any of their minds that before long, somewhere around the next corner, a terrible, unknown fate lay in wait. At each turn, they collectively held their breath as they travelled further and further, into the lair. Nearer to an attack, closer, they knew, to death.

TWENTY-FOUR
STONE'S TORCH

S tone hoisted the weapon onto the soldiers back.

'Let's see what this baby can do—might even eat through this fog – help us make up for lost time.'

The seconds ticked by. Shortly, the radio crackled. 'We're ready when you are, sir.'

Kemp and Sue crouched lower behind the stone.

Suddenly the roar of the flamethrower burst over them, tearing a hole into the fog, the stench of fuel filling the dank air, the gushing, whirring noise of the deadly fire machine blowing out its fury. Then it ceased, and the heat of the flare retracted.

'Bloody hell,' Stone said under his breath, but loud enough for everyone to hear. He picked up the radio and pressed the button, his voice filled with excitement. 'Did you see that? Ripped a hole clean through this stuff.'

'Affirmative, sir,' came the reply.

'Was it similar to the event Mills saw earlier?'

The radio went silent. 'Affirmative,' the voice came back. 'Pink and orange colours accentuating the white fog. We reckon it's the same, sir.'

Stone cursed. 'Right, that means someone else is on these hills, probably with the same idea. Keep your eyes sharp and your ears peeled,' he said into the radio. 'They may have spotted us, too. Team two, do you copy.'

The radio crackled again. 'Team two here. Yes, we copy. Would you like us to lay out some further devices now we've completed the perimeter, over?'

'Yes, why not. Use your flamethrower from now on; one blast and the fog melts like butter until it folds back in. You'll make far quicker progress that way. Should have done it ages ago, especially on those damned fish.'

Stone's radio went silent.

'OK. Roger and out.'

Stone spoke into the radio once again. 'Dickinson. Dickinson only. To channel ten please.'

Moments later, the knobs on the machine moved, Dickinson responded.

'Dickinson here, sir, over.'

'Right,' Stone said. 'Between you and me, I've got a better plan.'

'I'm all ears, sir.'

'Geddis thinks he recognises our position. We could be nearer to the cottage than we thought. If he's right, we can make up some of the time we lost and approach the cottage in sub-one hour.'

'Yes, sir, I understand.'

Stone continued, slowly, his voice level. 'Here's the new plan, Dickinson. I'm going to head directly towards the cottage and torch the whole damn place with this little beauty. That'll bring them running, like rats out of a nest.'

The radio went quiet.

'Dickinson, are you there?'

'The radio crackled again. 'Yes, sir.'

'Well?'

'Are you sure about that?' Dickinson replied. 'I mean, what if there are others in there? What about Mrs Pye—she's innocent, as is the headmaster and the two kids. They might be in the house.'

Stone grinned as he stepped up on to a boulder. 'They're

all involved,' he said. 'My guess is they all know more than you think. Let's burn the place and see what happens. To be honest with you, Dickinson, there's nothing to lose from this, but a hell of a lot to gain. Over.'

The radio remained lifeless. Then the static came over again. 'Just for the record, sir, I'm not sure such a move—'

'I don't give a crap what you think, soldier. Just remember, I'm your superior officer, and you will obey my commands. Do you copy?'

'Sir.' The radio went silent.

'Good. Let's get on with it. Switching channel.'

Stone stepped off the boulder, moved into the clearing and spoke into his radio. 'I'm taking a small team directly to the buildings,' he said. 'The rest of you have twenty minutes to set as many traps as you can. Then I want all personnel to start moving towards the buildings. Understand? There's going to be a little wake-up call for them when I get there, and I want you lot to see what comes wriggling out of their den. I'll let you know the timing of my little surprise.'

Stone smiled. Then we'll see what the de Lowe family are truly made of.

TWENTY-FIVE

THE TEMPERATURE RISES

I sabella draped her arms around the neck of her unicorn, her face nestled in its silky, soft mane.

The delicate fibres seemed to glow in a range of colours and had a curiously soothing effect that doused the feelings of dread that had consumed her. Now she rode with her eyes closed, every so often opening them, peeking out as though from behind a sofa. At every turn, she shook and moaned in expectation of a gory, violent meeting with the beast.

'This is what it feels like to expect death,' she said quietly. 'It's like the moment when the hangman puts the noose around your neck, knowing at any moment you're going to slip through the trapdoor. We've got a better chance of reaching the moon than we have of surviving this—'

'Will you stop thinking about dying Bells and try to concentrate on living,' Archie muttered. 'If you keep droning on, I will personally offer you up—'

'Bagsy her mobile phone,' Daisy said, loud enough so that Isabella could hear her. 'You can have her precious diary—'

'Diary and tablet?' Archie bargained. 'You can keep her phone. It's rubbish.'

'Deal,' Daisy said. 'As long as I get first dibs on her library, now that I'm officially a boffin like her.'

Archie chuckled. 'Talking animals, riding unicorns and Daisy the nerd. Not sure which is stranger.'

'You wait,' Daisy said. 'This learning thing is a doddle. I'm good at it, Archie. Better than misery guts over there.'

Isabella sat up. 'Give it a break, you fools,' she said. Did the twins have no idea how dangerous and insane this was?

She leaned into the mane of the unicorn and, to take her mind off the others, thought about her best friend Sue. Sue and Gus had been stuck out in their tiny boat in the sea with the rain cascading down on them hour after hour. When they came to, they found themselves, cold, isolated—without a speck of land in sight. Sue had beaten impossible odds, she thought, so she had to pull herself together and do the same. She closed her eyes, conscious of her thumping heart, wishing she had eyes in the back of her head and on the sides of her head, too.

The animals shifted position as they rounded another corner.

'Know your neighbour,' Old Man Wood repeated. 'Concentrate only on the matter at hand.'

Old Man Wood and Isabella, surrounded by animals, positioned themselves towards the front of the column, Daisy behind and Archie nearer the rear. Birds flew above their heads, occasionally flashing further forward, checking that the path was clear, returning to rest on the animals' backs as another flock took off in its place.

The procession ground on, its rhythm steady, like a heartbeat, on and on and on. At the fourth bend, there was still no sign or sightings of the beast. No sound of it either.

At every turn there was a growing unease that it would be waiting for them. Then, finding nothing but a long, empty passage ahead lined by the fire-torches, they breathed a sigh of relief and hurried on, the pace picking up.

Three passages and four more corners and still nothing.

The cavalcade turned again and, as the collective relaxed, Daisy started sniggering.

'Daisy, really?' Isabella demanded, giving her a hard stare.

'Yeah, sorry Bells,' Daisy snorted. 'Nerves. And a bird has poo-ed in your hair,' she said, 'it's dribbling.'

Archie burst out laughing as Isabella combed her hands through her hair, her face contorted in disgust.

'Well, I don't know why you think it's so bloody hilarious. It's the same with the both of you.'

Archie didn't believe her until he felt a slimy slug-like object slipping past his left lower hair-spike and behind the back of his ear. Daisy, now a little more restrained, tentatively patted her hair only to find a deposit right on top.

A red-breasted robin fluttered down. 'It is good luck you know. It really is.'

'Thank you,' Daisy said, the smile removed from her face. 'Just what we need: lucky bird droppings.'

But as the procession marched along, a strange thing was happening.

'Hey, Daisy,' Archie said, wiping his brow, 'You thinking what I'm thinking?'

'The heat?'

'It's like we're walking into the middle of the Earth.'

'I know what you mean. But we're not even going down-hill,' she said. Daisy plucked her shirt from her back and loosened her leather jacket. From the increasing volume, she noted how unsettled the animals were getting.

'You never know,' Archie continued, 'Perhaps there's a volcano here under the Yorkshire Moors.'

'Impossible,' Isabella retorted. 'Geographically it can't happen. Trust me.'

Daisy mimicked Isabella's voice 'Impossible, isn't a word I can trust anymore.'

Archie removed his coat, exposing a wet T-shirt underneath. 'I'm boiling.'

'You think that's bad,' bleated a sheep to his left, 'We're stuck with ours. I could do with a long drink of cool stream water.'

'Me too,' another bleated.

'Oh yes,' said the large heifer. 'A refreshing drink.'

On they went, the temperature rising. At the ninth turn, the sense of unease had deepened and the noise level had escalated.

Daisy turned to Archie. 'Hey, Arch,' she whispered sniffing the air and arching her brows. 'Have you noticed?'

Archie creased his brow. 'No. What is it?' he said, his voice filled with alarm. 'Have you seen it?'

Daisy held her nose. 'No. The pong. Think of the sweaty armpits of these hundreds of animals, all those glands—'

'I'm not interested, Daisy,' Archie said, concentrating. 'I have a strong feeling something is just about to happen.'

TWENTY-SIX

TIME FOR A DRINK

Old Man Wood, his face dripping with sweat, removed his big old coat, folded it over the rear of his unicorn and, just as the column of animals finished along one passageway he heard a cry of 'Halt!'

The procession shuffled to a stop.

'What is it?' the old man asked.

'Listen,' Himsworth said. 'Sounds like a trickle of water winding its way over the rocks at the Cod Beck.'

'Well, I never, so it is,' said a bull, known by the family as Burger. Others around him pawed the ground in agreement.

'There's water somewhere around here, that's for sure,' sang some little birds darting to and fro around their heads.

Daisy turned to the others her head cocked to one side as she listened intently. 'But I can't hear anything? Can you, Archie?'

'No, but I could murder a drink too,' Archie said. 'Anyone else?'

A volley of grunts and barks and other animal noises came back at him.

'Please, please find it, pleeease,' bleated several sheep over and over again. The pleading spread and in no time at all the other animals had joined in until there was a cacophony of bleating and mooing and twittering and quacking echoing down the passage.

Moments later, a mixed group of animals split from the central group, hurtling down the passageway in search of the water source.

They rounded the corner and disappeared out of sight.

'Silence!' Old Man Wood boomed.

The animals quietened.

'The sound is there to confuse. Do NOT listen to what you think is water. It is an illusion. The beast is playing tricks with your minds. Think about something else: the long grass blowing in the meadows or the swishing of wind in the trees.'

'Bless my curls! He's right,' said Himsworth, the ram standing next to Archie.

The animals re-grouped.

'Know thy neighbour,' they said.

As they turned the corner, a heap of animal carcasses lay prostrate, necks slit, blood spilling over the floor, eyes staring at the ceiling.

Isabella screamed and almost slipped off her mount, as the surrounding animals nestled closer together, warm blood washing over their hooves and paws as they moved slowly past the dead bodies of their comrades.

TWENTY-SEVEN

THE WAITING ENDS

'Quickly now!' Old Man Wood ordered, ushering them down the passageway. 'Know your neighbour.'

Daisy, who had been concentrating until her head hurt, her senses deeply tuned in, suddenly heard a tiny sound, like a gecko walking on the ceiling dislodging a crumb of earth. And the noise, she reckoned, was coming from directly above her. As subtly as she could, she slowly bent her head slightly back and flicked her eyes up scanning the ceiling.

Nothing. Phew. Her body uncoiled.

She breathed a sigh of relief.

'Arch,' she whispered, 'I think I heard something. Keep guard.'

Archie leaned forward, his hair spikes aside the unicorn's neck, a bevvy of animals surrounding him. He scoured the floor.

'Archie,' she repeated, as she turned to see if he'd heard her. 'Did you hear me?'

'Yeah,' he said. 'I'm checking the floor.'

From nowhere, a set of long, sharp, yellow teeth in a set of saliva-filled jaws flashed out of the darkness. Sharp claws flailed savagely at everything in their path.

Pandemonium broke out. The crowded passage erupted in terrified bellows and calls.

Archie and Daisy slipped off and crashed to the floor, hitting the surface just before the unicorns bucked and kicked out, once, twice, three times—then instantly swivelled and charged, head down, their spiralled long tusks flashing like swords.

Moments later, a flurry of wings clouded past, aiming at the beast's head, directly at its eyes, checking its progress.

'Run!' the birds urged as they regrouped for another attack on the snake's head like kamikaze pilots flying to their deaths, the monster clawing them off its face, many thudding into the walls.

But where one moment the beast was thrashing and clawing, the next, it had entirely vanished from view.

Archie's unicorn, immediately twisted back towards Archie who grabbed the mane and hauled himself up.

They galloped to the next corner, slowed, caught their breath, and, along with the others, searched for a misfit.

'Know thy neighbour,' they said as one, looking around, nervously.

Around the next corner were the remains of another encounter. Rodents, cats, geese and other animal remains lay strewn upon the path, the carnage of brutal death all around them.

In front of them, littered with corpses, was the longest passage so far and, at its end, a high vaulted room. In the middle stood a large stone plinth, like a grand square altar, with five-foot-high pillars supporting each corner. Underneath, water ran around it.

'Daisy!' Archie cried. 'Daisy, can you see the tablet?'

Daisy stared into the distance. 'Yup, it's there. Bang on top of that altar thing! Hurry.'

A smaller group of animals flashed past them down the long tunnel.

'GAGOG, GAGOG, BARK. GAGOG—BARK!'

The sickening, ear-piercing sound of Gorialla Yingarna

made them turn. At the far end of the tunnel, an immense beast rounded the corner like a train, filling the passage; it's face that of a prehistoric dinosaur, blood staining its long, sharp fangs.

'Go,' she shouted. 'All of you.'

'OH MY GOD!!' Isabella screamed.

The beast was making up ground, fast.

'Where are the animals and birds?' Archie asked as the unicorn started to run, Daisy on hers, next to him.

'They're lying in wait—in sections,' she replied.

Archie flicked a look down the passageway to see the bushy white tails of the rabbits, lying still on the hard earth floor.

'The rabbits have a plan. But it's madness,' Daisy yelled.

The beast, its massive head filling the tunnel, was crushing every animal in its path. The snarling face tight, its bloody eyes wide with fury.

Isabella heard the voice in her head again, this time icy cold and calculating. 'You cannot win. Give up…'

Suddenly the trance stopped.

The beast roared and beat its head on one side of the ceiling, and then the other, the sound reverberating like an earthquake.

The unicorns, as one, lay down inviting the Heirs to dismount. Archie, Daisy and Isabella ran towards the middle chamber.

'**BARK, GAGOG A GAGOG**,' echoed through the tunnel, the beast smashing its head on the passage surrounds, stone tumbling into the corridor.

'What's going on?' Archie whispered.

'It's the rabbits and smaller creatures, Daisy said, looking back. 'They've clamped over its eyes holding on for dear life digging their little claws in as hard as they can.'

As the beast tore at one rabbit, stripping it alive, another rabbit took its place. Now another one held on, then another —every one refusing to be pulled off—until the innards and blood and fur layered over its eyes blocking its vision.

A nauseous stench of entrails and guts filled the passage.

'Bells, Archie, run for it!' Daisy shouted. 'Go as fast as you can straight to the plinth.'

'Oh hell,' Archie shouted. 'It's coming.'

The unicorns, now in a line, faced the serpent while the other animals closed in around the Heirs.

'There's that burning noise again,' Daisy yelled. 'Dive!'

A blast of flame spat out of a very different looking creature. But the unicorns stood firm, absorbing the heat, the flames never reaching the Heirs.

In a flash, the beast charged at the unicorns, like a battering ram, but the unicorns charged back, heads down, jabbing at the reptile with razor sharp horns, forcing it back.

'Now it's a small snake,' Daisy said, 'and it's trying to bite … watch out!'

A flurry of activity above them—a mass of beating wings like a flock of starlings, flashed past, dive-bombing the snake, each one with claws outstretched aiming for its eyes.

Suddenly, the snake disappeared.

For all the beating of wings, and the confusion, and the stench and the searching of so many pairs of eyes, the beast was nowhere to be found.

'I don't like this one little bit,' Daisy murmured.

'Where's it gone, sis?'

'I don't know. I'm looking for it.' She scanned the walls. 'It can't have disappeared.'

'Was it killed?' Archie said. 'Did the unicorns get it?'

Daisy scoured the passage, from side to side, her eyes blazing.

'What do you see?'

'Little lumps and bumps, which could be anything. There's nothing. It's vanished.'

Isabella said, 'Do you think the unicorns will find it?'

Daisy rounded on her. 'Thing is, Sis, they've disappeared too.'

They stared down the long empty passageway.

'Maybe they've chased it around the corner,' Archie said.

Daisy shook her head. 'I'd have seen it. Anyway, remember what Leo Magna said. "They will protect us from our greatest peril".'

'That's not good,' Isabella's voice trembled. 'What could be worse than this?'

They ran on in silence, their hearts thumping and their minds in a state of high alert. As they neared the chamber entrance, a sense of deep vulnerability filled them.

Now less than a half of the original band that had set out remained.

TWENTY-EIGHT

STONE'S NEW PLAN

K emp and Sue stared at one another as the soldiers moved away into the fog.

'Bloody hell,' Kemp said. 'He's going to burn them out. He's an even bigger lunatic than I thought.'

Sue looked crestfallen. 'Yes, I know. That flame-thing was horrible.' A thought struck her, and she stiffened. 'Kemp, the only person at the cottage, is Mrs Pye.'

Kemp stood up and then, realising where he was, crouched down again. 'I've got to get her out; there's no way she'll move until it's too late.'

'But you'll never beat the soldiers, even if we follow them. We'd still have to work our way around them, and the worst thing that can happen is that we get caught—'

'Is it?'

'Well, yeah. Of course, it is,' Sue said. 'Stone will figure something's up and I'd bet money he'd torch the place anyway—and make us watch.'

Kemp rubbed his bald head. 'Where's Solomon?' he said. 'Isn't he there too?'

'No,' Sue replied. 'I got separated from him when I fell down the bank. With any luck, he went on towards the ruin.'

'Perhaps he'll stall the other group?'

Sue twiddled her thumbs. 'That was the original plan,'

she said. 'But it's impossible to see anything so it'll be pure luck if he stumbles on anyone. He's got an old radio, he calls it a wireless; they found it in one of the bedrooms. I'm not even sure he knows how to turn it on. The thing is, it's still not going to stop Stone.'

Suddenly she remembered the tablets. She ceased her twiddling and went stone-still.

'Sue? What is it?'

She caressed her forehead. 'The first two tablets are in the cottage. What if they get ruined? I'm going to have to get them before they get there.'

'It's impossible.'

'We've got to do something. We have to risk it.'

'It's not worth it,' Kemp snapped. In a flash, Kemp knew this was his chance. 'Look, Sue. There is another way. It's a bit of a mad one, and you might think I'm crazy but, you know that spirit I was talking about, he's the one who can save you...'

Sue gave him a sideways look. He took it as a sign to continue.

'Well, we could go with him—he has this way of being able to go absolutely anywhere.'

'What are you talking about?'

'He's not from here—'

'You're telling me he's an alien?'

'No,' Kemp cringed, realising it sounded absurd. 'I mean, yes—kind of. Look, he's a spirit who comes from another place, another planet very like Earth, I think. Because I agreed to go with him, he saved me from the storm. In return, my body gives his spirit substance, so he can do things, like walk and see a bit. That's all there is to it.'

Sue shook her head. If it were anyone else, she'd have walked away already.

'He'll help,' Kemp insisted. 'I mean, it's a bit uncomfortable at first—if you relax it'll only tingle a little, I promise it won't be too bad.'

Sue shot him a look. 'Kemp, after everything you've done

to ruin my life, why on earth should I trust you with this frankly ludicrous scheme now.'

'Because it's the only chance you'll get to save these tablets and even yourself. For me, it's the only way I've got any chance of being with my mum.'

Sue shook her head. 'I take it this is the same thing, the same spirit that led you and Gus up to the ruin? How did Gus know?'

He nodded. 'Yeah. I was coming to that. Gus found out when we had a fight in the attic room. Gus had me by the neck and nearly killed me. He only let me go when he learned that I'd travelled via the ghost. Gus insisted that he went with the ghost and afterwards, Cain—the spirit guy—decided we needed to fight each other to see who would have the right to go with him. That's how we ended up at the ruin.'

'You really expect me to believe that?' she seethed. 'You've made it up.'

'On my mother's life I haven't,' he said. 'Gus only did it because he wanted to save you. He wanted you to be together. He was trying to protect you.'

'You are so full of crap, it's unbelievable,' Sue said, eying him suspiciously.

'No, not this time Sue. Believe me. Everything I've told you is the truth. Why would I hide it? Why would I go to these lengths to tell you lies? Gus would have wanted you to be safe, more than anything. He did it for you.'

Sue chewed her bottom lip. 'But ... how does it work?'

Kemp shrugged. 'It's simple; you put on a coat and a hat, that's all there is to it. Then go with whatever the ghost does. The less you resist, the less painful it is.'

'Painful?'

'Yeah. Burns,' he said, patting his head. 'See? If you think my hair simply fell out, you're sorely mistaken. My barnet burned off, all of it—and every single hair on my body, because ... because I didn't understand how the ghost worked. And,' his voice slipped to barely a whisper, 'because I was afraid. I resisted.'

Sue wavered.

'Look, I know,' he said, 'it's a huge shot in the dark, but it's the only plan we've got going right now that won't jeopardise Archie, his sisters and my mum. I don't even know if the ghost will agree, but I do know that we haven't got much time.'

Sue didn't reply.

Now the soldiers were out of earshot, Kemp stood up. 'I'll walk over there and have a little chat with my friend just to make sure he's cool with it, OK?'

Sue didn't say anything. The news of his body-burns filled her with a dread that hit her right in the gut.

Kemp moved away. He looked back over his shoulder, 'I'll be back in a tick—so don't worry or go walkabout. If Cain agrees, then it's up to you. Only you can decide what you want to do. This union thing only works if you are prepared to go absolutely willingly.'

TWENTY-NINE

TEMPTATION

As they reached the end of yet another straight section of the labyrinth, a new passageway to their left appeared at an obtuse angle, merging with theirs. It flooded them with bright, natural light.

A fresh wind blew over the hot animals, who stood still letting the cool air wash over them. Instantly they perked up and, almost as one, stared in wonder and longing down the new passage where they could see, not too far away, a meadow of lush grass and butterflies and flower heads nodding in the breeze. In the distance, native trees of oaks and ash, their leaves fresh and plentiful fluttered from side to side.

A bird flew by in the distance and twittered.

'Right well, good luck,' Himsworth the ram said, as he headed down the opening.

'It's an illusion, Himsworth,' Old Man Wood said – intense concentration on his face, his branchwand trembling in his hand. 'Don't do it. It's not real. Do not go there.'

'With respect, sir, but I do know my field thank you very much! Besides, we've done our job. The beast has gone,' his head turned from side to side. 'Look around—there is no beast.'

'You don't know that, Himsworth. Gorialla Yingarna is

cunning and lethal. This field you see doesn't exist. It cannot exist.'

But the remaining cattle and deer and many others now joined in and shuffled further down. Himsworth continued. 'You just need to get across that chamber, pick up the tablet and put them all together, just as the legend says.'

'STOP!' Old Man Wood pleaded, screwing up his face. 'PLEASE! DON'T GO THERE. It is fake. It is temptation.' He desperately tried to think. 'The trees at home have no leaves ... it's a trap—it wants you to believe ... I can't ... it is too strong—'

Before Old Man Wood had a chance to finish his sentence, the remaining group of animals, some of Old Man Wood's cattle and a few smaller birds and creatures sped off towards the imaginary pastures.

In vain, Old Man Wood tried to go after them, but Archie held him back.

'NO!' Archie yelled. 'Don't follow them!'

The children, their faces expressing the terrible shock at what was happening, watched helplessly as, like lemmings off a cliff, the collective animals that had guarded them for so long, simply vanished without a trace.

THIRTY

A PERFECT DISGUISE

From the side of the passageway, a tiny, miniature tortoise, its stone-coloured shell no bigger than the palm of child's hand, ambled slowly by. It had been so, so easy. Childs-play.

By the time he'd changed his cover, and a layer of dust had settled over the floor, he was no more than a tiny bump in an altogether bumpy passageway. And more importantly, it had given him the chance to stop, to rest his exhausted body and consider his options. Sometimes, the most innocent things stare you in the face, Gorialla Yingarna thought.

And, here they were, alone, the pathetic Heirs of Eden entirely at his mercy, devoid of their animal shield; naked, like fresh-born babes.

The animals and those damnable birds, he hadn't been expecting them to be quite so … sacrificial. Perhaps he should have taken his time, picked up nourishment as he went.

Killing was such hungry work.

And what of the unicorns with their sharp horns? He flinched. If he remembered rightly, they were protectors. Why, then, did they suddenly run away? Was there something of more harm to them out there on this awful Earth, than him? More likely they'd realised how futile their quest was, and given up. Simpler to run, he supposed, than dying while looking after infants?

The tortoise raised its head and peered out through bleary, damaged eyes, at the children above him. Blurs, all of them.

Smart to attack the eyes, he supposed. After aeons, they'd had plenty of time to come up with a plan. But really, was this the best they could do? He ambled on, each step on his soft, leathery pads made in perfect silence.

How quiet his labyrinth passages were, now that they echoed only to the hushed voices of those pitiful Heirs of Eden. He listened from under his tiny shell. They were confused. Wondering why the unicorns had fled and why the stupid animals had deserted them. And by the wavering, troubled sounds they emitted, they were afraid. Very afraid. And so they should be. How troubling it was that the universe had sent children.

He'd show them no mercy. He'd fry one so intensely that its flesh would melt into its bones, and he'd pull another apart bit by bit, cracking every bone one by one in such a way that it made a tune. The other, he'd separate, offering different body parts to scavengers who would pick at the carcass. Then again, weren't children delicious to eat?

Maybe he'd eat the lot of them.

His mood lifted. Time to get back to the plinth, to guard his tablet, to see off the Heirs once and for all. He looked through his damaged eyes. Hazy vision, but nothing he couldn't cope with. He'd wash them in the water that ran around the stone. It would cleanse the gunk, the blood and the grime.

Instantly, he turned into a small chameleon blending in perfectly into the dusty floor and rocky surroundings.

They'd never see him, not as they were, fretting and fearful.

And then, just to think, when they turned up to claim their prize, he'd be there, waiting, like the perfect, unwanted surprise.

Now the games could really begin. He could hardly wait.

THIRTY-ONE
CAIN'S PLAN

'I'm here, boy,' the ghost, Cain said, as Kemp stumbled through the white sheet of air.

'Where?'

'Right by your side,' Cain whispered in his ear.

'Don't do that,' Kemp flapped. 'It's really bloody annoying.'

The ghost chuckled.

'Did you hear any of my conversation with Sue?' he asked. 'She'll come with us. She's got nothing to lose. She wants to get the tablets out of the house before they torch it. Why don't we get them first?'

'I like your thinking,' the ghost crowed. 'But, regrettably, now that the two tablets are joined together we cannot touch them. Only those associated with the quest may do so. But it would be beneficial for the house to burn to the ground with the tablets buried under a heap of smouldering rubble, should it come to that.'

'But I need to get my mother out. It didn't sound like they'll show her any mercy.'

'Indeed,' Cain said. 'Tricky. I have to say, so far, you have acquitted yourself excellently. With your mother, boy, it may be better to wait until we are sure the Heirs have failed. It will not be long now.'

'But you promised—'

'I will keep my promise to you,' he snapped. 'But let us be sure because it will be so much easier to get her to come willingly with us when the world is falling apart and when there are no other alternatives. Do you understand?'

Kemp nodded.

'Good.' Cain draped an overcoat-arm around Kemp's shoulders. 'Our mission now is to get the girl. Perhaps I should show her what lies ahead.'

Kemp wavered and moved away. 'What did you have in mind?'

'Let us go to her and explain. Sometimes there's nothing like the truth to persuade a person.'

'If she does come,' Kemp said, 'you mustn't hurt her.'

'Why would I do such a thing?' Cain said, as though pained. 'If we play this right, she will be an important part of our family. The next mother of all.'

Kemp breathed a sigh of relief and called out. 'Sue, I think we can sort this out.' He listened for a reply. 'Sue? Where are you?'

There was no reply.

'Sue, give us a yell. I can't see you.'

He waited, but even as he strained his ears and eyes, no voice and no words returned from out of the void.

THIRTY-TWO
SOLOMON'S TEST

S olomon ambled blindly in the white-out. Every so often he reverted to crawling, often bashing his head on unseen branches that dangled down as if suspended in mid-air. Even worse were the holes in the ground, filled with water, where trees, uprooted in the storm, had left behind small craters that he couldn't see. Solomon now slightly regretted bringing the radio that was tucked under his shirt and wondered—if the time came—whether it would still work after such a hammering.

By the time he'd been going for an hour, he was wet through, bruised all over and exhausted. Time to stop, take a bearing and grab a swig of water. He wished it was something stronger.

As far as he could tell, he'd started up towards the ruin before cutting down the steep banks towards the water. Finding a fallen bough of a tree, he sat down, wiped his brow with a handkerchief and pulled out a compass attached to a key ring. He examined it and stared out at the white sheet surrounding him. Suddenly, he heard a roar, like a waterfall, accompanied by the fog in front of him blurring to orange.

Moments later, the acrid stench of petroleum filled his nostrils, making him nauseous.

Now that he thought of it, the sound wasn't the noise of

roaring water, more likely the drone of something combusting; a flame-powered torch, perhaps?

His brain snapped into gear. Someone was blasting a path through the fog. On full alert, he listened, his ears attuned to every snap and squelch in the mud.

Suddenly the roar blasted out, this time much closer, coming directly at him.

He moved fast as the possibility of incineration dawned upon him. Crawling on hands and knees, he scrambled across the hillside and found a spot in which he felt sure there was a piece of open ground. He placed the radio behind a fallen bough and, as the flame-thrower tucked into the fog once more, he switched the dial and scurried away, on hands and knees, behind a thicker fallen branch.

A strange, static-like noise whistled through the air.

Solomon hadn't anticipated this and for a moment wondered if he shouldn't rush back and tune it in. But there were too many unknown factors involved, so he snuck behind the branch and listened as the footsteps approached.

'OK, ready for another one,' said a thick low voice. 'Stand back. Three, two, one.'

VoooOOOOOM!

Just to his right, a vicious tongue of flame licked out, engulfing everything in its path with furious fire. Heat and vapours the deadly by-products.

Solomon buried himself low in the ground covering his eyes and mouth.

The troops followed the blazing trail a couple of metres away from him and, as Solomon listened to the footsteps trundling by, he feared he hadn't turned the radio's volume up high enough.

But to his relief, the platoon came to a halt, leaning on some nearby branches.

'Right, a couple of minutes, gents. Piss and drink, then back to it.'

Solomon recognised the voice of Dickinson immediately.

'Sir,' came another voice. 'For the record, I'm unhappy

with Stone's order of burning the house down, especially if there are geezers in it. Can't we enter the building first to warn the occupants to remove themselves?'

'I couldn't agree with you more, Talbot,' Dickinson said. 'But we can only do that if we get there first. However, as Stone took the most direct path and is now burning his way to the top, I don't think that's likely. Furthermore,' he added, as if to cover himself, 'Stone is the commanding officer. Those are his orders.'

Solomon sat up—the news profoundly revealing. They'd split into groups—two, three, possibly—and Stone was leading his group directly to the cottage.

In the silence, as they caught their breath, the old wireless radio crackled into the gloom.

'Sir, did you capture that?'

He sensed the troops ducking.

Silence suddenly consumed everything.

Excellent—Solomon thought—just loud enough to send a shiver up the spine.

'Coming from nine o'clock,' one of the men whispered. 'Behind a tree. Could be a device.'

As if by magic, the troops dispersed into the fog.

Solomon tucked himself under the branch as much as he could and held his breath.

Moments later, the sole of a boot appeared at eye level. Then, and like a stalking cat, it moved away. Solomon exhaled.

Several minutes passed.

But as Solomon lay there, his initial idea of stalling the team now felt like the wrong idea. The information he'd garnered about Stone burning the cottage down and the general reaction of the soldiers made him consider a different course of action.

Solomon wondered if he could make Dickinson understand that what he was doing was hindering and not helping. If he could explain, and not be on the receiving end of the soldier's ridicule, or a bullet, perhaps they might send Stone on a wild goose chase instead.

The moment he first met Dickinson in Stone's study, he sensed the young officer saw things a little differently to his commander. If anyone might be turned, it was him. Solomon weighed up his options and sat up wracking his brains.

A cold, metallic object pushed into the middle of his bald patch.

'One move, and I'll blow your brains out,' a cold voice said. 'Understand?'

'Oh dear,' was the best Solomon could muster, in a voice that sounded very unlike his own.

'Sir,' the voice called out. 'Over here! I've found someone. Doesn't look particularly harmful from where I'm standing. Pretty sure he's unarmed.'

Solomon winced. 'Can you please take that thing away from my head. I'm hardly going to run away.'

The soldier weighed up the situation. 'One false step, Grandad...' he grabbed Solomon by his collar and pulled him to his feet.

Solomon shook himself down.

'Hang on,' the soldier said, in a slightly disbelieving voice. 'You're that schoolmaster from Upsall. Stone's cousin?'

Dickinson arrived on the scene. 'Goodness,' he said. 'With respect, headmaster, what on earth brings you out here?'

Solomon had the rough outline of a plan. 'I'm frightfully sorry, Dickinson,' he began, smiling his finest headmasterly smile and propping up his half-moon glasses, 'but my aim was, quite simply, to hold you up. And that hissing radio was to stop you in your tracks and make you falter. Oh, dear. Do look at me,' he said inspecting his damaged and muddy clothes, 'I'm not really cut out for this kind of thing, am I?' For a brief moment, the sight of his torn clothes reminded him of Archie. 'Bit of a bumbling idiot compared to you chaps.'

Dickinson took the bait. 'Why did you want to hold us up?'

Solomon moved quickly to his most serious face. 'Because I know what's going on. And I know that it's vital you chaps don't meddle— '

'Meddle?'

'Yes, get in the way,' Solomon said, his eyes moving from one soldier to the other. 'You see, he's been absolutely correct.'

'Who?'

'Your commander, Commissioner Stone.'

'Stone? Correct? What are you talking about?'

'Stone's sensed that the de Lowe children are deeply wrapped up in the calamity. He's spot on.'

'Really?' Dickinson said, his face betraying a look of confusion. 'Then, you lied to him,' he said disbelievingly.

'Not entirely. You see, at the time I didn't know what was what. In fact, it was Stone's intuition that helped me figure out that something a little other-worldly was going on with those children.'

Dickinson slipped back into his officer role. 'Then, I take it you know where they are?'

'The de Lowe children?' Solomon said, rubbing his chin.

'Yes, of course.'

Solomon grinned. 'Well, funnily enough, I'm not sure I do. I've been led to believe they're in a labyrinth not so far from here, trying to find a tablet.'

'What? Like an iPad—as you said in Stone's office?'

'Of course not,' Solomon chuckled. 'That, dear fellow, was a lame ploy to mislead you. Look, if I tell you any more you probably won't believe me—'

'So, what is this tablet, then?'

By now, the three troops had gathered around Dickinson and Solomon, just as Solomon had hoped.

'These are ancient stone tablets,' he began, 'three of them, hidden from humankind for more time, I daresay, than we can ever comprehend. They hold the secrets to a legend from antiquity about humankind's place and our role on this planet.'

One of the soldiers harrumphed.

Talbot laughed. 'What a load of old bollocks—'

'Now, here's the thing, young man,' Solomon said, rounding on him. 'It is indeed a story which begs for mockery. And yes, you might quite easily regard it as a load of old balls. In fact, I would go so far as saying that this story is as easy to ridicule as the air we breathe around us. But...'

The headmaster nodded sagely to himself, working the pause. 'But, to truly understand, is to look around: Yorkshire lies in ruins, the world is suffering an incurable, violent and wholly unknown disease, and the Americans are about to launch a bomb that will wipe out northern England. The annihilation of our planet is imminent. So, with these nuggets of information in the back of your minds, please feel free to discredit everything I'm about to tell you.' He gazed at each soldier in turn. 'Alternatively, you can open your minds and hear the truth.'

Solomon waited. 'So, go on,' he said, milking the attention. 'Walk away now before you hear the nonsense, the "bollocks", that I'm about to dispel.'

The troops fidgeted uncomfortably. The school-masterly telling-off had rendered them speechless.

'Jolly good. Then I will continue,' Solomon said. 'There is no time for dilly-dallying, gentlemen. What I'm going to tell you, however absurd it may sound, is nothing less than how things stand at this precise moment in time.' He paused for a beat, before adding, 'so if anyone wants to say something, please do it now, before I begin.'

Dickinson smiled. 'We thought you knew something. What kind of person throws themselves into the foul water of an old chapel looking at stained-glass windows without a particularly good reason?' He studied the faces of the troops. 'Well, go on. But I'll warn you; be brief—Stone has ramped-up his enthusiasm to find the de Lowe kids. I'm afraid he's going to either kill them himself or torture them or do something pretty unpleasant.'

'As I feared,' the headmaster said. 'And this is exactly what isn't needed.'

'Why?' Talbot asked.

The headmaster faced the soldier and raised his eyebrows. 'Because, my dear fellow, if the de Lowe children fail in the matter which has been tasked to them, then I'm afraid to say the whole world is going to go up the spout. It is no lie to say that they hold the key to this entire muddle.'

The soldiers stared at him with looks as if to say, you must be—but maybe you aren't—utterly insane.

'You're bloody kidding,' Talbot said at length.

'I wish I were,' the headmaster replied. 'The problem is, they have a seven-day deadline which coincides with the time limit of the Americans and their savage idea of razing Yorkshire to dust. Those children are running out of time and if Stone interferes in the slightest way—and I do know his intentions are noble—then I promise you one absolute certainty: this entire planet is up for a gigantic overhaul. And this means, in no short measure, that everything humankind has achieved up to this point will come to a rather ugly and abrupt finish. That includes the demise all of us standing here. The death of every loved one you have and the destruction of everything on this Earth.'

'How come you know this?'

'I was assigned to work it out. When I saw the children yesterday, they decided, on trust, to let me in on their secret. Now, either you're going to help me, or you're not.'

The headmaster pursed his lips and dabbed his forehead. 'Arrest me or believe me. The ball is in your court, Dickinson.'

THIRTY-THREE
ISABELLA'S DARING

F or a room deep underground, the large domed chamber was surprisingly bright. Beneath the raised table structure was a pool of clear water, which flowed around the structure and was fed, by water dripping continuously from a ledge high above into the stream. Over time, a channel had been carved from the edge of the cavern to the pool in the middle.

As they wound their way around and around the long, brazier-lit labyrinth, Isabella had barely opened her eyes and, when the animals charged off down the illusionary path, a wave of utter revulsion swept over her followed by a surge of heat that rushed through her body. The veins in her temples throbbed as her brain went into action.

'I'm going to get it,' she cried. 'It's only there on the plinth.'

'Get what?' Archie said.

'What do you bleeding well think? A chocolate bar? A newspaper? The tablet, you numpty.'

Before anyone had a chance to move, Isabella, her legs like a blur, rocketed across the cavernous floor to the plinth, Archie after her, the distance between them increasing at every step.

She jumped into the pool that circumnavigated the plinth, the cold water reaching up to the top of her calf muscles.

Moments later, with the water above her knees, she reached the stony base and the first hand-hold, pulling herself clear. With her legs dangling above the rocks, she levered herself up and onto the bottom lip of the frieze.

'One more bit, Bells,' she heard, as Archie appeared at the edge of the stream. 'Grab the overhang. Swing your legs over.'

Isabella reached up, her fingers grappling with the stone perimeter. She took a deep breath and, swinging her legs to and fro, wrestled first one, then the other leg over. Her body followed until she was lying, on her side on top of the plinth, the tablet just out of reach.

'Throw it down.' Archie shouted up to her.

But Isabella froze.

'Go on,' he screamed. 'Do it!'

But she remained motionless.

Archie tried to see what was going on. He waded into the stream. 'What's going on, Bells. Throw it down, now.'

But staring at Isabella was a king cobra, its tongue flickering in and out of its mouth, its head tall and erect, baring fangs, hood extended, its body coiled behind it. The snake slithered forward from behind the tablet, its eyes boring into Isabella's, ready to strike.

So, you will be the first.

Isabella gasped as the noise reverberated in her head. What could she do? Fall off the pedestal? She'd break her back, and besides, a king cobra would be faster than that. She stayed as still as she could.

The reptile inched forward.

Isabella felt a drop of sweat fall onto the flat stone beneath her. She shut her eyes trying to blot out the presence of the snake. But she could hear hissing, feel the flickering tongue flitting in and out of its mouth, so close it almost tickled her.

She readied herself to roll and fall. Better to hurt herself than die of the cobra's lethal venom.

She prised open her eyes to see the snake's green marble-like eyes meet hers, cold laughter, hatred and death flashed through her. Then it reared.

Isabella knew a strike was coming. As slowly as she could, millimetre by millimetre, she began to slip back to roll off the edge when a blur of brown feathers and a rush of beating wings shot out of nowhere directly at them. The eagle they had first met in the entrance chamber swooped, its talons outstretched, snatching the head of the snake in one unbroken movement before soaring high into the air.

The spell broke.

Isabella gasped, her heart thumping, her sweating brow resting on the stone. Out of the corner of her eye, the tablet lay on the flat surface only a couple of strides away, hers for the taking.

She pulled herself up and made towards it.

'Look out!' she heard Archie shout.

She looked up to see an immense flying dragon diving towards her. Could she get it?

A moment later fire engulfed the plinth, the blast blowing her over the edge. She crashed into the water below.

Archie ran around.

The dragon swooped, circled, cocked its head and flew straight towards them.

'Dive,' he screamed, as he plunged into the stream, flames engulfing the water above him, steam hissing off the surface.

As the dragon circled away high into the cavern rooftop and onto the plinth, Archie and Isabella pulled themselves clear of the water and, without looking back, sprinted to the relative safety of the entrance.

THIRTY-FOUR
THE FORGOTTEN RIDDLE

They hid in a small alcove, the remaining animals surrounding them, with a clear view of the chamber and plinth.

Daisy shook her head. 'We're doing this all wrong,' she said. 'Look, apart from your unbelievably bold, but reckless attempt to get the tablet, Bells, we haven't actually done anything yet. We haven't had to lift a finger, and that's the point. These animals— all those creatures who got us here—sacrificing their lives for us —did so for a reason. They sheltered us to make sure we're fresh for this bit. Everything that happens from now on is up to us and, if my hunch about our powers is right, the longer we're still in this, the stronger we get. They've done their job, paying the ultimate price, now it's our turn to kick some serious butt.'

Isabella groaned. She hadn't stopped shaking since their return. 'You're getting extremely good at these speeches,' she said. 'Daisy, we haven't got a chance—'

'Of course we have. It's not as hard as you think,' she continued. 'There has to be a way. Otherwise, it wouldn't have been invented in the first place. Besides, the further we go, the greater our chance of survival. It's been the same all along. But the beast thing up there doesn't know that. He thinks we're a bunch of school kids—'

'Actually, we are,' Archie said, drolly.

Daisy wasn't giving up. 'NO, I mean it,' she implored. 'That thing up there thinks we're useless, frail bambinos and I'll bet it wants to play games with us, teach us a lesson. It's been hanging around like forever, so why get this over in one quick burst?'

'What do you suggest?' Isabella said. 'A game of chess? A quick kick-about?'

Daisy's bright, red-lit eyes bore into her sister. 'None of the above,' she said, coolly.

'Let's try and be a bit smarter. Firstly, we've entirely forgotten one hugely important thing. I'm sure we've got to send something.'

The others pulled faces.

'Dur. The riddles. The poems. Remember.'

Archie and Isabella blushed.

'Archie,' Daisy continued, enjoying herself. 'Can you remember how it goes?'

Archie stuck a finger in the air and scrunched his eyes.

'The third one you search for is under your nose.
It's clear, pure and cold.
In order to draw it out…
You'll need to send a rose.'

DAISY TUTTED, and mimicked Isabella. 'God, we've been so stupid,' she said. 'We've come all this way, killed hundreds of animals and yet we haven't even bothered to follow some simple instructions.' She smiled at her siblings in a snobbishly superior kind of way, before exploding: 'Where the hell are we going to find a rose? Look around; there isn't a hint of life in this horrible place apart from that monster over there. What were we thinking!'

Isabella butted in. 'I'll sprint back and pick one from the garden.'

'You can't do that!' Daisy snapped. 'You can't slip off while we sit here trying to entertain a very violent beast. In any case, it's autumn. If you hadn't noticed, it's rained—a lot. There aren't any leaves, let alone flowers on any plant this side of Tokyo. There are no roses.'

'You got a better idea?' Isabella responded.

'Listen,' Archie began. 'The poem is a riddle, just like Blabisterberry jelly,' he turned towards the old man as an idea struck him. 'Old Man Wood—what can you do with that magical branchwandy thing? Can you grow a rose?'

'I don't know. The branchwand connects with inner energy. I suppose I could if I concentrate.'

'Well, TRY!' they chorused.

With a look of intense concentration on his gnarled old face, Old Man Wood whipped the twig up, circled it in the air and pointed it at the ground.

'Branchwand,' he ordered. 'A rose!'

They looked on in hopeful silence.

'Why doesn't it work?' Isabella whispered.

'I don't know. I told you I hadn't used it in years. It probably doesn't like me, or it's cross with me or something.'

'Cross with you?' Isabella wondered out loud. 'How come—'

'Maybe you're just doing it wrong,' Daisy added. 'Wrong words or something … don't you have to say something in Latin or magic language?'

Old Man Wood started again. 'Branch of Knowledge, grow me a rose, please.'

Isabella spluttered. 'That's a bit desperate?'

Old Man Wood glared at her. 'Manners, Bells. Energy generally responds to good manners.'

'This is absolutely ridiculous,' Isabella stormed. 'We need to do something, or that thing over there is going to slide over and tear us into little bits. And we're not even half way … oooh! Look!' Isabella pointed at the floor.

A tiny bundle of leaves started growing out of the ground. But when it was little more than a small bush, the plant withered and died.

'Rats,' Archie said, stroking his foremost hair spike and staring in the direction of the plinth.

'How about a rose stem, you know, like the ones Dad gives Mum on Valentine's Day,' Isabella said, looking at his blank face. 'Rose cuttings that you arrange in vases?'

Old Man Wood held his breath and shut his eyes. Then, as before, he whipped up the twig:

'Branchwand, please form a rose stem, with a full flower.'

The shining twig glowed and instantly produced a startling red rose.

'That's it!' Isabella squealed, 'you've done it!'

'I told you it was all about manners,' Old Man Wood said, triumphantly.

But before their eyes, the beautiful flower faded and the petals separated and floated to the floor.

'Why is it doing that?'

Old Man Wood shook his head. 'Don't know. Some other power most probably.'

'I've got an idea. Bit random, but I'm sure I'll work,' Isabella cried. 'Anyone got a pen?'

They searched their pockets.

'Old Man Wood, make a pen! Magic me a pencil, charcoal, chalk—something to write with. Please! You can do that?'

The branchwand flashed. Isabella gasped as a thick, gnarly pencil tinkled on the stone floor.

'Paper, as well—a notebook or something.'

Sheets of thick, creamy paper thudded at their feet.

Isabella picked it up and thrust in her sister's direction. 'Daisy you're good at art,' she said. 'Draw a rose.'

'You're kidding.'

'Do I look like I'm kidding?'

Daisy sighed. 'I'm rubbish at art. The thing is, I always get Annie to do all my drawings—'

'You cheat?'

The beast let them know it was there. **GAGOG GAGOG —BARK.**

Daisy fumbled the pencil and picked it up while stealing a glance at the plinth. 'Yeah, or I trace around Mrs Purvis' drawings. She's never bothered.'

Isabella frowned. 'Just try, please?'

Daisy's hand was shaking so much that the final result was nothing like a flower head.

'That's something a three-year-old would be proud of,' Archie said, grinning.

'Well, if you think you can do better,' Daisy said, thrusting the paper at him, 'you do it.'

Archie took the pen and started scribbling.

After a short while, he turned his sheet round to the others.

'OMG, that's even worse than Daisy's,' Isabella scoffed. She grabbed the pen and paper.

All three of them became engrossed as she very rapidly scribbled yet another disastrous flower that looked more like a dandelion than a rose.

Isabella studied it. 'Hopeless—'

Another yelp from the plinth.

'If we can't do this, we've had it,' Daisy said.

'Wait! Stop! You say you traced stuff,' Archie exclaimed as an idea shot into his head. 'I've got it!' He rummaged in his pockets finally finding what he was looking for in his back pocket. Then, with a broad smile, he pulled out the postcard with the glorious red rose on a white background. "A Rose of the Mesopotamian valleys" it read.

'Wow! Excellent,' Daisy beamed. 'Where did you get that?'

'The Italian painting of Mum's, when we were searching the house—'

'Sketch around it ... hurry,' Old Man Wood said. 'The beast's beginning to wonder what's going on.'

As Daisy scribbled around the flower, the others bent over,

engrossed. Soon, her pencil rounded the last petal, and she pulled away, admiring her work.

'Not bad,' Isabella said, inspecting it. 'It definitely passes, probably a B-minus. Any ideas how we might send Daisy's scribble?'

Silence

'Anyone care to volunteer an answer? Old Man Wood, Archie?' Isabella said,

Old Man Wood scratched his chin.

Daisy piped up. 'Use your branchy-thingummy-jig—ask your twig to wing it.'

'No,' Archie said. 'I've got a better idea. Daisy, draw as many as you can, quickly. Isabella, do you remember how to make paper planes?'

She nodded.

'Good,' he said. 'We'll turn each picture of a rose into a plane.'

The beast barked and, as they looked towards it, it had reverted to a dragon once more.

'Hurry. It's looking like it's going to fly over,' Archie said. 'Come on, before it breathes fire over us and burns the lot.'

THIRTY-FIVE

SUE'S CHOICE

S ue stumbled once, then again and fell flat on her face.
 Tears tumbled down her cheeks. She sat down on a
fallen tree trunk and wept. Gus hadn't deserved to be beaten
to death. Her frame shook. How could this have happened
after everything they'd been through together?

She'd never forgive Kemp. Never. Even if he was trying to
help.

And Daisy? Hell, she thought, Daisy had been consumed
by guilt over her choices. Choices that she'd had to make in
the heat of the moment. But why? Why had she rolled the
stone?

She wiped her eyes and filled her lungs with deep breaths.
She wouldn't give in quite so quickly to that oaf Kemp,
knowing that the de Lowes were in the labyrinth.

At the back of her mind lay a nagging doubt. What if
Kemp was right? What if they failed? It only took one of
them to die, and they'd already had such narrow escapes. And
what about this Cain spirit-thing? Kemp didn't think the
ghost was evil. And Kemp had told her that Gus had gone
with it, to save her. Typical Gus, she thought. Selfless to the
very end. Would Gus have wanted her to give in?

She slammed her hand down on the bark of the fallen
tree. 'What is the world coming to?' she said out loud.

A rich, croaky voice answered her back. 'You may well ask.'

Sue's body prickled. She stood up and twisted one way and then the other, but in each direction she found only the fog.

'Who's there?' she said. 'Who is it?'

'You cannot see me,' the voice said. 'But fear ye not, young lady.'

Sue thought quickly. 'Are you ... are you the thing with Kemp?'

The voice appeared to sigh. 'The boy and I have become acquainted,' it replied, 'though we are apart at the moment. He is wondering where you went.'

Inside, Sue seethed. She couldn't hold it back. 'You're the monster who is responsible. You made them fight each other, and now Gus is dead.'

'But you're all going to die,' the voice calmly replied. 'Don't you understand, my dear girl. I am a spirit, connected to the past, the present and the future. Right now, I alone can save you. No one else will survive.'

'But you don't know that!' she screamed. 'What if the de Lowes make it—then we're alright, then everything will go back to normal, and they've still got a chance.' Her voice quietened. 'But Gus won't ever come back, will he?'

'I've just been to see your dear little friends,' the ghost said. 'Check out how they're getting on. And, I am afraid to report that they're finding it a little punishing. Would you like me to fill you in?'

The ghost went quiet. Terrible unease like a chill swept through her. What if it was bad news? She ran her hands through her hair. 'Go on.'

'The Heirs of Eden entered the labyrinth with over three hundred animals of all shapes and sizes guarding them. Quite a sight, so I'm told. These brave beasts put up considerable resistance as they progressed to the middle chamber. But would you like to know how many survived?'

He paused. Then after a suitable break, he continued. 'No

more than twenty − maybe a few more if you include the rats.'

Sue wrapped her arms around herself and shivered.

'The passages run with blood, girl. Right now, they are alone in the chamber against an ancient killing machine. It has been toying with them, but soon it will tire of such games and tear them asunder. You see, it is only a matter of time.'

'You don't know them,' Sue yelled. 'There's more to them than meets the eye.'

The ghost laughed. 'Gorialla Yingarna has never been bested. Not by entire armies or by beasts or by ogres. He is too smart and too strong by half. When cornered, he disappears. One minute he is a fearless dragon, the next he is a tiny blimp on a rock, or a venomous snake or a beast that existed from before your time.

'I'm not telling you this to scare you, but to help you understand the truth. To help you make the right choice. Your friend Gus could see it—'

'Leave Gus out of it.'

'Oh, how the truth hurts. Even if the Heirs defeat Gorialla Yingarna, there is worse to come for your little friends. Rest assured, they will fail—'

'Why are you so sure? What makes you think they can't?'

'Because, dear girl, they, like you, are but small children. And children cannot do this thing.'

'What thing?'

'I cannot tell you—it is for them to find out.' The ghost paused, and his voice mellowed. 'I don't derive pleasure from all this, girl, I'm only telling you because there is another way for you to survive, an opportunity for you to thrive and prosper.'

'Never,' she cried. 'Find someone else!'

The ghost tutted. 'There is a tiny problem; at any moment one of your friends might, how should I say it, "expire". And when that happens, the destruction of your planet will come quickly. There will be no salvation for any living thing on

Earth. Why do you think so many animals sacrificed their lives for your friends?'

The ghost paused for a little while Sue worked it out for herself.

'Your type of human will be eradicated and, in time, a new one will take your place. This is the way of life.'

'Who are you?' she said. 'What do you want?'

'I am from another place, a planet far from here. A long time ago my body was taken away but my spirit, dear girl, will remain on forever.'

'But if you're from another planet, how did you get here?'

'A-ha,' the ghost said. 'A good question. I happened upon a great slice of fortune, which meant I could travel to and fro from Earth. My task was to find a human who might willingly share a body with me—a trickier mission than you might imagine. However, when I rescued the boy, we combined as one body, and the child was saved. The other one, the friend you mentioned, was within a moment of taking over from him.'

The spirit stopped and inspected the girl. 'Tears, my dear, of loss and stubbornness will not help you now.'

'I don't care,' she mumbled.

'I'm sure you know the human expression; desperate times require desperate measures.' The ghost lowered his voice. 'Do not throw this precious life away. You have great qualities. You alone have the opportunity of a new life. A wondrous beginning is within your grasp.'

Sue closed her eyes. 'And if I was to go with you, then what would it be like? Who else is there?'

'The boy and his mother.'

'You want me to go to this alien place with Kemp? You've got to be joking.'

The ghost chuckled. 'The boy said the same thing too. It is a shame. He is not the same as the boy you once knew.'

'He killed Gus—'

'What else could he do?' the ghost said. 'Your friend Gus wanted to win but, perhaps, he missed his opportunity. In any case, it is not Kemp that you should blame but rather the hand of another.'

'You're talking about Daisy, rolling the stone?'

'Indeed. That girl interfered,' the ghost paused for effect. 'She made the difference to their struggle. And what was the boy to do? Lie back? Accept defeat? Give in and die? Both boys knew what they were taking on, but her action, girl, enabled the killer blow.'

Sue's heartbeat quickened. 'But Daisy? Why?' she cried, as much to herself as to the ghost.

'Daisy recognised that the boy you call Kemp had changed. All his life he had no parents and no love and now he has a mother and his heart has stirred. Daisy has unearthed a different person.'

Sue stared into the fog and heard the roar of the flamethrower up the hill. She noted how the eerie veil of white briefly shaded from pink to orange. Sue shifted, remembering the troops setting out to burn down the house. Her head told her this was wrong, madness, contrary to all she'd ever believed or felt. But, in her heart, she observed one honest truth; survival. And when she did that, Gus's face appeared, and his toothy grin smiled back at her.

'I cannot wait forever,' the ghost said. 'And I cannot force you. You will have to make a choice. You must *want* to do this.'

Sue groaned. 'If I was to go with you, and the de Lowes do manage to do this impossible thing? Would you return me here?'

Cain stifled a smile. 'Why, of course, my dear. There will be no point in my hanging on to you. After all, I am only a spirit.'

'Do you promise?'

The ghost hummed, thinking. Then, with a severe and cautious tone in his voice, he spoke. 'I cannot promise a thing like that because the process of transporting you is not up to me. It is done by another creature. I cannot bargain promises on their behalf. You will have to trust my word that I will do whatever I can to get you back in one piece.'

Sue shifted on the bough of the tree.

His tone lightened. 'Perhaps, dear girl, I might make one small suggestion?'

Sue's silence told him to continue.

'If you are in any way interested, let me show you where I'm from and what you might expect. It is not such a bad place and who knows, you may choose to stay, regardless of the outcome here.'

Sue took a deep breath and was about to speak when she heard noises coming from the side.

'Sue!' Kemp's voice rang out. 'Sue, where are you?'

'Here,' she cried out. 'I'm over here.'

Before long, the heavy tread of Kemp's feet negotiating the debris moved closer until, guided in by her voice, he appeared.

'What happened?' he said. 'Are you alright?' He noticed her arm. 'You're cut.'

He ripped off the bottom of his shirt. 'Not sure it's the cleanest but, here, hold your arm out…'

Kemp wrapped the bandage around her forearm knotting the ends neatly together.

'Is everything OK? I—I didn't mean to scare you.'

'I needed to think. It's not everyday this kind of thing happens and the last few days have been so full on, I don't know where my brain is right now.'

Kemp dipped his eyes. 'The soldiers have moved on; they're probably nearing the house now, so … well, you know, you don't have to do anything, but I really need to get my mother out.' He looked up, searching her eyes. 'Have you thought about my suggestion?'

She nodded.

'No one can force you to do anything,' he continued. 'Certainly not me. It has to be something you totally get.'

'I know,' she replied. 'But, I still don't know.'

'If it's any help, I've been thinking,' Kemp said. 'Now that you understand what's going to happen if they fail, think what Isabella and Gus and all the people who care about you would want you to do?' he paused. 'Die, with everyone else, or make a fresh start? I know what my choice would be if it were me. I'm pretty sure the others would feel the same way too—'

'Kemp, shut up,' she interrupted. 'I've made my mind up. I'm not going to do it for you, or for the de Lowes or for Gus or whatever. If you're right, and the world goes down the sinkhole, there's one weenie thing we've overlooked. Humanity. Humanity has to survive, Kemp. If that burden rests on my shoulders, then so be it—even if it means I have to spend the rest of my life with you.'

Kemp hadn't considered this. 'Oh,' he said thickly. 'So, does that mean you're—'

'Yes. I'm prepared to take that chance.'

'Great—'

'I said, shut up,' Sue looked him firmly in the eye. 'First things first, Kemp. Understand this; this is my choice and, from now on, you will do exactly as I say. That's the bottom line. Get it?'

Kemp frowned. He hadn't figured her response would be so assured. 'Er, yeah, sure.'

'Right. Ghost, or whoever you are,' she said into the fog. 'I think it's time you showed me this world of yours. Then, and only then, will I make up my mind.'

THIRTY-SIX
PAPER DARTS

When Daisy had traced several copies and converted them into paper darts, Archie took back the original postcard and neatly folded it into a tiny paper plane. He nudged Old Man Wood.

Archie counted up the darts. Eight in total. 'Can your Branchwand make the darts fly quicker?'

'I'll certainly try, young'un.'

Archie glanced towards the plinth. 'Good, OK. So here's the plan. Bells, you go in the middle directly towards the beast and start distracting it—'

'Sounds like a great idea,' Isabella said, sarcastically. 'How?'

Archie shrugged. 'I don't know, make it up. Then, when you get a chance, throw a dart towards the plinth. Old Man Wood will try and give them a bit more oomph, right?'

Old Man Wood stared anxiously at his branchwand.

'What if it fires a fireball?' Isabella said.

'If it blows fire, Daisy will tell you it's coming and then you do that protection-bubble thing with your hands.'

He turned to Daisy. 'Got it? Go with Isabella. When the time comes, run out and throw more darts. It's a bit of a gamble because I'm not sure you can deflect stuff like her, so after it's blasted a long fireball, run like crazy. And then try to get it to talk to you—'

Isabella nodded. 'Smart idea, Arch. It speaks inside your head about how it's going to tear you to shreds—'

'Sounds like a totally awesome plan so far,' Daisy said, sarcastically. 'And while we're getting incinerated, what are you going to do?'

Archie smiled. 'I'm going to sneak around the other side and outflank it. When I'm ready, I'll give you the sign—'

'What sort of sign?'

Archie rubbed a hair spike. 'I'll hoot, like an owl. You'll know—so use your listening skill, Daisy. If it latches on to me, fly the remaining darts with the roses on to the plinth.'

'Seriously, Archie. Will this work?' Isabella asked, incredulously. 'I mean, when ancient man was preparing for this exact moment to determine the future of the worlds, I'm not sure they had paper planes in mind.'

Archie shrugged. 'Have you got a better suggestion?'

The silence said it all.

Suddenly a beating of wings made them look up at the jagged domed ceiling above. The beast flapped high above them.

Archie sensed his moment. 'Run, Bells. Go for the plinth. Old Man Wood, get ready.'

With that, Isabella raced into the open, Daisy trying hard to keep up.

The beast dived.

'Look out!' Archie cried.

The girls threw themselves to the floor as the talons of the dragon narrowly missing them, wind from its wings brushing dust over their faces as it returned to its position on the tablet.

Daisy was the first to her feet. Moments later she launched a dart. It flew up and glided, nearing the plinth. But there it remained; floating, suspended, high up in the air.

'Bells, throw another!' Daisy said.

Isabella cocked her arm and released. The dart flew straight, but instead of remaining motionless, the beast, now back on the plinth, reverted into a coiled snake, extended upwards so that it reached high into the air like a stretched spring. Then it leaned out towards the paper dart, opened its jaws and gobbled the dart up.

A strange, high-pitched screech filled the chamber, the sound crashing into their heads.

Your answer to getting the tablet of the labyrinth is to throw thin, wooden birds. I am most amused. Is this what the old man taught you?

The beast, now a small dragon, sat on the edge of the plinth staring down at the girls. Then, with a puff of smoke, the suspended dart burst into flames, its charred remains dancing to the ground.

Laughter resounded.

Look at me; I'm a baby dragon, fighting baby children.

'Don't listen to it,' Daisy yelled, shaking her sister. 'Think of something else, anything.'

'I can't. Its voice vibrates right through to my toes.'

'I'm going to run for the far side,' Daisy said. 'To the exit passageway on the over there—'

She heard a strange clicking noise. 'Incoming fireball! Isabella! Now!'

Isabella reacted fast. Her hands reached up as a stream of fire flashed out of the dragon's mouth. Isabella pushed back sending the flames back from where they came.

The dragon roared, confused at being engulfed by its own flames.

Daisy slipped out from behind Isabella and ran, stopping only to launch another dart before sprinting off across the floor. This dart lacked thrust and crash-landed short of the stream.

Three down.

Isabella stood alone in the middle of the cavern, trembling. She looked up. Now, on the plinth, sat an enormous beast, four times the size of the baby, smoke pouring from its nostrils, snarling back at her.

All she had to do was run twenty metres and throw the

dart—if Archie's theory held. And she could be there in a flash. But just as she readied herself, a voice called out.

I am bored of you, pathetic children, it said, the noise rattling around her brain rendering her helpless.

The beast reared up on its hind legs.

Time to get rid of you once and for all.

It took off and flew directly at Daisy, its razor-sharp claws outstretched, menace blazing from its eyes.

THIRTY-SEVEN
A STRANGE NOISE

Although the going had been treacherous and exhausting, Stone willed them on, the blast of the flamethrower displaying rocks and upturned trees and holes in the ground before the fog wrapped around them, like a blanket.

'Sir,' Lambert announced. 'Buildings dead ahead. Got a glimpse of stonework on the last burn.'

'Excellent,' Stone replied. 'Quicker than I hoped. Any idea of distance?'

'Fifty metres at a guess, could be more. These things reach a hell of a long way.'

'How much fuel in the tank?'

Lambert inspected the weapon. 'Three or four more blasts, sir, if we keep them short.'

Stone shook out a leg. 'Reserve fire until we're up there. Reckon you can find a path?'

'I'll do my best, sir,' Lambert replied. 'Don't think there's much in the way. Straight on up.'

'Good. No time to waste, soldiers, Let's move.'

They began their ascent to the cottage, each following close on the heels of the man in front. The only sounds were the clinking of metal and boots squishing in the mud.

A short while later, Geddis stopped and called out 'Halt!'

He bent down, the others following.

'What is it, Geddis?'

'A strange noise, sir. Listen.'

Instinctively the soldiers remained statue-still, straining their ears.

Stone stroked his moustache. 'Sounds familiar. Like animals.'

He pulled out his radio. 'Come in units.'

A radio crackled back.

'We've got a strange noise heading our way. Have you come across anything…'

'Sir,' one of his men yelled. 'It's a stampede, heading directly towards us.'

The noise of hooves pounding the ground, was coming up fast.

The men squatted. Lambert shuffled the flamethrower around his torso and pulled out his handgun.

Stone's fingers gripped the cold metal of his automatic too.

'No animal would be crazy enough … Get down!' Stone ordered, but his words were lost amidst a crashing of hooves and whinnying and neighing.

The men scattered in all directions.

'What the bleeding hell was that,' Stone roared. 'Missed me by a millimetre.'

'Horses, sir,' returned Geddis, panting.

'I know that, you dimwit. Why are they charging us?'

Geddis cocked his head. 'They're coming back, sir,' he said, his eyes darting from side to side. He ran.

'We'll see about that,' Stone said, and he pulled out his weapon, loosening a couple of rounds into the fog.

But the thunder of hooves didn't abate and, before he knew it, the animals flashed into view. This time, instead of galloping through, the animals stopped, reared up, and kicked out, bucking furiously.

Stone felt the full force in his chest, propelling him down the hill. He crashed into a pool of mud, pain ripping through his midriff. As the animals tore off, Stone reached for his weapon and fired randomly into the gloom. He sank back, listening to the sudden quiet.

As he inhaled, pains, like sharp knives, stabbed his rib cage. A crack or two, he thought. Nothing more. Nothing he couldn't cope with. He folded his left arm across his chest making it bearable. Where was that damn flamethrower? Lambert had it.

A groan from nearby caught his attention.

He crawled on his hands and knees, picking his way to the noise.

Rolling over a large tree bough, he held his sides until the pain faded and moved on. The moaning, now sporadic, sounded close.

'Sir!' he heard, the cries laced with agony.

Stone found the soldier lying under a boulder.

'Everything all right?' Stone asked.

The man blinked slowly as Stone's face came into view.

Stone checked the man over, finding blood seeping from a wound in his upper breast. 'Blimey, caught you a cropper, didn't it?' Stone said.

Pulling out his knife, Stone cut open the fabric to inspect the wound. Then he realised what had happened.

Stone whistled. 'What's your name, lad?'

The soldier, his face pale and his eyes wide, stared back, struggling to form his words. 'Vincent, sir.'

'Got any family, Vincent.'

Vincent's breathing laboured and momentarily, he closed his eyes tight. 'A little girl, sir.' He grabbed the commissioner's arm, digging in his fingernails. 'Tell her,' he breathed, a desperate sense of urgency filling him, 'tell her that I saw a unicorn. A beautiful white unicorn.'

Stone shook his head. Death and delusion, hand in hand. He pulled out his automatic and placed the barrel to the soldiers head. 'Sure,' he said, 'I'll pass on the message.'

Then, he squeezed the trigger.

THIRTY-EIGHT
ARCHIE'S PLAN

'Archie!' Isabella screamed. 'What the hell are you doing?'

Sensing Archie's move to the other side of the chamber, the beast changed tack.

'Look out, it's coming your way—'

Archie was running when a ball of fire engulfed him. He threw himself to the floor.

'Hell!' Isabella said, her eyes bulging. Flames danced on Archie's jacket.

Isabella flashed over and smothered the flames.

'What is it with you, Arch, you reckless lunatic. What about the plan?!'

'Daisy was attacked. I couldn't watch without doing something. She took a claw to the shoulder. Lucky it didn't take her head off.'

'Look out!' Daisy screamed from across the chamber. 'Incoming!'

Isabella stood up and faced the beast, extending her hands in front of her. The flames curved around them in an arc. The dragon flapping close, roared, blowing Isabella to the floor.

'Send another dart, while it circles,' Daisy yelled, clasping her throbbing shoulder. 'NOW.'

Isabella dusted herself off, pulled out the paper dart, straightened it as fast as she could and jerked her arm forward. Old Man Wood flicked his branchwand, and the mini paper-plane zoomed towards the plinth.

'And another,' Daisy yelled.

'We only have two left!'

'DO IT!'

Isabella fumbled, straightened the dart and sent it on its way.

In a flash, she pulled Archie up and together they ran, the noise of flapping wings closing in on them.

'Incom—'

Archie dived into a narrow gully pulling Isabella with him. Flames licked the stone behind them.

Isabella studied their position. 'We're trapped, Archie,' Isabella said, her voice shaking. 'All it has to do is fly over.'

'No, we're not. Look,' he said. 'New plan. You've got one more dart. On my signal, sprint into the middle of the room as fast as you can, directly towards the plinth, get as close as you can and let go. Physically put it on—if you can.'

Isabella looked appalled. 'That amounts to suicide, Archie. And what are you going to do?'

Archie winked. 'Trust me,' he said, before haring across the chamber towards the far side.

THIRTY-NINE

SUE YIELDS

'Don't struggle, whatever you do,' Kemp said. 'Just try and go with the flow. I mean, that's if you can.' He didn't intend for it to sound like it did.

Sue shot him a look. 'Sure,' she said. Her arm shook so much she couldn't find the entrance to the coat sleeve.

Trying to compose herself she glanced at Kemp, seeking reassurance, but all she saw was Kemp's smirk. The one he used on her and Isabella whenever trouble was lurking.

She hesitated.

The ghost growled his impatience. 'Is there a problem?' he said.

'What if Gus is still alive,' she blurted out.

The ghost chuckled. 'I can vouch that more likely than not, Gus is already in the digestive tracks of the beast. I tell you this, so you are not fooled into believing there is any hope he is alive.'

She bowed her head, the pain of his loss sharper every time she thought of him.

'Are you ready,' Cain said, his tone softer. 'My dear girl, the universe waits for no man—or girl.'

Slowly, Sue pushed one arm into the sleeve of the overcoat. Instantly, a cold freeze enveloped her, tingling her nerves. She twisted as her other arm dived in, and she drew the front of the coat around her frame. Exquisite feelings of cold, yet burning, treacle-like sensations flooded into her heart, as the liquid ice poured through her veins and into every sinew, taking her breath away. The feelings crept down her midriff, through her groin, washing, like thick oil, into her legs and down to the tips of her toes. She groaned as the intense feeling took hold of her.

The ghost's hat rested on her head, and the burning liquid continued its journey up, through her neck and into her brain.

Sue cried out as the cold flashed through her skull and around her head quickly turning into a heat, like molten iron, which plunged into her eyes. The pain, like nothing she'd ever experienced before.

She winced but, as the discomfort subsided, she remembered Kemp's advice to relax as much as she could. She breathed deeply and let herself go.

She soon realised she could hear, in a muffled way, as if cotton wool had been crammed in her ears. And as she dared to open her eyes, her vision was distorted as if a film of privacy glass had been coated over them.

She stood still and a tingling sensation in her legs, like mild sunburn, left her wondering what it meant.

The pain grew, so she moved, alleviating the pain. The same happened to the other leg.

So, she thought, this was walking.

Her arms suffered the same sensations, and she learned that resisting movement resulted in a burn, just as Kemp had shown her. At least he hadn't lied.

She closed her eyes, relaxing as best she could, feeling for nudges of heat and reacting accordingly. In no time, almost as if by second nature, she could tell exactly what was coming.

FORTY

AN UNEXPECTED WEAPON

Isabella heard a breathy hooting sound. *Archie's signal!* She took a deep breath and, armed only with a paper dart, climbed out of the gully and ran directly at the plinth her feet taking her at full speed.

Archie watched her go. In a flash, he fished out the original postcard, now a card-sized paper-plane and kissed it.

He scanned the chamber. He could just make out the head of the beast, distracted by Isabella's suicidal run.

Excellent. If he could just sneak a teeny bit closer.

He tiptoed.

Then he glanced up.

A head, suspended by an impossibly long, thick neck, with smoke snaking out of its flared nostrils, and huge, marble-like, green eyes bore into him. He felt momentarily winded, as if his soul was being sucked out of him.

But how? The head he'd seen had gone towards Isabella who was, to all intents and purposes, shielding him from a flame attack. His heartbeat quickened and dizziness washed through him.

Isabella screamed.

The beast had multiple heads.

This wasn't in the plan.

He carried on running, his head in turmoil.

The beast arched its neck. A blast was heading his way, but he wasn't nearly close enough to let go.

As he heard the roar of angry fire, his foot snagged and he tripped flat on his face, the dart slipping through his fingers.

Archie's head hit the floor, and then he rolled. Needles of fire pushed through him, his clothes flaming orange. He continued rolling and rolling, his body tingling as if boiling oil had been poured over his skin.

He came to a stop not far from the plinth, at the full mercy of the beast. Quickly, he ripped off the remains of his coat and there, strapped across his torso, were his collection of knives.

'Fantastic plan, Arch—extremely well thought through.' Daisy yelled over, conscious that blood from her wound now seeped over her hand.

'Yeah, thanks,' he said through gritted teeth. 'I reckon it's going pretty well.'

'Any idea what we should do now?'

'Old Man Wood might have a plan.'

'Old Man Wood? You're joking.'

He twisted around to see Isabella catching her breath, gawping at the two-headed beast who remained on the plinth. 'Bells, what do you think.'

Isabella, her hair stuck to her forehead, regarded Archie with nothing less than animosity.

'Archie de Lowe,' she seethed. 'If you so much as breathe another word about a plan, I'm going to personally offer you up—' She spotted his knives around his chest. 'Your knives! Do feel free to use them. For once, you have my complete authority.'

The beast's head jerked towards him.

It was now or toast, Archie thought, as he reached into his knife holster and weighed up a knife. Then, darting forward as the beast's heads lowered towards him, his arm flashed forward. The weapon zinged through the air, slicing into its neck.

A terrible roar filled the cavern as the beast reared up. Archie let another go, this time the blade disappearing into its chest.

Suddenly the beast vanished.

Instinctively, they turned and sprinted back to the edge of the cave entrance where they huddled together, edging backwards.

'You're quite good at that,' Isabella said.

'Years of practice,' he smiled, 'when you weren't watching.'

'Any paper planes remaining?' Daisy asked.

'Nah, all gone,' Archie answered. 'Didn't really factor in the fire-breathing bit.'

'Your planning skills leave a lot to be desired, 'Isabella said. 'I should never have trusted you.'

Archie shrugged. 'It was worth a try.'

Isabella noticed Daisy's lacerated shoulder and ran her hands over the wound, halting the blood flow. 'Looking at the state of us, Archie,' she spat, 'I'm not sure it was.'

'There's one dart left, a duff-shot,' Daisy said. 'It's lying on the ground...' she pointed towards the plinth, 'over there.'

'What about the postcard?'

Archie coughed. 'Oh yeah. The postcard ... well—'

Isabella rounded on him. 'What happened to the post-card, Archie?'

'I dropped it,' he said.

'You did what?!'

Archie reddened. 'I tripped, which kind of helped me avoid a full frying. As I fell, it slipped out.'

'Where did it go?'

He shrugged. 'I don't know. Could have gone anywhere. It's probably been incinerated, like most of me.'

'Great,' Isabella said. 'Now what?' She suddenly shuffled backwards faster. 'OM bloody G.'

Archie whistled. 'It's a pulsing yellow mishmash of a triceratops, a gigantic toad and a—'

'Diplodocus,' Isabella finished off for him.

'And it smells,' Daisy volunteered, 'like rotten eggs, with a touch of spirit, like alcohol, infused with dung.'

By now, they'd retreated even further down the passageway and re-joined Old Man Wood.

Isabella felt agitated. She sniffed the air again and crouched down.

'Daisy,' she said, 'Scour the air. Look for anything unusual.'

'Like what?'

'Gas particles.'

'What the hell do they look like?'

'Different, Daisy. The particle structure won't be the same.'

'Not really very helpful,' Daisy said, her red eyes scanning the air surrounding the beast. 'Actually, I think I've got something. A-ha, a yellow, spiky mixture of elements.'

'It's gassing us, Daisy. It's going to subdue us—make us helpless.'

'Old Man Wood, can you please do something with that branch thing?'

'I'm trying. The beast is too powerful—'

Suddenly a large puff of yellow gas cloud sped towards them.

'Get down!' Isabella ordered. 'Right down, on the floor. Closer,' she ordered. 'Heads together.' With a swirl of her hands, she forced out a pink cocoon. She closed her eyes and gritted her teeth, holding the protective film as the musty, swirling gas cloud filled the chamber and leeched down the passageway.

'I don't know how long I can hold this.' Isabella cried.

The bubble began to deflate like a balloon with a tiny pin prick in it.

'Keep going,' Archie said. 'As long as you can.'

Beads of perspiration rolled off her brow.

The bubble soon circled only their heads and, as the gas sank lower, drowsiness began to fill them.

One by one, their eyes closed, and their breathing shallowed.

With one final effort, Isabella forced the bubble to expand once more, giving them a last, desperate supply of oxygen, but now she too struggled to keep her eyes open.

Daisy stole a look towards the plinth. She noticed that the beast had changed into a huge T-Rex creature and was sniffing around the plinth, its head darting here and there as though agitated, nervous.

Maybe, she thought, *it's readying itself to get us.*

With that finally thought, she joined the others and slipped away.

FORTY-ONE
SOLOMON UNDERSTANDS

'Quiet!' Dickinson said. 'Listen.'

Not far away, the beat of hooves patted the ground, walking.

'They're coming closer. Maybe it's the gunmen.'

'Are they dangerous?'

The soldiers and Solomon crouched down, as still as statues, waiting, as the hooves and snorting of the beasts approached through the fog, their hooves occasionally catching stone or clipping bits of wood.

'Put that weapon away, Talbot,' Dickinson ordered.

'But you heard the shots?'

'I don't care,' Dickinson said. 'These animals don't mean any harm. They're probably scared to death and looking for company. There's no point intimidating them.'

'What about the gunfire, who was that?'

'That was way off, Talbot. If you hadn't noticed, it's impossible to see out there and, as you are fully aware, you never fire guns when you can't see.'

Talbot slipped the automatic back in its holster as a head broke through the fog.

'Goodness gracious me!' Solomon exclaimed. 'Well, would you look at that!'

Into the clearing emerged a long, ivory-coloured, spiralling horn followed by the snow-white nose of a horse.

'Hey! It's a pretty horsey,' Talbot said. 'And some joker's stuck a tusk on it.'

Solomon smiled. 'Quite right, Talbot. I wonder what else that sort of creature might be known as?'

Dickinson scratched his nose. 'A horse with a spike on its head,' he mused. 'That's unusual—handsome enough beast though.'

Solomon burst out laughing. 'Don't get me wrong, but horses with spikes on their heads are generally known as "unicorns".'

'Oh, that's bleedin' hilarious,' Talbot said. 'A unicorn, right here in Yorkshire? My arse. Next you'll be telling me there are two-headed dragons kicking about, or animals that can talk.' He laughed at his words, as another glimmering unicorn entered and stood by the first, both of their horns shining like polished needles. The first unicorn whinnied, then backed off, nudging its head to one side.

Talbot whistled. 'Bleeding heck. It's like a cartoon round 'ere. Next thing you know there'll be a handsome prince swanning along with a sword and armour 'n all.'

'What do you think it wants?' Solomon asked.

Dickinson pulled his jaw from the floor. 'Want? What do you mean, "want"?'

'Well,' Solomon began, 'in my experience, unicorns don't exactly show up every day, do they?'

'Good point,' Dickinson said, recovering his wits. 'This lot don't look as if they would harm a fly.'

'Maybe they want feeding?' Talbot said.

'Or, maybe,' Gates, the scrawny young soldier said, 'we're dead. Coz, these are, like, heavenly creatures, ain't they?'

The second unicorn retreated and disappeared into the fog. Then the first did the same, before returning.

This curious action was repeated.

'By George!' Solomon said. 'I think they want us to follow them.'

The unicorn whinnied and pointed its horn towards Solomon before retreating again.

'Well, there we have it,' Solomon said. 'Come on. These things don't happen without a reason. Let's try, eh? See what happens?'

They gathered their bits and, as one unicorn moved in front of the other, the party did the same, making a single file. Dickinson behind the unicorn followed by Solomon and the other troops.

Dickinson noticed it first. 'The tail,' he half-whispered to Solomon. 'Look how it shines?'

Even in the fog, wisps of fine hairs glowed like threads of brightly coloured luminous tinsel. Following this strange beacon proved easy and, for the first time, the section found themselves walking rather than scrabbling and tripping up the hillside.

Soon their footsteps were surer as the ground became stony and solid as though they had moved onto a track or a path. Moreover they noticed that instead of climbing they were on a level, walking along the brow of a hill.

'I do believe,' Solomon said, 'that they're taking us to the cottage.'

Dickinson turned briefly. 'Really, headmaster? But why?'

'I would have thought the reason was obvious,' Solomon said, catching his breath. 'Right now, who is the most considerable threat to the success of the children?'

'Stone?'

'Indeed. And, if I'm right, these beautiful animals have entrusted us to sort Stone out before he does any further harm.'

FORTY-TWO

GAIA FINDS A DREAM

G aia, the dreamspinner, flashed through her electric maghole into the chamber.

It wasn't long before she recognized she wasn't the only dreamspinner checking up on the Heirs of Eden's progress. Tiny flashes from other dreamspinners bursting in and out told her and soon she could see many suspended in the air high above in the cavern ceiling and also on the sides.

Looking into the chamber she noticed a yellow substance mingling with the air. It reminded her of the mixture used by the traitor, Asgard, with his poison-filled dream powders that had spread plague to humans as they slept.

Was this the same lethal matter? Whatever it was, she knew she had to do something. The old man had regained his branchwand, but, she realised, he still had no idea how to use it.

Immediately she inverted and arrived beside the bodies of the three children and Old Man Wood, who lay prostrate on the ground with an almost deflated bubble surrounding their heads. Reverting into her visible form so that other dreamspinners wouldn't see her unless they did the same, she stretched a long, thin claw into her maghole in search of some dream-powders. Moments later, she *knitted and spun* a dream about fresh air that she had used for those trapped under water or in the airless reaches of space.

She pushed a tiny needle at the end of her leg through the barrier and applied the powder the moment he drew in a breath.

Before sealing the hole Gaia pushed in a body of fresh air particles. Enough to keep them alive while the powder set to work.

A sound from nearby made her turn.

Asgard appeared in his visible form. Immediately, his legs hummed together in speech. 'Gaia. Do you meddle?'

'I check if the Heirs are alive, Asgard. For gas and poison is such a miserable and cowardly way to die, isn't it?'

'How would we dreamspinners know such a thing?' he responded. 'The Heirs of Eden have little time left in this world,' he said, his legs vibrating fast. 'Join me. Let us be rid of this world and start afresh in another place where dreams can still be made.'

'Havilah is a last resort,' Gaia retorted. 'There is still a chance, Asgard.'

'You still think they can win, don't you, Gaia? Did you not see how the Heirs of Eden in their great wisdom sent flammable birds to defeat the beast? A sick universe is one that sends children instead of men. Meddle if you must with the old man. It will not matter.' Then, with a tiny flash, Asgard vanished.

Gaia waited until the dreamspinner's vibrations had departed.

Sending thin, wooden darts was indeed ludicrous, but these Heirs were selected because they were strong and fast and smart. There had to be a reason for their actions. But what was it?

She scoured the floor and noticed the sheets of paper and the thick writing implement and two abandoned pieces of paper nearby. Moving over she examined them.

Flowers?

Then it dawned on her. *The riddle*. The riddle said they needed to send a rose—wasn't that it?

Gaia suddenly understood what they'd been trying to achieve.

She scoured the room and saw a strange shape hanging high up in the cave.

Beneath her, the old man fumbled for his stick. *Excellent.*

Gaia dipped two legs into her maghole. Perhaps, she thought, the infinite wisdom of the universe still had other ideas.

FORTY-THREE
ARCHIE GETS STUCK

J ust as Old Man Wood shut his eyes, the clear idea of a fresh-air spell zipped into his mind, and, with one last effort, he blew on his strange stick and uttered the words: 'Vooosh swisshes woozoom-shhh.'

Moments later the group stirred.

Isabella sucked the atom-wide material back into her hands and breathed deeply.

Archie yawned. 'Aw. My head hurts.'

'Mine too,' Daisy said. 'How long do you think we were out?'

'No idea. To be honest, I'm amazed we're still here. I wonder what made the gas disappear?'

The others had no answer.

'What's it up to now?' Archie said, as they sat up.

'Looking for something,' Daisy said, squinting at the pedestal.

'For what?'

'A bag of nuts? A hot date? How should I know,' she said. 'Don't ask stupid questions.'

The beast barked and sprang from one leg to the other then changed into a huge snake, which slithered around the plinth swinging its head to and fro, like a pendulum.

In a flash it was a small lizard running over and through

the cracks and then it changed into a vast brontosaurus, its body over-spilling the plinth, its elongated neck bending on itself, blowing air into the smaller nooks and crannies.

On the ground, just in front of the plinth, the air whipped up a small cloud of dust. A paper dart briefly fluttered up and floated down.

'There!' Archie exclaimed. 'Your paper plane! I thought they'd been burned…'

A whoosh of flame raged from the beast's mouth.

'Oh.'

'Terrific,' Isabella said, kicking out at the side of the tunnel. A pile of gravelly earth spilled out. 'Right back to where we started. Old Man Wood have you got the pen and paper?'

'They were burned too. The only things left are your dreadful pictures.'

'Can you make more?'

Old Man Wood prepared his branchwand but Archie stepped in.

'There's no point, we don't have the postcard to trace around,' he reminded them.

As if reading their minds, the monster blew a burst of fire into the chamber.

Daisy ignored it and stepped inside the chamber, scanning the ceiling. She thought she'd seen a tiny flicker, like a bat … or a large spider? She stared at it for some time and then scratched her chin with her less painful hand. 'I may be mistaken,' she said, 'but I have a feeling your postcard's hanging from a rock in the ceiling directly above the plinth.'

'It can't be. I fell over.'

'It's a paper-plane, Arch. It could have soared up into the sky—'

'Really?'

'Yes. On a thermal, like vultures,' Isabella added. 'The hot air could easily have made it rise. It's not impossible with its aerodynamic shape. You did make it properly, didn't you?'

Archie looked injured. 'Yeah.'

'If it is,' Daisy said, her full gaze upon it, 'it's caught in something, like a spiders web.' And then, as she zoomed-in even further, she added. 'And there's a kind of weird-looking spider on it, trying to cut it out—'

'Which means it might fall at any second,' Archie said. 'And, if it goes, it's our—'

'Very last chance,' Daisy finished off for him.

Isabella brushed her foot over the floor. 'Another distraction?'

'Yup, looks like it.'

'The postcard's wobbling,' Daisy exclaimed. 'Do something. NOW!'

Archie marched out into the open.

'No! Archie!' Isabella shrieked. 'You damn fool.'

'Oi!' Archie yelled towards the plinth. 'Why don't you and I have a little chat.'

Cold laughter reverberated as an echo through their heads.

Archie ignored it and continued 'If you give up now and hand over the tablet, I might be prepared to spare you.'

The beast, now a huge dragon, fixed Archie with a cold stare, then it reared up.

'Incoming, Arch,' Daisy yelled.

Archie dived out of the way as the bolt of fire flashed past. He picked himself up and dusted himself down. 'You see, we know your tricks—you're no match for us.'

'Another incom—'

Archie dived again, like a goalkeeper in a penalty shoot-out. He guessed correctly, stood up and faced the dragon.

But the beast morphed into a huge snake and reared up.

You won't escape this, little human child.

'Different noise, Archie,' Daisy said. 'Don't know what it means—'

The snake opened its jaws wide showing long, glistening fangs. It leaned over.

'Poison,' Isabella screamed. 'Venom. Don't let it touch you.'

Daisy scoured the ceiling for the post-dart. She couldn't see it. Her heartbeat quickened. She ran out into the open. 'It's behind you!' she yelled to the serpent. 'He's right. Give up now, or else.'

Isabella shook her head. *Idiots!*

The beast studied Daisy, its eyes fixing her with a look of extreme hatred.

'Seriously,' Daisy said. 'The thing you're looking for is behind you.'

'It's behind you!' Archie yelled.

It's like a bleeding pantomime, Isabella thought as she ran out. 'It's behind you!' she bellowed, pointing with her arm.

Momentarily, the snake twisted towards her, wondering if it was a trick.

Then, resuming its position, venom gushed out of its long fangs like a hose.

Daisy heard it coming. 'Scram,' she whispered to Archie who dashed to the side as the poison jetted out, fizzling on the ground.

The beast twisted.

'GAGOG GAGOG BARK GAGOG!'

The noise was so loud it dislodged small rocks and earth from the ceiling.

Then, it shuddered, as if shaking itself dry. Now it howled like a dog, furiously until all three were pushing fingers into their ears.

'Snakey's freaking out,' Archie said, joining the others, 'something weird is going on.'

They backed off and crouched down.

A noise like a waterfall grew and grew as if getting nearer.

They scoured the chamber and ran back to Old Man Wood in the entrance.

Suddenly, Daisy squealed. 'Over there! It's a ... plant.'

'What?'

'A climbing, spiky plant, like a rose.'

Tendrils shot up from the water surrounding the plinth on

all sides, flashing out so fast that by the time the beast had any idea what was happening it was too late.

It wriggled, then swayed, first one way then the other, but the barbs of the rose covered its scales so rapidly that in no time the beast was coated in a bush of needle-like, thorny creepers.

The beast shrank but tendrils flashed out horizontally directing its growth towards it at astonishing speed. Believing the tablet was at risk, the beast expanded into a huge monster, shrieking and screaming as the tendrils dug deep and rushed up and over its vast body. The more it struggled, they sensed, the thicker and tighter the tendrils became, the more the spurs appeared to work into its flesh, tying the monster up as if it were snared in barbed wire.

And now as they looked up at the plinth they could see white blood flowing down its scales. And, even from a distance, they could smell its foul odour.

'COME ON,' Archie yelled.

In no time, all three together with Old Man Wood were beside the pool.

Without hesitating, Archie splashed through the water, looked up at the thorny tendrils. As he reached out to touch the prickly stem, the spikes turned into smooth bark in front of his eyes.

'Get me up there! Old Man Wood, give me a leg up ... higher.'

Old Man Wood waded in and hoisted Archie up to the stone ledge. In one movement Archie pulled himself up.

'What can you see?' Daisy yelled.

The serpent barked and tried to thrash out.

Archie slipped, almost tumbling into the stream.

'It's sitting on the tablet!' he shouted down. 'But it's totally tied up ... I think,' he said, giving the netted beast a light shove. The beast rocked, fractionally. He fell onto his stomach and tried to reach under the scaly bulk to the tablet. He gave up. 'I'm going to have to push it off!'

'Then do it!'

Archie shoved. The beast wobbled. Archie put all of his strength into his next push, jogging the beast further to the edge.

'It's coming!' he said, as the huge scales moved a fraction more. With another shove, he inched it even further. At last he saw the edge of the tablet. Success was a couple of mighty shoves away.

'Can you get it?' Daisy shouted.

'Give me a chance!' Archie said, his face twisted by his efforts. 'This isn't exactly easy.'

In frustration, Archie stood up and swung his foot at the belly of the snake as hard as he could. There was a slurping 'thud' followed by an ear-shattering BARK.

'What was that?' Old Man Wood shouted.

Archie howled. 'Oh NO! NOOO!'

'What is it? What's going on up there?' Old Man Wood called out.

'My foot ... it's my foot.' Archie yelled. He was hopping up and down as if on pogo stick.

'What about your foot?' Daisy asked.

'I kicked the snake a little hard. My foot—'

'Archie?'

'It's ... it's stuck.'

'Stuck? Where?' Isabella called out. 'Archie, what on earth are you doing up there? Can you see the tablet?'

'Yes,' he groaned. But I can't get it out—because I can't get my foot out. And ... oh boy.'

He squealed.

'Archie!' Isabella said, 'speak to us.'

'I'm trying to move it ... nearly there...'

The stone tablet slipped over the edge of the plinth and splashed into the water in front of Daisy.

She grabbed it just before it sank. 'I've got it!' she shouted. 'Get out of there!'

'I told you. I can't. My foot's stuck like a vice.'

'You've got to, Arch. NOW!' Daisy pleaded. 'Rip it out!'

'What do you think I'm trying to do?'

Archie howled.

Old Man Wood pulled himself up the plinth until his head popped over and he could see the situation. 'Push the snake off the plinth—it's the only way you'll release it.'

'But if I push it off, it'll escape.'

'Have you got a better idea?' Isabella yelled back at him.

Archie weighed up his options. Then he started heaving. Slowly the bulk of the beast moved ever closer to the edge of the dais.

'Aaaarrrggghhh! My leg!' he screamed, as a slurping, 'POP' resonated, as if a cork had been blown out of a champagne bottle.

'Archie!' Isabella screamed.

There was no reply. The children held their breath.

'Archie, are you OK? Archie, answer me!' Isabella cried. 'Old Man Wood, DO something.'

Archie's head appeared over the plinth, a big smile covering his face. 'I got my leg out. Boy, it stinks.'

FORTY-FOUR

GUS AWAKENS

G us hadn't slept so well in ages.

He yawned and stretched his arms out wide. As he opened his eyes and they began adjusting to the dim light falling through a small hole high up in the roof above him, he saw a stony slide angling down towards him.

Smells of animal dung, hides and the tang of urine filled the air. On the far side a brazier flickered soft, orange light.

It came rushing back. The fight. Kemp beaten, lying on the ground, moaning. The pain. He'd waited, told Kemp to run away and get out of there, but then, as if from nowhere, Kemp had smashed him. A stone, a rock. The memories, hazy though they were, began rushing back.

He thought of lovely Sue. *Did she think he was dead?*

Gus flexed his leg and noticed the tightness in his muscles. Pulling up his trouser leg he fingered the tender, rotund, blue bruises on his shin.

Instinctively, he ran a hand over his body and then his scalp touching bruises as tender as juicy figs. As he stood up, his head hummed and a terrific pain started behind his eyes. Nausea filled his stomach. Had he been knocked out cold? Even if he had, how had he arrived here, of all places?

He noticed a stone basin and a trickle of water dripping

into it from the rocks above. He sniffed it, wary of its contents and, satisfied, he cupped his hands and drank deeply, splashing water over his head. The liquid refreshed him better than he'd dared hope. Almost at once the clouds in his head cleared and the pain behind his eyes softened. After another draught, his bruises and aches lessened.

Gus stood up, stretched and strode around the empty, quiet room, wondering where he was. Had Isabella and Daisy and Archie been here? Had Sue been here with hundreds of animals? And, had each one made the journey down the chute before marching off down the one corridor. If so, why?

Removing a sconce from the wall, he inspected the ground with the firelight.

Hoof and paw prints, deer and rabbit imprints, birds' talons and webbed feet. And then he noticed a large cat print. A lion?

For a minute the image of every animal in a zoo slipped into his mind. In here? Really?

He followed the direction of the prints near the entrance further down the chamber. Passing the corridor, he noticed a mixture of hoof, paw and claw marks, and then he saw what had previously puzzled him. Shoe prints, as clear as anything. Three or four types of boot design, imprinted like clay-moulds into the muddy surface.

Gus set off, his brain whirring. His long strides turned into a jog, which, as his blood began to pump, turned into a run. But while the corridor was a blur of every hoof and print he could imagine, there was no sign of footprints. Had they been carried? Had they left?

At every corner, Gus slowed, peering round to see what, if anything, lay in wait for him on the other side.

Several turns later he approached another bend. A darker colour stained the floor. He touched the silky liquid and, when he put it up to the firelight, the colour was a deep red. Almost black.

Blood.

He turned. Carcasses lay heaped to the side, necks split, guts spilling.

Gus reeled. He held his nose and made a cursory examination of the bodies. Necks slashed by a sharp blade. A huge claw, or sharp teeth?

He tiptoed through. What kind of person, or beast, could kill on such a scale, with such brutality?

He studied the patterns of hooves and paws in the floor. A footprint... then half a footprint.

At the next turn smaller animals, rabbits, weasels, rats and mice, almost unrecognizable with their guts shredded, their fluffy coats ripped, and their remains stuck to the walls and ceiling. Further on, blood-soaked feathers, some downy, some long and in all shapes and sizes followed a similar pattern.

Whatever had done this monstrous deed, he realised, wasn't to be messed with.

Two more turns and he found himself staring at a corridor, which led towards a green field, with blue sky and trees in full leaf.

Hoof marks followed the path. But, the more he studied it, the more the scene didn't add up. The outside world didn't look like that and Gus had been out there long enough to know it. The world he remembered was beaten up, scarred, full of smashed trees, landslips and water and fog.

As he hunted around, looking for clues, he spied a large outdoor coat. He held it up as memories of the ghost rushed in. He swayed, recalling his journey through the spirit. The memory knocked him with a sense of awe and, equally, revulsion.

Gus understood that the only person a coat of this size might belong to, was Old Man Wood. But why had the old man discarded it? Why leave it here of all places amongst the blood and the carnage? *Had he died?*

Gus rifled through the pockets: one small apple and a jar containing white sugar grains. He twisted off the lid and sniffed. Sugar?

Gus pushed the jar back into the pocket and rubbed the

apple on his jeans, shining the peel. He bit in, savouring the curious mix of sour and sweetness. Immediately, his body fizzed as a curious sense of vitality rushed through his frame.

He looked out into the chamber in front of him and took another bite. Time, he thought, to investigate.

FORTY-FIVE

ALTERNATIVE TUNNELING

'Jump!' Old Man Wood cried. 'NOW!'

Archie threw himself off the podium bombing into the pool below. As he rubbed the white gunk off his leg he said, 'Bells use your speed, take the tablet to safety, we'll follow.'

'I can't!' she replied.

'Go!' he said, staring at his already swollen foot. 'I won't make it all the way back.'

Isabella shook her head. 'No, Archie. We do this together. You know it, and I know it.'

The huge rambling rose containing the beast towered into the air. It creaked like the branches of a tree in a storm. Nervously, they stumbled towards the exit on the far side of the chamber, diametrically opposite to the one they'd arrived in.

Old Man Wood supported Archie on one side and Daisy on the other, holding her arm.

They looked back to see the rose sway first one way and then the other.

'Move… run!'

With a thunderous crash, the thorny rambler slipped off the podium, water spraying in every direction.

'I've got a better plan,' Isabella said. 'The tunnels go

round on themselves—up and back, up and back—and so forth. If we go through the walls—it'll be quicker.

'And how do you propose to do this small engineering miracle,' Archie asked. 'A mechanical tunnel mole?'

Isabella rolled her eyes. 'We dig.'

'Dig?' Daisy said. 'With what?'

'Whatever we can find?'

'You're crazy! It'll take months,' Daisy said. 'And besides,' she smiled, 'it'll ruin my nails.'

'Daisy,' Isabella fumed, 'no it won't, we'll use the...' the metal torch holders caught her eye. 'Those burning sconce-things on the wall. Old Man Wood can magic something up with his wand-thing, can't you?'

Old Man Wood tipped his head as though it was possible.

She gestured towards Archie's damaged leg, 'Arch, this has to be the best way, so don't argue with me—every second counts.' Isabella marched off to the side, grabbed one of the burning braziers in her hands and ripped it off the wall. 'Archie, divide them into picks.'

'You're mad,' he said. 'They're red-hot.'

'Wrong,' Isabella replied. 'I've taken the heat out. Try it.' She kicked at the wall. A mini avalanche of stone tumbled out. 'The walls may look like stone, but they're not. Daisy, what material are they made of?'

Daisy trained her eyes at the wall. 'It isn't thick rock—more like gravel or sandstone or something.'

'As I suspected,' Isabella replied. 'Then it shouldn't be a problem. Now, get out of my way!'

She hacked at the first wall and in no time at all they had made a hole large enough for them to squeeze through.

'Quick!' Isabella cried, helping them through. Shortly, she was attacking the second wall, her hands moving like a blur.

'How many more?' Daisy asked, noticing a fresh trickle of blood running down the inside of her jacket and over her fingers.

'Nine or ten. I wasn't counting,' Archie said.

Breaking through the next wall they ran across the

passage. Isabella resumed her whirlwind digging. Archie watched amazed. Half way through he pulled her back.

'Let me,' he said, and before anyone could move, head down, he charged, limping at the wall like a bull, smashing through with his head and shoulders and finding the new passageway. He tossed the debris free.

As they tunneled through the next wall an ear-splitting noise filled the labyrinth.

'Good Lord,' Isabella said, dread in her voice. 'It's free…'

She returned to her digging re-doubling her efforts. Sweat, mixing with mud and rock, caked their bodies.

Another ear-splitting noise reverberated down the passageways.

This time it wasn't a bark. This was the noise of a wounded animal; deeper and longer in pitch, wilder, furious. It was followed by a heart-stopping **YELP**.

Then silence.

'Either it's a cry of deep despair… or it's coming to get us,' Daisy said. 'How many more?'

'At least five,' Isabella said, nervously. Her hands, now shaped like various digging implements, flew at the tunnel, mud and rocks spraying all over the place, until the hole was deep enough for Archie to bash his way through again.

One at a time they climbed into the new passageway. Archie pulled the old man through.

Daisy listened again. Her face pale and drawn as she struggled to make sense of the distant sounds.

Isabella marched over to the wall.

'Wait!' Daisy commanded.

'What is it?'

Daisy tuned in, her eyes closed, concentrating.

'Well—'

Her frown gave it away.

'My God. It's coming, isn't it?' Isabella said, as she made to attack the next wall.

Then, as if Gorialla Yingarna had heard her, its voice bounced around the passageways and into their heads.

Strange, high-pitched laughter filled the hallway.

You're only half-way, children of man. Would you like to do a deal?

Isabella ceased digging. 'There has to be another way—'

…Which of you will watch me tear the others into pieces…

'Like, what?' Daisy said, wincing, the pain of her wound throbbing through her body.

Isabella swivelled towards Old Man Wood. 'Can't you do something with that branchwandy thing of yours?'

Old Man Wood shook his head.

'You must be able to. Why isn't it working?'

'The beast has one too, littlun. The branchwands appear to have struck a deal to cancel each other out.'

Isabella studied him curiously. 'The branchwands "talk" to one another? Great. I don't mean to put a dampener on it, but I don't fancy our chances alone in these tunnels without all those animals.'

'I don't know,' Archie piped up. 'What if it's bluffing? It has to eat—it must be starving. Think about it, we've had it on the run for hours and it's cold-blooded. It'll have to go directly for its next meal.'

Isabella rounded on him. 'Don't you get it, Archie. *We're the next meal.* If it's got any sense, it's going to eat us!'

Daisy ears pricked, her face twitching as distant sounds came to her.

'Daisy, what is it? Is it coming?'

'Yup,' she said quietly. 'Bit smaller this time, and slithering.'

'Where?' Isabella demanded.

'En-route … three tunnels behind'

She swore and resumed her earthworks. 'Come on!'

'Wait!' Daisy said, a faraway look on her face. The corners of her mouth turned up. 'You want another way out of this?'

They nodded.

A smile spread over her increasingly pale face. She nodded sagely as she listened, and her eyes twinkled. 'Well, my dears. I do believe transport is on its way!'

FORTY-SIX

GUS FOLLOWS

G us cautiously pushed his arms into Old Man Wood's coat and rolled the sleeves up, the coattail brushing the passageway behind him as he set off again.

When Gus arrived at the entrance to the chamber, he spied the footprints again. Relieved that they appeared to have survived up to this point, he checked the area out for signs of life.

But once again, nothing but burnt animal and bird carcasses littered the ground. Fire marks bruised the floor and the walls.

Quietly, Gus crept into the chamber and sidled around the edges, keeping close to the sides.

He followed the stream to a pool in the centre where, in the middle, there was a classical-styled stone construction like some kind of stone sacrificial altar.

To the side of this lay a vast, strange plant spread out all over the ground in front, blanketed in tiny sharks-teeth-like thorns. A dog rose Gus supposed, on a gigantic scale? Looking at the stem, he could see that the rambling rose had, at some point, fractured and fallen, crashing from a great height.

Furthermore, a great struggle had ensued within it. Streaks of a curious white liquid stained the stone looking like a severe case of mildew. Thorns were dislodged from their stems and lay scattered over the ground.

Peering inside the confines of the creeper, he spied a gigantic, white skin.

Gus froze. *A snakeskin?*

For some time he stared at it, baffled, trying to envisage what had happened. And the more he stared, the more he kept coming back to the same conclusion. It had to be a snake. But this was one hell of a snake. A super-anaconda? But even a beast of this size wasn't nearly big enough for the extensive tracts of skin. Was this the creature that Cain had told him and Kemp about? The creature that had never been bested?

He followed more tracks to the opposite side noticing how, in places, the rock appeared scorched. From here, and from the markings on the dusty surface, he wondered if, at some point, they'd thrown themselves into the gully that he now found himself looking at.

He jumped in and touched the surfaces. Warm, like the outer edges of an Aga cooker.

Gus heard the swift sounds of hooves going at full tilt down the passageway. He ducked down.

Moments later, four horses, like a white blur, flashed into the chamber. They stopped as though inspecting the damage, reared up and shot off down the exit passageway on the far side.

Gus wondered if he was seeing things. The sparkle, the energy, the twisting, straight spikes on their heads? Were they what he thought they were?

Gus followed. Footprints interspersed with galloping hoof marks followed the passageway to its end. To his astonishment, the wall directly in front had a hole through it. Had a massive snake simply bulldozed through the walls? Thinking about it made his blood run cold. As he pushed gravel to one side, he noticed a black stain smearing the limestone rock.

Instinctively he reached out to touch it, but he found this wasn't the same as the liquid stuck to the rose; this was blood and more likely human blood. His hairs prickled. The blood hadn't yet hardened. Gus was no pathologist, but he knew it couldn't be more than an hour old.

Were his friends injured?

Gus hurried through the hole, noting a smaller snake's tracks, like twisted rope, over-lying the boot prints. In the new corridor on the other side, the pattern repeated itself. The hoof marks with large distances between strides, and on the wall in front, a hole smashed through to the other side.

Gus sensed that he had to hurry. They were clearly being followed by an ominous, and absolutely lethal creature.

If they were alive, and by the footprints and blood he'd spotted, they were, he still had a chance to help his friends. He revved up his pace.

If he could help them to get out of here, in due course, he might be able to forewarn Sue about Kemp and the ghost. His heartbeat quickened. Yes, he'd have a chance to tell her to keep well-away from the spirit, at all costs.

FORTY-SEVEN

SUE AND CAIN DEPART

'Absolutely exquisite,' the ashen figure of Cain said, sitting down after a small walk, trying to ascertain the girl's spirit within him. 'She is a wonderful human specimen,' he said. 'In a moment, I will show her around my palace.'

Kemp looked on, his face pale. 'But you'll come back for me, won't you?'

Cain grinned back. 'Only if there are sufficient Dreamspinners willing to help. You know, boy, maybe I should take this girl all for myself. I'm sure we could find a way of procreating a new world. I'm beginning to wonder if you are necessary.'

Cain felt a transient surge of energy from within him as though the girl had derived pleasure from his comments.

'But you said...'

'Dreamspinner, dreamspinner, dreamspinner,' Cain shouted.

Two, tiny blue electrical flashes winked out of the white fog.

'Ah! There you are, Asgard. I have the girl. To Havilah this instant.'

'And with speed,' the dreamspinner said. 'There is little time.'

Cain turned to Kemp. 'I will return, boy. Then, we will seek out your mother.'

Kemp sighed with relief. 'Dreamspinner,' he managed to ask. 'What's going on in the labyrinth? Are they dead yet?'

'Believe you me,' Cain tutted, 'if they had died, you would know.'

'But what's happening?'

A reedy voice from the blue light replied. 'The Heirs, and one other, are alone against Gorialla Yingarna. The battle has been long and difficult—'

'There,' Cain said. 'I told you it would be over soon.' Then casually, he asked. 'I take it there are enough dream-spinners for the boy and his mother?'

Asgard replied. 'There are fewer than before.'

Kemp felt his knees weaken.

'How so, dreamspinner?' Cain replied. 'The children are with Gorialla Yingarna in the labyrinth. Is he still playing games with them?'

'The Heirs are more powerful than they know. But now they tire. The end is nigh.'

'It must be the most one-sided battle in all history. Tell me, why do more dreamspinners not flock to you, Asgard?'

'For one very simple reason, Master of Havilah. The Heirs of Eden have the third tablet.'

FORTY-EIGHT
STONE FIRES INTO THE FOG

Stone bungled and bashed into the wreckage of trees and rocks on the hillside. Shortly, he heard muffled voices.

'Lambert, Geddis?' he boomed. 'Is that you?'

'Who is it?'

'It's Stone. Has everyone made it OK?'

Stone heard mutterings.

'I dispersed those horses,' Stone said. 'Scared them off with a couple of rounds.'

Lambert's voice came back out of the fog. 'Not sure those were exactly horses, sir.'

Stone moved towards the noise as quietly as he could, noting that the overall vision had improved slightly, the fog not so thick.

'Want my opinion?' the voice croaked. 'I'm not sure we should be here, sir. It's getting a bit too bloody weird—reckon someone's trying to tell us something—'

'Tell us what?' Stone said, muffling his voice. He winced at the barb of pain in his chest as he reached over a fallen tree trunk.

'Not to go any further, sir. Not to mess—'

'Is that so,' Stone replied. 'But, lads, I'm telling you, we need to get up to that cottage. Now.'

Stone heard whispering. 'So, come on,' he continued, 'find your things and let's get about it.'

'We're not going, sir.'

Stone's tone changed. 'I'm sorry? What did you say?'

'We ain't going,' Lambert repeated. 'We're not welcome here.'

'Are you disobeying my orders, soldier?' Stone said, withdrawing his gun. He emptied the cartridge and added another. It clicked into place. He knew the soldiers could hear.

'It isn't right, sir.'

'What isn't?' Stone replied.

'This whole thing. It stinks, like it's rotten.'

'You don't know that. We're involved in an international incident of the highest degree, and we're closing in on the prime suspects. You know nothing about this.'

For a brief moment, in the silence, Stone wondered if they would come out. He waited.

'So, either, you come with me now,' Stone said, pacing his words, 'or you drop your weapons right where you are and put your hands up.' He moved quickly towards them hoping he'd catch them out, his gun raised.

'I'm not afraid to use it,' Stone bragged. 'That last gunshot was Vincent. Claimed he'd seen a unicorn but I soon put him right. Do you understand where I'm coming from, soldiers?'

To his right he heard the clank of metal and a scampering of boots, squishing in the mud, as they tore away.

'I've warned you,' Stone yelled. 'Leaving is an act of desertion.' He levelled his gun and fired two shots towards the noise. The second met with a sickening thud followed by a low-pitched groan.

'Two down, one to go,' he said. 'Damn fools.'

He spied the long barrel of the flame-thrower and smiled. 'Better to arrive late, than not at all. Time to torch that old cottage—'

An explosion turned his head. Stone laughed. 'Useless fool ran into his own trap. The scoundrel deserved it.'

Bending his knees, he grappled with the strap, hoisting it over and around his body, gritting his teeth as the weight of the armoury attacked his ribs like a blunt knife.

Then he noticed a pin-prick flashing red light.

Stone stared at it for a while, bending his knees to take a more in-depth look.

'Clever,' he said. 'The damn swines.'

Straightening, he aimed his weapon and blew the radio into several pieces.

Looking up, Stone noticed the fog had cleared further. Visibility was over a few metres. But, having previously followed the soldiers, now a feeling of disorientation hit him.

With no tracking device, moving only a few degrees or in his case, steps, in the wrong direction would lead to a significant deviation at the top of the hill.

He rubbed his chin and twisted the end of his moustache. He'd go directly up. And, when he reached the top, he prayed that the fog might have cleared so that he'd get a clear run in on the cottage.

Then, he'd burn it to the ground and, if his instincts were right, the de Lowes would come running out, straight into his hands.

FORTY-NINE

SUE HEARS CAIN'S STORY

Now that she'd quickly worked out how to operate within the outline of the ghost, Sue was overwhelmed by a sense of peace. She'd made her bed, she thought, and now she had to lie in it.

But the revelation that the Heirs of Eden had the third tablet festered in her mind. Had she given up on her friends too easily? Hadn't she trusted them enough?

And when Asgard, the strange creature they'd dived through, mentioned that they were with one other, fleetingly her heart told her that it might be Gus. But then she knew the creature could only have meant Old Man Wood. Hard as it was to swallow, she tried to push the thought out of her mind, even though it niggled like an itch craving for a scratch.

They'd arrived in the place that Cain called Havilah. Cain removed himself from her, the feeling, she thought, like being peeled out of a tight, rubber mould. Bearing only a long scarf around his neck the spirit showed her around. Later, he encouraged her to look around for herself, to make herself at home.

For some time she wandered through the old, crumbling palace, whose walls were dotted with sparkling rocks. She'd never seen anywhere so unusual in her whole life. Along one entire length, the building seemed to butt onto a cliff-edge, its

rock seams flashing with colour, its higgledy-piggledy forma-
tions twinkling back at her. Along the other, ran a neat, almost
classical stone facade, with pillars and friezes, looking out over
a vast canyon.

Libraries, drawing rooms, receptions, ballrooms. The
palace went on and on. Wherever she went the creatures were
almost, but not quite, human, she suspected. When she
looked carefully, their bodies and heads were wrapped in
simple sackcloth as they cleaned away piles of dust, and
polished the stones and rubbed the glass in the huge windows.

Even the majestic fireplace, a grand construction the size
of a small house, had a team of these strange people working
on a wooden scaffold rendering the stonework. When she
moved closer, the strange creatures huddled together and
turned away as if they were in fear of her.

Her stomach rumbled, and when she mentioned food, the
small, long-bearded servants, with black eyes and bushy
eyebrows, like elves, led her to the dining room where delicious meals were in abundance. She gorged herself.

Later, intrigued and rejuvenated, she found her way into
the library, a vast room, with shelf after shelf piled high with
either boxes or ancient scrolls or thick leather-bound books.
Ladders scaled high up—almost as far as she could see—and
she noticed many boxes had been half pulled out, or broken
and patched back together.

A round, murky pool, like an old, rustic well, sat in the
middle of the room. Sue touched the water, amazed to find it
fizzle, like a chemical reaction. She moved on, finding rooms
containing atlas-globes and another containing an armoury
full of dusty dull-coloured weaponry. Through another wide
doorway further on, she came upon a broad stone courtyard
surrounded by high walls and turrets. Dotted on the floor
were curious, rock-hard glass-like puddles, each the size of a
large dish and smeared with mud and thick with dust.

She rubbed one to see the reflection of a man's face
smiling back at her. Wondering if it was a reflection of
someone standing above her, she peeked over her shoulder.

She was alone. She rubbed a little more. The kindly man smiled back, though his dark, tired eyes were dim and his frown lines told of some faraway sadness.

She moved onto another glass puddle. A girl much the same age as herself, her skin smooth and radiant, confidence radiating from her, her eyes glimmering and her pupils large it was as if she was in love. The next showed a young boy whose large blue eyes sparkled mischievously, she thought. She smiled back.

The next puddle showed a handsome, middle-aged woman with plump lips and neat, combed hair and skipping to the next, she found a man with hard eyes and a snake tattoo on one side of his face. In the following puddle, she saw an elderly man with silver eyebrows and a plump, bald head that reminded her of her grandfather. Beside him a wizened-looking man with a long grey beard and watchful eyes, the many years of experience etched into the lines of his face, reminiscent of Old Man Wood.

And now, at every step, she found more puddles. And these strange puddles contained people, people, she realised, who weren't so very different to the ones she knew.

Sue wondered if these magical, living gravestones were some kind of Havilarian graveyard, or a memorial to Havilah's dead. The more she thought about it, the odder she found it, and the less she wanted to be there.

'Come to spy on my lost souls?' Cain's voice said.

Sue stood up smartly and flicked her head towards the voice.

'Lost souls? Oh. Is that what they are?' She started towards the door, as if, somehow, she'd encroached. 'Are they dead?' she said.

'They're frozen in time, dear girl.'

'Wow. Whatever did they do?'

'In a rage,' Cain sighed, 'I put them there.'

Sue looked appalled. 'And you left them, like this?

Cain sighed. 'One of the side-effects of losing my eyes

meant I had no means of turning them back into their usual selves.'

Sue moved along to another puddle and dusted it off. 'How long have they been like this?' she asked.

Cain sensed her confusion and her unease. 'Right at the beginning of all this, a long, long time ago, I had my eyes taken away from me.'

'Removing eyes is pretty barbaric, isn't it? It sounds like you probably deserved it.'

'My thoughts too, dear girl. I'm not sure you'll know this, but eyes are the source of pure magic. Used in the right way, to the right person with the right training, they can generate remarkable power. When mine were scooped out, I lost that power. And subsequently, I was never able to change these people back.'

'That's an awful story,' she said. 'Did it hurt?'

'Oh, the pain of having eyes removed is nothing compared to the agony of losing an entire people.'

Now that she scanned the courtyard, she noticed hundreds of flat puddles littering the floor, mostly concealed beneath a film of dust.

'There are so many,' she said.

'Many millions—across Havilah, from pole to pole. Though I am blind, I see their souls every day. I can almost hear them,' he said bitterly. 'And worse, even though I hover over them, they do not see me because I don't really exist.'

Sue sensed the sadness and deep sorrow in Cain. 'What happened, what made you do this to them?'

Cain sighed. 'The ones in this courtyard were my finest and most loyal companions. These men, women and children were the cream of my court. When I was summoned for execution, or, perhaps more accurately, incineration, I used the population of Havilah as a means of bargaining. I told them that if I were to be no more, then the same fate would befall all Havilarian people. No one believed I would do it. But I did.'

'You did it as revenge—?'

'At the time, great sacrifices were made, girl.'

'But you froze the entire population of a planet? That's insane.'

'Indeed. Now, it certainly feels that way. But back then, feelings ran high and, chances are, those same emotions will stir again someday soon.' Cain tossed a length of his scarf around his would-be neck. 'Those you see here had been summoned for a celebration. They did not know that our enemy had taken me. They did not know that I'd been tried and sentenced to burn. I told the officers of the trial that if flames licked my torso, I would remove all human life from Havilah.'

'I take it they thought you were bluffing,' Sue said.

'Precisely. The moment I burned, their bodies crumpled into these watery, glassy puddles, trapped, but preserved, until the spell is broken. The same thing happened to every household in Havilah. Together we have been stuck for eternity, while the planet has succumbed to the lesser beings who once inhabited the caves and the deep crevices of the land.'

Cain floated over to the doorway and felt for a stick. Pushing the stick ahead of him, he felt his way over to a puddle towards the middle.

The ghost bent down as if to look at the puddle. 'This child, inside here, was one of my sons.'

Sue looked down at a small infant; its blue eyes bulging, bubbles forming on its lips. Sue's hands moved to touch it, finding a glass-like shield over the child.

'You see, the magic applied even to babes.'

'Haven't you tried to break the spell?' she said.

'Of course, I have,' Cain snapped. 'Do not take me for a coward: Every day for eternity I have searched for my branchwand to break them out. But strong bonds were put in place, beyond my control.'

Sue kept her silence but eventually, she couldn't help herself. 'What, in heavens name, did you do to get yourself incinerated and leave your very own population to everlasting damnation?'

She noted a puff of dust nearby and sensed Cain sitting down beside her.

'I've had a long time to ponder these things, my dear,' he began, sighing. 'My dear girl, life is a process of movement, of continuation, of balance. These people stuck in time are, I suppose, no different to rocks and trees and waters. They survive by living off the complex energy particles that our suns and moons throw at them. But living is different. We move and change over the course of many generations. I suppose it comes down to how the inhabited places of the universe evolve—'

'You haven't answered my question,' Sue said, with more confidence. 'Tell me, what awful thing did you do?'

'I disagreed,' he said, flatly.

'Disagreed?'

'Yes, I disagreed with others.'

'You argued?' she said, incredulously. 'About what?'

'The process,' he replied. 'In simple terms, I objected to the direction in which the universe was heading.'

FIFTY

TAKEN TO SAFETY

R elief filled their faces at the sound of pounding hooves. Suddenly, a blur of white flashed towards them down the dimly lit passageway filling each of them with a sense of awe. Prickles of excitement darted into their minds that a way out was suddenly within reach. They were going to make it.

The unicorns stopped abruptly in front of one another.

Instantly, Daisy's whinnied and stared at her intensely with its large, blue eyes. In the next moment, the unicorn nestled up to her and licked at her wound through the tear in her coat. Then it lay down, inviting Daisy to climb on top.

Daisy, could barely keep her eyes open. Her shoulder throbbed like crazy, but the saliva of the unicorn congealed the laceration, and she sensed the wound healing.

She fell over the animal's sleek, white back and buried her head in its sparkling mane then stretched forward grasping the horn. The unicorns stood up as one and, with a quick look at one another, tore off, hooves pounding the earthen corridors like drums, their pace relentless, slowing only marginally at the turns.

Soon, they arrived in a chamber almost identical to the one in which they'd entered the labyrinth but, instead of a chute coming down from the ceiling, a stone stairway ascended, and a glimmer of daylight flickered down.

The unicorns pulled up. As one, they sat down allowing the four to dismount. Daisy fell awkwardly to the dusty floor.

Dipping their heads low, as though in a bow, the unicorns turned and raced up the stairs, disappearing from view.

A strange, tired silence filled the end chamber.

'Why didn't they take us?' Archie asked.

'Probably,' Old Man Wood said, 'because we must leave the labyrinth with the tablet all by ourselves. They have fulfilled their role.'

'Well, come on!' Isabella said, helping Daisy to her feet, 'let's go.'

'Daisy?'

She lay clutching her side.

Archie removed the tablet from his pocket and handed it to Isabella. Then he hobbled over to his twin and picked her up gently before squirming in pain himself. Isabella took her by the hand as Old Man Wood rushed over to Archie's side. 'Not far now,' he said, 'Think you can make it?'

Archie grinned. 'What, and give up now? We've only got to get up the stairs. Of course I'm going to make it.'

FIFTY-ONE
CAIN'S STORY OF CREATION

'I don't understand,' Sue said. 'What process are you talking about—?'

'The process of creating life, girl. I didn't think the means of developing creatures and living things to sustain planets should be continued.'

Sue frowned, her brain swimming with questions. 'Why not?'

'Because the evolution of species was working just as well —if not better.'

Sue shuffled around, needing to move. She brushed more dust off another glassy puddle and waved at the trapped incumbent. 'So, you're saying that there was a place which was making creatures for the planets?'

'Yes, my dear. The Garden of Eden created all things and sent them to planets around the universes when they were ready.'

'Like… a scientific laboratory?'

Cain didn't entirely understand. 'If you mean that the Garden had special powers to design creation, then, yes.'

Sue shook her head and remained in thought for several beats. 'You're telling me that this Garden of Eden place built everything. Plants, soils, seas, living things?'

Cain examined her. 'The Garden of Eden has all the

apparatus of generating life. It is the birthplace of everything. It was designed to do such things,' he said, with a sigh. His scarf fell to the floor.

'Right at the very beginning, when there wasn't a great deal of life, my father said, "Let us make a place to live. Let us make creatures and animals and shape the landscape." Using gases and particles and all the energies of the infinite, he began to make and shape things. One day he blended various gases and waters and elements and along came tiny grains of bacteria that liked to dwell in soils and these were followed by plant life, followed by insects, and so on and so forth. A great deal of time later—when we were young and had learned how to use the power in our eyes to shape and mould— we began to understand the qualities of the elements, the particles and the gases. We joined in with my father's work, beginning with life in the waters. Soon, the waters were quickly populated—they were considered more accessible, I suppose, and mistakes could be hidden. Do you still have a creature on Earth that they call a shark?'

'Yes, there are many types, I think,' she replied.

'Oh, I am glad to hear it. One of my better ones. Clever little brutes. 'And eels?' he asked.

'Yes, we have those too,' she said.

'Who do you think put the power in their ends?' he said. 'A very tricky bit of engineering at the time,' he crowed. 'Now where was I?'

'Something about gases,' Sue said.

'Ah, yes. The thing is, the creation of life creates a continual knock-on effect. Make one thing, and you need to make another to feed it and another to feed that and so on and so forth. It becomes complex beyond reason. After some dreadful mistakes, there were rules by which we monitored our creations. One was that all things required a purpose. If they didn't benefit others, they wouldn't succeed. Another was called the chain of life—'

'Where one species becomes a link in a chain to support the rest,' Sue finished off.

Cain, although invisible, smiled. 'Indeed. How smart you are, young lady. And all of this happened over a great deal of time, dear girl. When these organisms passed the test of selection, they were sent to different worlds to develop.'

Sue was rendered numb but eventually summoned her brain. 'It's a great story, but seriously, you are kidding me, aren't you?' she said. 'Everyone knows that living things evolved from tiny bacteria, from sea-life from particles over millions of years, bit by agonising bit, changing, evolving, piece by piece.'

'Yes, this is true,' Cain said, 'but in the first instance, and I am talking an awfully long time ago, much of life did not develop on its own accord. That was the remarkable thing.'

Sue ran her hands through her hair. 'So, what was the massive argument about?' she asked. 'Must have been pretty drastic for you to do what you did?'

'Yes, I suppose it was,' he said, bitterness in his tone. 'Creation, girl, is the greatest of all gifts. But those in the Garden of Eden grew tired of merely upgrading and tweaking species. They set about developing entirely new ones. At first, it worked. New, smaller species were welcome throughout the worlds. The great reptilian experiment—I think you humans named them dinosaurs—was finally closed down—awful, cumbersome, stupid beasts—and the Garden developed a new master species, humankind. After several prototypes and plenty of tweaks, the eventual outcome showed immense promise. After all, it was, in essence, modelled on ourselves.

'At long last, we had a deserving species that worked. Humankind passed the tests and spread to different planets where, over time, just as we suspected, it thrived without interference. But, buoyed by its success, the Garden had new ideas and announced that it would supersede humankind with a better version, a more original model.

'As you can imagine, this met with furious opposition because, over time, humankind's development had exceeded everyone's expectation. The proposal was scandalous. The Garden had no right.'

'I take it you disagreed?'

'Absolutely,' he spluttered. 'Evolution was working! There was no need to play around anymore.'

Sue swirled her hand through the dust on the floor revealing another glass puddle with the image of a girl her age smiling enthusiastically back at her. 'OK. Then what happened?' she said.

'What does everyone do when there is an unbreakable impasse?'

'They fight, don't they?' Sue said.

The ghost sighed. 'Indeed. And so, we went to war. The consequence of this action is what you see all around you. And it affects not only these people here but your friends on Earth too, I'm sorry to say.'

Sue frowned at the girl who frowned back. 'Then, I take it you lost,' she said.

'In brief, dear girl, two of the planets annihilated one another, the Garden of Eden was shut down, and every species was moved to dull, bland Earth—a relatively unpopulated place at the time. Earth was left to its own devices in the knowledge that one day, a test would be given to see if humankind and those on earth might have evolved sufficiently to warrant their station, essentially putting the argument to bed, once and for all.'

'And these are the tests my friends are going through?' Sue said, as she stood up and curled her hair over her ears. 'Their actions are connected to you here?'

'Yes, my dear. Of course.'

'But, then surely you'd want Archie and Isabella and Daisy to survive? To win.'

'If humankind were successful the Garden of Eden would re-open with terrible consequences for all life. Creations would begin again when there is no need. Creation would dominate once more, because that is what it tends to do. In my opinion, life has matured enough to earn its way.'

'And what if they fail?'

Cain's voice perked up. 'If they fail, the citizens of

Havilah will, in due course, wake from their rest. Then, the test of the Garden of Eden will come to Havilah. Strangely, putting a spell on my people may yet prove to be a triumph.'

'No wonder you want them to fail,' Sue said. 'But at the cost of seven billion people and countless trillion creatures on Earth?'

'Life is never straightforward, girl. What happens to one, affects another: every action creates a reaction. One person's loss is another's gain. It is the same with power. It is the same with worlds and universes.'

Sue stretched and breathed deeply, trying to wrap her head around all the information Cain had given her.

'The people and the species of Havilah are,' the ghost continued, 'in every way superior to those on Earth. If you're worrying about Earth, re-population is necessary on every planet every once in a while. It happened here once. It is life, my dear. It is simply the way of the universe. Earth will, in the long run, be a great deal better for it.'

FIFTY-TWO

PITCHED INTO DARKNESS

I sabella took Daisy by the arm and guided her towards the steps. Following them, a little way behind, Archie limped on, supported by Old Man Wood.

All of a sudden Old Man Wood and Archie were pitched into blackness. They stopped, grappling at the dark.

'What's going on?' Archie whispered.

'I don't know,' Old Man Wood replied. 'Appalling smell.'

Archie's mace-like hair turned steely as a disturbing thought shot through him. 'It's the blood of the beast,' he said, gagging on the stench. He reached out. 'It's moving in on us,' he said, touching the cold scales. 'We're enclosed!'

Stretching their arms out, Old Man Wood and Archie found alternating layers of coils moving in opposing directions, sliding inwards towards them.

Soon they were pushing against them with all their might, their legs on one side of the tightening coils, their hands on the other.

'Branchwand—please push,' Old Man Wood whispered closing his eyes, but the contraction still continued, if fractionally slower.

'We're going to get crushed,' Archie spluttered, struggling for air. He strained against the coils, hammering them with his head, denting them, using every ounce of his strength, doing everything he could to temper the movement.

For a brief moment it worked, but holding the relentless sideways-sliding walls proved impossible.

'Daisy!' Archie yelled as loudly as he could. 'Daisy! HELP US! HELP...!'

His body and moreover his sharp hair spikes pushed into Old Man Wood.

'Archie,' the old man gasped. 'Move your head.'

'I can't... it's jammed.'

Old Man Wood groaned as Archie's head spikes began to cut into him.

Archie screamed again, but his sounds were muffled by the snake's vast bulk. Slowly but surely, the snake's barrel-sized coils began to squeeze the life out of them.

FIFTY-THREE
SUE HEARS THE ALTERNATIVE

Sue shook her head. 'But I don't understand what kind of universe would choose the de Lowes to take the test—'

'My thoughts exactly,' agreed the ghost, 'especially after such a long time and when their mentor has forgotten the lot of it.'

'You're saying Old Man Wood is supposed to be their mentor. He's part of this?'

Cain chuckled. 'You did not know? You didn't even suspect his involvement?'

'No. I just thought he was a bit of an old oddball, that's all, looking after his cattle and his apple trees.'

'That old man has been wandering the Earth for thousands and thousands of years. Are you telling me no one noticed? Between you and me, it is a miracle your friends have gone as far as they have with his useless guidance. That old man has forgotten everything, and he should not be trusted. Not by them, not by you, not by anyone—'

'But he's a lovely, gentle old chap...'

'It's a simple trick to be forgetful and gentle, girl when you have time on your side. But that's isn't the half of it; there is more than meets the eye where he's concerned.'

Sue looked flabbergasted. 'So you know him? How come?'

'This man,' he spat, 'who you daintily call Old Man Wood, is my father. He controlled the Garden. He controlled the processes of creation.'

Sue took a sharp intake of breath. 'You're bloody kidding me!'

'I am afraid not. Why would I lie?'

Sue scratched the ground with her hand, thinking. 'You're saying, in a funny, roundabout way, that Old Man Wood is God?'

'Only if you believe in such a thing,' Cain replied, suppressing a laugh.

Sue didn't know what to think. Her heartbeat raced. 'You fought your very own father in a battle between creation and evolution?'

Silence set in as she rubbed the dust off another glassy puddle and peered in.

The ghost noticed her discomfort and changed the subject. 'If your friends were to unlock the key to the Garden, there is only one other way for the people of Havilah to awaken…'

Sue, too, was pleased to leave the topic. 'If there's another way,' she said, sitting up. 'Surely, it's got to be worth letting them win and trying it.'

'To release the humankind in these patches on the floor,' Cain said, dryly. 'Either the Heirs of Eden fail or…'

Cain's voice indicated he was moving away.

'Or what?'

'Or there is a birth here, in Havilah, of a human child…'

Sue's forehead crinkled. 'I'm not sure I follow—a human child? But everyone here is frozen. I don't understand,' she said.

But when no answer returned and as his words sunk in, Sue began to grasp the full meaning of his words.

FIFTY-FOUR
AN IMPASSE

'D id you hear that?' Daisy said, as they climbed the stairs. Isabella looked at her curiously. 'No, I didn't hear anything. You're probably hearing things.'

'Where's Archie?'

'Behind us,' Isabella replied casually. 'Come on, let's get out of here.'

Daisy heard it again.

She turned and tugged on Isabella's arm. Her voice wavered. 'No, he's not. We have to go back.'

'Seriously?' Isabella quizzed. She turned around. 'Oh, hell.'

'They're in terrible danger,' Daisy said, looking up at her sister, her brow creased. 'Trust me. I think they're trapped.'

'What about the tablet?'

'It's all or nothing. You know that and there's nothing we can do about it.'

Retracing their steps, a vast coiled snake sat in precisely the spot where they'd last seen Archie and Old Man Wood.

If you are looking for your friends, the serpent said. *Death is but a few twists away. Return the tablet and you may get them back.*

'How can we trust you,' Isabella said without talking, as if the conversation were taking place in a slightly different part of her brain.

You have no option, child!

'Don't flatter yourself, you repulsive slug,' Daisy replied. 'We have the tablet that you cherish so much.'

Well, if you're going to be like that—your little family dies. And then, of course, you'll die too, because if one of you fails, you all die.'

'But, if the tablet leaves the labyrinth,' Isabella said, 'then you will die too. The freedom you've waited for, for so long, will have been utterly in vain.'

The snake's coils stopped twisting.

Then we have an impasse.

'Yes, we do.'

For several moments, both were locked in a will of minds.

We could strike an agreement, the snake said, its eyes bulging towards Isabella, twisting and twirling around and around.

Isabella found she couldn't release herself from its gaze. 'An agreement,' she repeated. 'Yes.'

Daisy nudged her sister. 'Bells—?'

Give me the tablet, the snake said.

'Yes. Give you the tablet,' Isabella repeated.

'Bells, what are you doing?' Daisy said, her impatience growing. She glanced up at her sister's fixated stare. *Oh God, it's hypnotising her again.* She waved her hand in front of sister's eyes. Not even a blink.

Daisy watched in terror as the coils began to slither again, the muffled cries from within increasing.

Summoning her energy, anger building fast, she faced the beast.

'Let go of them now!' she roared.

Really? The beast replied. *And what will you do?*

Two beams of light flashed out of her eyes, smashing the snake in its head.

The snake's head recoiled.

Isabella gasped and collapsed, the spell broken.

'Want another one?' Daisy said, her eyes glowing.

The snake hissed back.

Daisy fired again this time at the coils, burning a hole.

White globs of flesh spat out of the snake. Instantly it uncoiled the top two loops and flew at Daisy.

Daisy was too quick. Her eyes shone, another flash striking its neck.

The snake retreated nestling back on its cone of coils, its smoky marble eyes glaring at Daisy.

They stared intensely at one another, anger sizzling through the air.

You do realise, the snake finally said, *that if I were to die while I surround your friends, you would never get them out in time.* Gorialla Yingarna closed its eyes. *Perhaps, I should rest awhile.*

In the silence, Daisy thought she heard something familiar, like heavy breathing and the pitter-pattering of running. Was it Archie and Old Man Wood trying to beat their way out?

'Maybe the beast's right?' Isabella whispered, at length. 'Maybe we should do a deal.'

Daisy glowered at her. 'No bleeding way! Let me finish it off.'

Isabella squeezed her sister's healthy shoulder. 'We can't leave them, Daisy. I don't think you have the strength to zap it to death like Superman. One way or the other, we have to get out of here, and we have to take the tablet. A stalemate doesn't help anyone.'

Deep down, Daisy knew she was right.

'Hell-ooo!' Isabella called out. 'How about I put the tablet over here by the wall.'

The snake opened an eye.

'…but only when you release them.'

Are you talking to me, child?

Isabella repeated the request.

The snake flickered its tongue. *In the interests of fairness, why not place the tablet halfway from you, and halfway from me. Wouldn't you agree?*

Isabella and Daisy caught each other's eye. 'OK. Seems fair,' Daisy said. 'But I'll be the judge of where it goes.'

Excellent, the snake crowed. *Put it wherever you feel is equitable.*

'How can we trust you'll let them go?'

You have my word. Furthermore, I will wait for you to reacquaint yourselves.

Daisy had a better idea. 'I'll draw a line in the dust. When Archie and Old Man Wood cross it, you may go for the tablet. Agreed?'

Agreed, the snake said, its voice filled with mirth. *If that is how you wish to proceed, let our game begin.*

FIFTY-FIVE

STONE'S PLAN

S tone laughed. The fog had lightened and he found himself walking briskly, dodging fallen trees and mud pools and low-lying branches. Even the stabbing in his midriff had lessened, especially when he bent over and held his arm tight around his chest, the weight of the flamethrower and the fuel rucksack over his back somehow dulling the sudden spikes of pain.

Moving along, he hummed to himself, thinking of his approach. Two or three blasts worth of fuel, that's what the soldier said. One would do, he thought: a long one, tracing into their house, torching everything in its path. But would they dash out of the front door, or slip out of the back? He toyed with this thought. If he set fire to the front, it had to be the back, in which case, he'd need to move fast around the house.

And what of the other units? He didn't really care. Without a radio, he'd take matters into his own hands. If other soldiers appeared, he'd move them into position, get them to assist.

And, when he found the de Lowes, to show them how determined he was, maybe he'd put a bullet in the old man. He was expendable. Now he thought of it, so was the girl,

Sue, and her friend Gus, and also, he figured, the headmaster —even if he was his cousin.

He'd line them up, shoot them, one after the other, depending on the answers they gave. After the first one, he suspected they'd sing like birds. Maximum fear for a maximum return. Fear worked; it always worked.

Afterwards, he'd tie the boy up. Maybe, he'd beat him up first. Or perhaps, he thought, he would get them to the boats and navigate the flooded Vale of York back to Swinton Park. No, there wasn't time. He'd start the interrogation the moment he found them. It depended, he supposed, on who flew out of the wasps' nest first. And, of course, how much they decided to tell him.

And, after they'd let him in on their secret, he'd take this tablet or whatever it was they cherished so much, and he'd contact the Americans and let them know that the situation had been resolved and tell them to back off.

Then, he'd reach out to the COBRA offices and let them know he had acquired the solution to the global pandemic.

Or maybe, he mused, mulling the thought around his brain, he'd threaten to use whatever it was that they had found. He'd assume whatever power it had, all for himself.

No, no. He shook his head. His first duty was to stop the bomb going off, and then he'd figure out how to halt the spread of the Ebora disease.

And after that, he'd be a world hero; the man who figured it all out. And, what's more, he'd have the tablet.

FIFTY-SIX
A LINE IN THE SAND

D aisy walked across the chamber and placed the tablet carefully on a stone.

As she walked towards Isabella, the huge coils began unravelling. Archie and Old Man Wood fell out, tumbling to the floor, wheezing and gasping for air. They crawled towards the girls, coughing.

'We've done a deal,' Isabella said.

Old Man Wood spluttered struggling to find his voice. 'A deal?' he wheezed. 'Gorialla Yingarna never stays true to any deal. Why didn't you go? The snake dies if the tablet leaves.'

'But so would you two—and that would mean we'd have failed. We couldn't go on without you both. We're in this together, remember.'

There. You heard it, old man, the serpent hissed. *Go and join your family.*

'Isabella, what is the nature of this deal?' Old Man Wood asked.

Isabella smiled and looked deeply into Old Man Wood's eyes. 'When you cross this line here,' she indicated it with her finger, 'there's going to be a race to get the tablet which is sitting on a rock over there.' She pointed at the stone. Her voice went barely above a whisper. 'So, stay right where you are, both of you. Catch your breath. Stretch or something.'

Then, in a small kind of huddle, Isabella whispered to Archie and Old Man Wood 'We've been working on a plan.'

Archie raised his eyebrows. 'Excellent. How's it going?'

'Actually,' Daisy added, 'it involves you two remaining the wrong side of the line.'

Archie's shocked expression said it all. 'Why?'

'Because we're relying on its natural arrogance, deceit and greed,' Daisy whispered. 'We're going to offer you as bait— we're pretty confident it will attempt to kill you again before taking the tablet. It's super-hungry.'

'Famished,' Isabella continued. 'Why have one, when you can have two?'

'Wow. Another super idea,' Archie said. 'Just out of interest, how long do we stay here?'

'I don't know. When it makes a move, Daisy blasts it and I run for the tablet and—'

'You are joking.'

'No—I think, this time, it's really going to work,' Isabella said.

Daisy tapped her on the shoulder. 'There's a bit of a problem.' She flicked her head towards Gorialla Yingarna. 'I think we've forgotten something.'

'What?'

'Look for yourselves.'

They turned.

'Lord Almighty. It's vanished again,' Isabella gasped, her heartbeat thumping like a drum. *'Idiots!'*

Their eyes searched the chamber as a shiver ran through them.

'Another exceptional plan,' Archie said sarcastically. 'Feels like we're sliding right back down the ladder to square one again.'

FIFTY-SEVEN

THE END OF THE BATTLE

How many more turns were there? Gus thought as he paused, hands on knees, panting hard, sweating. He unzipped Old Man Wood's coat and draped it around his shoulders.

He had to be close.

Then he heard it, and for a brief second, he thought his heart would stop.

His brow dripped. Daisy? Was that Daisy? Or Isabella? Or Archie?

He ran, sprinting. One corner, another. One more. At the end of the next, he heard them talking. Talking to something.

In the blink of an eye he saw his friends and the old man. In the next, the back of a huge scaly monster, like a dinosaur, filled his view.

He tiptoed to the side and watched.

Archie lay on the ground, his leg swollen at the ankle, trousers ripped, his spiky head covered in mud and rock and blood.

Daisy's left side was soaked dark red, her clothes and jacket lacerated almost beyond recognition.

As the creature moved in on Isabella, a strange bubble flew out of her outstretched fingertips at the exact moment a blast of fire blew over them, protecting them like a huge rubber shield.

He noted the old man, cowering in the corner. Terrified. Sobbing.

A moment later, the flames and the bubble gone, Archie limped towards the beast, and hurled himself head first at it. The creature faltered and rocked, almost toppling over, then roared so loudly Gus thought his ears would bleed. Then its tail flashed around and smashed Archie into the wall.

Archie's face told Gus that he hadn't given up. Whipping a knife out of a holster, he threw it at the beast, the blade lodging handle-deep in its throat.

Daisy's eyes flashed a powerful laser-like blast burning the flesh. The beast retreated, hurt, squealing.

Jesus.

Then the beast changed tack and flew at Isabella. She looked exhausted, struggling to hold it back with the red energy particles emanating from her hands. Daisy fired again, catching the monster in the throat but, from where he watched, he could tell the strike lacked the same power.

Unbound fury crashed out in its bark, in its roar.

It jumped at Isabella again, but now Archie rushed in, recklessly smashing into the beast with his spiky head. White blood flew everywhere.

Screaming, Archie took a blow to the shoulder only to run at the beast once more, sending it sideways.

Gus could scarcely believe his eyes.

This time the beast took time to adjust, shaking itself down, stabilising itself. It too was gasping for breath.

He thought of Sue, seeing her so identically in Isabella's face, so similar that it filled Gus with strength, injecting him with steel.

He had to do something. He had to help save the de Lowes—wasn't that what Sue would have wanted more than anything?

Now, a serpent-like monster reared over Isabella, hissing and roaring. Isabella kicked out, whacking the sides of the reptilian face. Daisy flashed another light beam out of her eyes, sending the beast reeling.

Gus felt in the pockets of the coat. A penknife, and the strange jar. He pulled out his Swiss Army knife, took off Old Man Wood's overcoat and, holding it under one arm, crept as quietly as he possibly could, hugging the wall, to the far side of the beast.

Head down, the beast surveyed the Heirs, saliva dripping from its mouth, its sharp teeth ready to plunge. Then, in an instant, it changed.

Smaller, faster, menacing, just like a raptor.

As one, the de Lowe children shuffled backwards, the beast flashing its head from one to the other.

Gus knew he had to act now. And then, from the corner of his eye, he saw it. An oblong block of stone lying on the floor, next to where the previous monster's feet had stood.

He crouched down hardly daring to breathe.

Commando-style, on hands and knees, Gus crept forward. He stretched out a hand, grasped the stone in his fingers and began to pull it ever-so gently towards him, trying to keep his breathing even, his face buried in the ground, praying he wouldn't be noticed.

A strange, high-pitched bark crashed into his ears and made him stop stone-still. The beast was ready to attack, he could sense it.

Gus crawled forward and kept pulling the tablet as though in ultra-slow motion. With a gentle release of breath, he dropped it into one of the large coat pockets.

A plan formed in his mind. Reckless and crazy, yes. But he had to do it.

The beast had moved further forwards towards his friends, snaring them in the corner.

With a deep breath, Gus stood up, and, remembering his words to Sue on the boat, he summoned the haunting theme tune from 'Titanic' into a whistle, stepped out from behind the monster, and started walking.

FIFTY-EIGHT
SUE MAKES A DECISION

To Sue, it felt as if hours had passed. She walked around the vast palace, dusting off corners of paintings and the edges of rocks discovering sparkling stones that glowed back at her, most bearing a colour and depth such as she'd never seen before. The more she walked, the deeper her mind churned. Besides not saying farewell to her loved ones, especially her mum and Isabella, her thoughts returned to Gus.

Her dear Gus. Heroic and fabulous and funny and talented. Sue's heart ached as if it might shatter at any moment. An intense sorrowfulness she'd never considered possible filled her bones until she reminded herself that it was nothing short of a miracle that she was still alive. Wasn't that in itself worth treasuring?

Gus had made her life possible. More than anything, he would have wanted her to live, and to live in a way that captured the sparkle and dynamism and love that he'd shown her on their brief, yet exhilarating adventure.

Perhaps, she thought, this was his gift. A special underestimated gift, just like him.

And when she thought of Kemp, the gut-wrenching revulsion she previously felt for him faded like a stain coming out in the wash. Sure, she could never—would never—love him like Gus. He was just an insecure boy, she figured, shy and sensitive, masked by a bully's shell. She recognised that he'd understood the luck of the cards in this strange game of survival. *Funny how things turn out.*

And here she was, wandering about on an alien planet. A place beyond imagination, scarred by a tragic history that concerned Earth and the unknown accounts before the known dawn of humankind. And all she could do was wait for news of Earth's demise and the loss of numberless souls.

She walked on and on. In every room and along every dust-filled passageway, she noted the glass-like, plate-shaped puddles covered by layers of dust. And, when she stopped and bent down to wipe them, she discovered that each one bore the face of a person who stared back at her; some smiling, some waving, occasionally a wink, or a brief upturn in the corner of the mouth.

Did they know they were trapped? She wondered. The more she examined them, the more she saw in each face the flicker in the eye of yearning, a look that cried out to be loved.

They were waiting, she thought. Lost in space, floating in an empty void.

Sadness consumed her. The visions of lost souls swept through her mind and pulled on her heart strings. She ran hard, crying until she had no more tears, collapsing into a corner of what she imagined must have once been a kind of stable block. More puddles, larger puddles.

She wiped away the dust.

In front of her, nodding, a horse's face looked back at her.

Horses too? She thought. That was unexpected.

From her dark place, she noted a pinprick of light in its eye.

She smiled at its long, white, nose and the way it tossed its head. She put her hand on the puddle and ran it up and down as if stroking, petting the animal.

It seemed to respond to her touch.

'I think I'll call you "London"' she said. The thought warmed her.

'And you,' she said, sliding over to the next one and

brushing the dust away, 'can be "Edinburgh". In no time, she'd named twenty-five patches and, just to make sure she wouldn't forget she went round each one calling out their names.

On the third circuit, she was sure she detected a form of recognition, as though they could hear, as if they knew they were being spoken to.

Maybe, Sue thought, if they could hear her, she might be able to learn the names of not only the horses, but the people, so that when they woke up, she wouldn't be overwhelmed or distrusted. Indeed, she might even gain their friendship as she waited.

She liked the thought that she could enable change. Maybe she could do something significant here. Make a difference.

The more she churned around in her head what Cain had told her, the clearer her mind became.

She would stay here for the people in the puddles and for the horses in the stables. Not for Kemp or the ghost.

Soon she'd know. One more day, that's all the time they had left.

As she waited, petting a grey horse she'd named "Paris" she figured she'd need to work on a plan for both outcomes.

FIFTY-NINE
KEMP TRIES TO EXPLAIN

When Cain didn't return, Kemp assumed that his previous instruction meant he should get to the cottage and, at the very least, try and talk his mother into willingly going with him. He knew she had to be persuaded one way or the other, or his entire purpose would have failed. Besides, if it went badly, this would be his last chance to be with her. And he wanted to be with her more than anything else right now.

Shots rang out—he couldn't tell from where, but it urged him on faster, uphill—the fog lifting bit by bit.

Sensing he'd reached the top of the rise, he turned to the right and followed the outline of the track, climbing logs and straddling puddles, negotiating fallen stones as quietly as he could, making sure that he wouldn't be found and taken in by the soldiers.

It felt like ages before he saw the linear outline of a rooftop. He realised he'd travelled further round than he would have liked, but it had kept him out of harm's way. As he approached the old, grey courtyard, he hid among the scraggly bushes listening, watching, waiting.

From here, he knew it took only a quick dash up the staircase to his mother's apartment.

Tiptoeing across, he arrived at her door, knocked briefly and then, without waiting for an answer, let himself in.

Mrs Pye sat in her chair, rocking backwards and forwards, her eyes staring wildly at the door.

Her alarm disappeared when she saw Kemp, and her face beamed, as much as her facial expression allowed. 'I knew you'd be back,' she said. 'I had a feeling, deep in here.' She pointed to her chest.

'Couldn't keep me away,' Kemp replied, moving in for a hug. 'Can I make you a cup of tea or something?'

'Don't you be silly,' she said. 'What can I get *you*? It's not every day I find out I've got a little one all of my own.' She struggled out of her chair, Kemp helping her.

'I know what. Are you hungry? I'll make you one of my all-time specials,' she said. 'It's called a Mrs Pye Special. Those others love my MPS's.'

'I know about those,' Kemp beamed. 'They're famous.'

'And I reckon you is going to love them too,' she said. 'Come on. Let's go over and make one, together.'

In the kitchen, Mrs Pye tossed Kemp an apron, and they set about putting the huge sandwich together. All the while, Mrs Pye chatted, not about anything in particular, but mainly about the recipe and how kind everyone had been to her.

Finally, they sat down and began to eat.

'I am sorry,' she said when their plates were empty.

'About what?'

'Well, my little treasure, I'm sorry that I never saw you growing up. Now, look at you, all brawn and muscles and handsomeness. I imagine you must have been a right beautiful boy, huh?'

No one had ever commented that Kemp could be in any way either handsome or beautiful before and he swelled with pride. 'I don't know. No one has ever said such nice things,' he said.

Kemp knew this was his chance.

'There's something I need to discuss with you, mum,' he

said, before adding, 'I can call you "Mum" can't I? Or would you prefer "mother" or something else? Maybe just Mrs Pye?'

Mrs Pye reddened, she'd never given any thought to it. She chortled in a slightly embarrassed way. 'Mother, for now, I think,' she said.

'Mother,' Kemp said, relishing the shape of the word in his mouth.

'Now, go on. What's this thing you want to talk about? Is it about Archie and his sisters by any chance?'

Kemp nodded. 'Yeah.'

'I'll tell you for free; they're acting most queer, them lot. Out of the ordinary, like they're trying to save the world.'

'That's the thing,' he said. 'They kind of are. And there's good news and bad news on that front.'

Mrs Pye leaned forward. 'Keep going.'

Kemp picked his plate up and placed it in the sink. 'Let's go back to your room, and I'll tell you everything, I promise. It's complicated, but I don't think it's safe to talk here. There are soldiers on the hills right now, looking for them. If they find me, I won't be coming back, I promise you.'

She stood up and moved quickly to the door. 'Can't leave me on tenterhooks. Come on, I'll lead the way.'

Inside Mrs Pye's snug room, she sat down on her chair while Kemp perched at the end of the bed.

'It's a strange story,' he began, 'but it's all true, however daft it sounds,' he began. 'Thing is, you've got to believe me, because, without these weird things happening, I would never have found you, and I wouldn't have lost all my hair and the headmaster wouldn't be here and the soldiers wouldn't be turning up asking questions and the telly would work and then there wouldn't have been this unreal flood and the disease and the pandemonium everywhere.' He stared at his mother. 'I take it you know about all this stuff?'

Mrs Pye eyed him curiously. 'Yep. Nothing but terror-awful stories on my telly-box. And they're wanting my Archie and that girl Sue too. I wondered if it was some kind of joke at first. But it can't be, can it?'

'No, mother, it is all very real,' he said, as earnestly as he could. Then he paused trying to work out how to begin. 'Look, don't ask me why, but the three de Lowes were chosen to save everyone.' He knew immediately that it sounded ridiculous and sniggered. 'Bit of a weird choice, if you ask me, but, so far, they've done better than anyone imagined.'

'Well, go on,' she encouraged. 'I'm all ears.'

'The thing is, they've got to solve three riddles that lead them to finding three stone tablets. If they don't, then the world will be wiped out by further rain and disease.' Kemp shook his head. 'Oh hell, you must think I'm crazy?'

Mrs Pye inclined her head. 'That would explain why they turned the house upside down looking at all them pictures,' she said.

He raised an eyebrow. 'Yeah, probably.'

'And why they pulled out those strange carpet thing-a-me's after I'd shoved them in the washing machine.'

'Yeah. That's right—Archie told me the rugs had clues to finding the riddles,' he said.

'And does all this explain why Archie has his hair sticking out and Daisy ruddy eyes and Isabella holes in her hands?'

Kemp nodded. 'Yes, mother,' he said. 'It's all to do with the same thing. But, you see, it doesn't finish with simply finding these tablets. Even if they succeed, they must do one more thing.'

'Something else, huh?'

'Yeah, and it's not good.' His voice went quiet. 'In fact, it's completely shocking.'

Mrs Pye scratched her nose.

Kemp hesitated. 'I'm not sure I know how to tell you—'

'They're my lot, they are,' she said, 'and if it's got anything to do with them, I'm needing to know. Go on, my boy. Tell me this awful-dreadful thing they've got to do.'

SIXTY
WHISTLING

'We're cornered,' Daisy whispered. 'Any ideas?'

'Not really. I'm almost on my knees.'

'LOOK OUT!!' she screamed.

Archie ducked and threw another knife, which lodged neatly into the beast's neck.

Now a fearsome dragon, its snake eyes filled with fury, the beast recoiled and then jumped, going at Daisy with open jaws.

Isabella flipped from her hands into a cartwheel and kicked the beast in the head.

The animal crashed to the side, quickly turning into a small slippery viper, Archie's knives falling out of the old body to the floor.

'What the hell...?'

'Music?'

Even the snake turned to follow their eyes.

From out of the shadows, Gus walked casually past, whistling the melodious, haunting tune from the film, *Titanic*.

He glanced up, giving them a remarkably big grin. 'Don't mean to disturb you, but mind if I let myself out?' he said. 'It's a little bit stuffy in here.'

'Bloody hell!' Archie said in astonishment. '*Gus?* What the...'

Gus threw the coat at Archie who caught it smartly. Then he smiled and winked. 'My friends, I think you'll find it's got everything you need—'

Gus stood little chance.

In a flash, to the shock of the onlookers, the viper shot at Gus's neck and in for the kill.

SIXTY-ONE
A DIFFERENT MOUTHFUL

I n a flash three knives lay buried up to their hilt, two in the beast's neck, which oozed thick, white blood, the other just above its thigh.

Burn marks sizzled around the reptiles neck from Daisy's lasers.

The beast fell but righted itself quickly, its jaws stained red.

Archie, with the coat tucked under one arm reached into his breast holster and hurled another. This time the blade sank into its chest.

The beast toppled and roared. It spun its head around and moved clumsily away from Gus. Turning, it sprang at Archie.

But, instead of running or ducking, Archie ran towards it to meet the on-rushing jaws of the monster. In one movement, perfectly timed, Archie extended his arm and thrust the coat straight down the serpent's throat, momentarily gagging it.

'Have your tablet back,' he said, removing his arm a millisecond before the jaws snapped shut.

The beast tipped its head back, chewing the remains of the coat with its sharp teeth, devouring it like a chocolate treat.

From the coat pocket, a glass jar span through the air.

Daisy studied it, her eyes tuning in. *The jar of Havilarian Toadstool Powder!*

In a flash she stood up knowing exactly what she had to do.

The glass jar caught the light as it bounced.

Daisy rushed in—the face of the beast following her movements, it's jaws opening.

Daisy knew she had one chance. Her foot connected perfectly, her aim true, the jar flashing like a bullet straight into the beasts mouth. A crunching sound, like breaking glass, the only noise.

In no time, Gorialla Yingarna had Archie pinned to the wall. *It is over,* he roared, triumphantly into their heads.

In a flash the beast changed into a smaller dragon. It levelled its foul head inches from Archie's, its large, hazy green gaze spraying him with an emerald-green light that probed deep into his eyes.

I have you now, the serpent said.

'DON'T LISTEN TO IT!' Daisy screamed. 'Hold on!'

Now the huge snake in front of Archie twitched, the movement reverberating along the length of its body.

'Archie! Close your eyes!'

But the hypnosis was already set.

Say farewell, child, the snake said, its forked tongue flickering in and out of its mouth. The snake bared its long, yellow fangs millimetres from Archie's face. *One nip is all it takes to extinguish your entire world.*

Its long, sharp, bloodied teeth made to bite him, but instead of doing so, a wave, like a gigantic hiccup rolled down the beast.

'WAKE UP, Arch! Wake up!' Isabella yelled.

Another spasm washed over the beast.

Isabella ran at Archie trying to wrestle him away, but the beast's tail whipped round and smashed her into the wall. She groaned, motionless. Old Man Wood, creeping up on the other side, followed her, but the tail twisted round and beat him to the ground.

As the beast opened its mouth, another spasm shuttled through the beast.

It coughed and thrust its head agonizingly into the air, twisting, groaning, shuddering, trying to inspect its body.

The spell broke.

Archie collapsed. 'What's going on?' he asked, looking up at the writhing snake in front of him.

Old Man Wood limped forward and pulled him up and out of reach.

Gorialla Yingarna twisted as if doused in acid, convulsing, withering.

Together, they hobbled as fast as they could towards the stairs, Archie collecting his knives as he went.

'The tablet! We can't go without it!' Daisy cried.

'Then,' Isabella said, 'one of us is going to have to slit the damn thing open.' She dabbed at a deep laceration on her head, blood spilling out. 'Leave it to me.' But Isabella's head swam and, filled with dizziness, she tripped landing face down on the floor.

The beast unravelled and advanced.

'Bells, MOVE!'

Isabella shivered, too shattered, too gone.

'Bells!' Daisy yelled. 'What are you doing?'

Isabella summoned her reserves and hobbled, on her knees, towards the steps. As the snake sprang, its jaws shutting on the torn rags of her trousers, Archie flashed another knife between the beast's eyes.

Daisy pulled her away as the snake collapsed in a heap on the floor in front of them.

Huddled on the steps, the four looked on in silence, as the beast twisted and writhed, white phlegm foaming out of its mouth, its eyes conversely shutting then bulging, red veins throbbing as if they might, at any moment, explode.

'Top tip,' Archie said, his breathing shallow and his heartbeat racing. 'Don't ever eat old people's coats.'

Daisy sat Isabella down and draped her good arm around her. 'Bells. Stop shivering, hun. It's going to be all right. You hear?' She ran a hand over her brow, inspecting her wound. 'It can't hurt any of us anymore.'

Daisy's pale face tried to smile. 'We've just got to figure out how to get the tablet out, that's all.'

They watched as the reptile lying in front of them decayed as if it was bathing in a bath of acid.

Daisy leaned in, squinting. 'Just as I thought,' she said.

'What?' Archie said.

'Weenie toadstools.'

'Toadstools?'

For a minute Archie wondered what Daisy was talking about, but then, little by little, multi-coloured toadstools popped out of the beast's scaly skin, covering it like a pin-cushion.

'It's nothing less than our sugary friend, Havilarian toad-stool powder,' Daisy said. 'I never, ever thought I'd be happy to see that stuff again.'

SIXTY-TWO

LEO

The beast surveyed them with its hypnotic eyes for one last time as a voice of terrible laughter echoed in their heads. Then, a strange, green goo belched out of its body; depositing filthy embryonic material, like stinking slime, onto the floor.

The toadstools quickly multiplied, the sound of decay like water splashing in a metal basin.

A giant, light-green and white-striped toadstool sliced itself out of the great body of the snake followed by three more, glowing and angry. They throbbed menacingly, growing fast, the beast shrivelling up before their eyes until it was little more than a flimsy sack.

'How fitting' Old Man Wood said slowly, 'that this Prince of Darkness, should die from poison of his own making. It is the death it alone deserves.'

As soon as the beast posed no possible further threat, they hobbled over to Gus' body.

For a little while, their thoughts were entirely lost as they looked at his face, still bearing his happy smile.

'Gus,' Isabella said, tears rolling down her cheeks. 'Thank you. No-one in the world ever did a braver thing.'

'Hear, hear,' Archie said. 'And no one in the universe ever did a more noble thing either.'

To their astonishment, Gus blinked and turned his head towards them.

'GUS!' they said.

He swallowed, blinked for a long moment and, clearly in discomfort and with great difficulty, attempted to speak. The words struggled to form.

They leaned in, waiting for him.

'Gus. There's no hurry, mate,' Archie said, tears in his eyes, 'Not now.' He turned to his sister. 'Bells, heal him—like you did with Old Man Wood?'

Gus shook his head a tiny fraction. 'Too… late,' he croaked. 'Goner.' He smiled again, swallowing, closing his eyes.

'No!' Isabella cried. 'I can; I can save you, Gus. Stay with us. Whatever you do, don't fall asleep—understand?' She thrust out her hands, but the energy she had used to save the others failed to materialise. 'It's not working,' she cried.

'Bad,' he said. His eyes flickered down.

Now that they looked, blood soaked his T-shirt.

Archie knelt down and very gently prised the cotton fabric aside from the tear made by the beast. Archie stared up, his eyes wide. 'Bad.' He repeated, blood draining from his face. 'Very,' he mouthed.

Focusing on Isabella, Gus said, 'Tell Sue…' he sucked in more air, 'it … it was fun.' He winced, the effort immense. 'Tell her she's … beautiful.' He tried to smile.

'Tell her… that her Leo's waiting…' he said, his blood-stained teeth trying to smile, his nose wrinkled in pain.

His head remained still, but his eyes switched towards Daisy. They shut for a longer period, his breathing shallow, gurgling a little.

Daisy could hardly bear it, swallowing, trying to hold herself together. 'Oh my God. I'm so sorry, Gus, 'she cried, tears rolling down her cheeks. 'I'm so, so sorry.'

'No.' He forced out. 'Don't… be.' He smiled. 'Nice… kick.' He coughed. Blood bubbled in his mouth. 'Fate, huh?'

His breathing stuttered. He desperately tried to find air to funnel into his damaged body.

He grasped Archie's hand.

Archie shook, his body heaving with despair. 'You're a total hero, mate,' he said, his eyes watering.

Gus sighed. 'You, same,' he breathed.

His eyes now bore into Archie's with a seemingly desperate look, as though, Archie thought, he was trying to tell him something.

Archie leaned in closer.

'Do it... for... Sue... promise... me?' he croaked, the final words barely above a sigh. 'Look... after... her.'

Archie held Gus's hand, pulled it to his mouth and kissed it. 'Sure, Gus,' he said, tears streaming down his cheeks. 'I promise.'

Gus's head sank back onto the cold cavern floor and as his breathing stopped his eyes lost their light. A death rattle made them realize that the big toothy grin had smiled for the very last time.

A stunned, hollow silence hung in the cave.

Isabella closed his mouth and pulled down his eyelids.

As the moment of bitter truth passed, Archie laid Gus's hand down on the earth and wiped his eyes. 'I promise you Gus Williams,' he said, 'when this is over, we will see you off properly, mate.'

Seeing the tablet through the remains of the skin of the beast, Archie climbed over the slimy remains and prised it out, wiping the stone carefully on the remains of his jeans.

He noted a flicker of metal by the dragon's swollen leg. He bent down and collected the knives he'd thrown, slipping them back in the holster around his chest.

Then, handing the tablet to Daisy, he bent down and picked Gus's body off the floor and followed the others, who, without looking back, shuffled wearily up the stairs.

SIXTY-THREE
WORKING IT OUT

Out in the open, sunlight strained through wisps of low cloud and threatened to break the mist that clouded over the valley below.

They gulped in lungfuls of fresh air and shielded their faces from the glare. In due course they sidled over to a large flat stone by the side of the ruin where they fell, exhausted.

Archie laid Gus' body down, covering it with the remains of his coat.

'We'll have to leave him here, come back and sort him out later. I'm too exhausted to carry him an inch further.'

Every part, from the tips of their heads to the nails on their toes, ached.

No smiles, no cheers, no talking. Lost in private, despondent thoughts.

'I still don't understand,' Isabella said at length, 'how the toadstool powder end up in the monster?'

Archie scratched a now-soft hair-spike. 'A sensational volley, I believe,' he said, winking at Daisy. 'It was in Old Man Wood's coat all along,' he said. 'We noticed it when we were trying to find the Resplendix Mix healing potion after you'd knocked yourself out?'

Even now, Daisy chuckled at the thought of it.

'Talking of Resplendix Mix,' Archie said, 'Look at my

arm. It's raked.' Three angry red cuts ran in neat lines from his elbow-join to his wrist.

'You think that's bad?' Daisy said. 'Check this out.' She removed the torn clothing around her shoulder to reveal a long, deep laceration.

Old Man Wood sidled over and whistled. 'Oh dear, that's not good young'un. I'll sort you out, just as soon as we get back home.'

'Did you drop your coat when the animals ran off?' Archie said, addressing the old man.

'Now, then. I'd draped it over the back of one of those fabulous unicorns,' Old Man Wood said. 'That terrible heat. Those poor animals, how courageous they were.'

'Gus must have found it on his way through the labyrinth,' Archie said. 'But how did he even end up in the labyrinth? I mean, we found it, but only by mistake.'

Daisy cleared her throat. 'Kemp and Gus fought. Kemp won. I thought Gus died, but instead, he must have fallen through the hole—'

'But we'd have seen him,' Archie said. 'Or he'd have been trampled to death.'

'Maybe he'd been hidden?' Isabella volunteered.

'Hidden?'

'Maybe the beast was saving him for later?'

They dropped the conversation and looked out over the strange wispy sky, grateful that the fog had already cleared on the hilltop.

'Bells, you're going to have to tell Sue,' Daisy said. 'Tell her everything.'

'I know,' she said forlornly. 'I'm dreading it already. To be honest, I think it would be better if we're all there—give his sacrifice the gravitas it deserves.'

Old Man Wood raised a hand in agreement. Then, groaning loudly, he pulled himself into a sitting position. 'Time to get on, my little heroes.'

They helped each other up and, linking arms, shuffled on.

Old Man Wood supported the two girls, in much the same

way as he'd done when they escaped from the cave, stopping now and then for rests.

As they went, more clouds parted, and shards of golden sunlight beamed down upon them, a kaleidoscope of colours enveloping them like a prism.

They said nothing, drinking in the glory of the light, the beauty of the sky and the rich colours of the hill that fell away into the white cloud.

Each one stumbled on, submerged in thoughts of the terrible end of Gus and Gorialla Yingarna and slowly thinking about the final task that lay ahead.

'Look at that!' Daisy said, pointing towards the cottage some way down the hill.

They stopped to admire a rainbow that arched overhead, one end seemingly finishing smack in the middle of Old Man Wood's vegetable garden.

'Flood, followed by a rainbow,' Isabella said. 'Straight out of the Bible.'

'Yes, indeed,' Old Man Wood said. 'Mother Nature's gifts are indeed complex and curious.'

'I don't mean to be rude Old Man Wood,' Archie began, 'but I've been meaning to ask you something.'

'Ask away, littlun.'

'Well, it's a bit weird,' he began, hesitantly. 'But… I think you're, you know, well, are you, like, Adam from the Creation story?'

'Funny you should say that,' Isabella said, 'but I've been thinking he's more like Noah from the flood story.'

Old Man Wood scrunched his eyes together. 'Hmmm. I suppose. I might, or mightn't be,' was all he said, unhelpfully. The furrows on his mud-encrusted forehead deepened.

'He's definitely Old Man Wood,' Daisy added. 'That's the most important thing.'

Old Man Wood stopped and sat down on a fallen tree branch. He eyed each one of them slowly and smiled. 'Well, if you must know, the thing is, the Noah story has always been a genuine mistake. You see, I was on this great big boat with a huge storm brewing, and some strange-looking man kept on yelling at me if I was someone or other, and so I screamed back, "NO!—Ah, I'm afraid I can't hear you." And of course, the man didn't hear and, as the story was passed down, I ended up being called No-ah – though of course, the language was different. And then this daft man drew up a family tree with No-ah in it. Madness the lot of it. And that wasn't even the REAL flood.'

His laugh boomed out over the quiet valley where, for the first time in ages, high, excited twitters of birdsong registered in their ears.

They walked on aware of little animal faces running into the path and looking at them before scurrying off.

For the stunned children, the penny had finally dropped that this blundering, loving, caring, great, great Grandfather many, many times over—or so he claimed—was beyond extraordinary, beyond comprehension of both the ancient and the mystical.

And, what's more, he possessed a magic branchwand from the original Tree of Knowledge that was contained in an ear-stud.

The difference was that this time, however crazy his stories, they absolutely believed him.

SIXTY-FOUR

SOLOMON'S WARNING

'Hull-oo!'

They stopped in their tracks and peered through the dim, white cloud that surrounded them.

'Archie! Is that you?' the voice said.

'Er, yes,' Archie replied. The children and Old Man Wood turned to one another, a look of confusion on their faces.

'Archie, Daisy, Isabella?'

'It's Solomon,' Daisy whispered.

Solomon heaved himself over a fallen bough and hurried over.

'Goodness, gracious me! You did it! You came out!' he exclaimed, recoiling at the sight of them. 'By the Gods, it would appear you need urgent medical attention—all of you. Can I offer a shoulder—or two? I'm afraid there really is no other alternative.'

They rearranged themselves so that Old Man Wood supported Daisy, while the other two spread their arms around the headmaster's shoulders.

As they found a rhythm, Solomon continued. 'I'm not sure you're in a fit state to talk, so let me do that,' he began. 'We've been beside ourselves with worry, but I'm afraid you're not out of the woods yet. I'll try and describe what's been going on. Our not-so-friendly Commissioner has gone a little, how do you say, AWOL.'

Archie glanced up. *'What?'*

'Absent-With-Out-Leave, dear boy,' Solomon said. 'I've been picking up the lingo from the soldiers. Stone's got it into his head that he has to stop you—and stop you at any cost. When I heard gunshots and his appalling manner on the radio, the soldiers and I concluded that he may have already put a bullet in a couple of his men. Luckily, I managed to persuade Dickinson that you need protecting, not detaining. He's gone on ahead with his men.'

They stepped over a broken branch, Solomon busily helping each one. 'Stone's plan is to burn the cottage to the ground so that you come running out. He doesn't even realise you're not there.'

'The cottage! What about Mrs Pye?' Archie said.

'Yes. Mrs Pye as well,' he said. 'He's taken hold of a flamethrower. Wretched, beastly thing—I don't think I've ever witnessed such a destructive and deeply unpleasant implement of war.'

'The other tablets are in the cottage,' Archie said, an edge of panic in his voice.

'Well then, let's hope Dickinson sticks to his word and gets that man out of the way before he manages to wreak more havoc.'

'Sir, Have you seen Sue?' Isabella asked.

'Sue? No, I'm afraid she fell rather early on. We were separated. We planned to get closer to the ruin,' Solomon said. 'But I haven't heard from her since, and I'm quite sure none of Stone's units stumbled into her. My guess is that she returned to the cottage.'

Shortly, Solomon couldn't contain the question any longer. 'I take it were you successful in sourcing the tablet?' he asked.

'We wouldn't be here if we weren't,' Isabella said, wincing. 'It came at a great price.'

'I can see that by the astonishing mess you're in,' he said, looking at theim. 'We'll get you patched up as soon as we get things straightened out with Stone.'

'Actually, sir, I'm not talking about us. You see, Gus Williams showed up,' she said. 'Gus saved us. In fact, it's probably more accurate to say that Gus single-handedly saved the planet.'

'Gus? Really?' Solomon stopped. 'Goodness me. What was he doing in there?'

'That's the thing. We don't know. We think he must've fallen in after his fight with Kemp. It's a bit of a mystery.'

Solomon continued on the path. 'And where is Gus now?'

For a while, the tread of their feet on the sludgy ground sounded louder.

Archie bowed his head. 'He didn't make it, sir,' he said. 'He made the ultimate sacrifice, helping us right at the end. Isabella was right. Gus did the bravest thing ever known, just as it was about to go against us.'

Solomon missed a step, righting himself before he pulled them over with him. 'Oh, my dear children! How dreadful. I'm so terribly sorry you have had to witness such a thing. What a sorry business.'

A violent whoosh and the roar of flames from a position below them, nearer the house, brought them to a sudden standstill. Tangy petrol fumes hit their nostrils.

'Drat! Stone and his infernal machine,' Solomon whispered. 'He's beaten them to it.' He glanced at them again, noting their beaten, shattered condition. 'In your circumstances,' he said, 'I would advise you to stay well away.'

'Where is he?' Archie asked.

'At a guess, he's just above the courtyard.'

The daylight surrounding them had further cleared the path towards the cottage.

'We face a tricky situation,' Solomon declared quietly. 'We can't have him destroy the house, and yet, it would be extremely unwise to face him. '

'But we have to go on,' Daisy said, 'especially if Mrs Pye and Sue are in the house. We promised Gus we'd protect Sue, and we've got to put the tablets together. We're running out of time.'

Solomon shifted and shook his head. 'But looking at you three, are you in any position to, how should I put it, use your gifts? For example, could you repel the flames of his flamethrower and stop a bullet?'

Daisy shook her head. 'I'm absolutely spent. Don't know about you guys, but I've got nothing left.'

'Me neither,' Isabella said. 'Though, of course, I'll try.'

They shuffled along, the earlier nervousness of travelling through the passages returning.

From nowhere, they suddenly felt the heat of fire and the choking stench of fumes that followed.

'Get down!' Solomon cried. They crawled behind the fallen bough of a tree and waited.

Emerging from the wispy fog, was a tall, lean figure holding a long metallic tube.

Then the man spoke, his voice hard and crisp and edged with a lilt of triumph in his tone.

'Come out Archie de Lowe. Your game is up.'

He waited.

'We can do this the easy way,' he yelled, 'or we can do it the hard way. Whichever you prefer.'

Still, there was no response.

Stone walked closer.

'I know you're there and I know you have the information about the storm and the disease. All you've got to do is tell me what's going on.'

No one moved.

'I'll give you until the count of three,' he said, 'to show yourself.'

'One.

'Two.' The rattle of metal could be heard on his body.

'Three.'

The machine whirred into action spewing fire left and right, the tree branch in front of them bursting into flames.

All of them gagged, coughing, their eyes watering.

'Archie de Lowe,' Stone called out, 'I am arresting you under the Terrorism Act on the suspicion of creating, or being party to, a world pandemic. You do not have to say anything, but it may harm your defence if you do not mention when questioned, something which you later rely on in court. Anything you do say may be given in evidence.'

'We can't stay here like this,' Archie whispered, as he scrabbled on the ground behind the tree stump as though looking for something. 'The man's bonkers.' He stood up. 'I'll face him.'

'I hope you know what you're doing,' Daisy said. 'Your last plan was rubbish.'

'Yours wasn't much better,' he whispered. 'This time, I know what I'm doing…'

Daisy looked into the light haze and frowned. 'Take the tablet. Show it to him. It's the only way there's a chance he'll be convinced.'

Solomon stood up too. 'I'll go with you, Archie. Let's see if we can reason with the man, get him to put that wretched thing down.'

They stepped out into the light, coughing the last particles of petroleum out of their lungs.

'For heaven's sake's be careful,' Isabella whispered. 'And Archie, stay out of the way of that machine.'

'It's me Solomon,' the headmaster called out. 'I have Archie here with me. We're coming down the track. Please, lower that ghastly weapon.'

Archie, supported by Solomon's arm, stumbled down the track stopping about thirty paces from the Commissioner. They faced one another like gunfighters in a duel.

'A-ha. Hello little Archie de Lowe. I can't tell you how nice it is to finally meet you. So, you've come out of your hiding place at long last. Tell me, what is it about you, huh? What makes you so damned special? Your headmaster here told me you were looking for some kind of a tablet. Is this true?'

'Yes,' Archie said. 'We need to find three tablets to save everyone. That's all you need to know.'

'You have these tablets?'

'Uh-huh.'

Stone grinned. 'Why is it *you*, de Lowe?'

'I don't know,' Archie replied. 'It just is.'

'What information, what little secrets are you holding?'

'It's nothing that concerns you,' Archie replied.

Stone paused. 'Now then, first of all, hand over this troublesome tablet-thing.'

'With respect, cousin,' Solomon said, 'the de Lowes have been through the most testing trials any human being could have gone through to attain these artefacts—'

Stone's icy voice interrupted. 'Let me remind you both that Archie is under arrest. Headmaster, right now you are aiding a suspected criminal.' His voice went softer. 'Please, Archie, hand over the evidence.'

Solomon's face was turning puce. 'Don't you understand, you nitwit, they can't—'

A shot rang out.

Solomon fell to the floor like a sack of coal.

'Nobody calls me a nitwit,' Stone said. 'Now, Archie, do as I say and give me the tablet.'

With a look of shock painted on his face, Archie stared at the prostrate figure of the headmaster, then back at Stone.

'Sure,' Archie said, coolly. 'I'll put the tablet halfway between us. How does that sound?'

Stone hesitated.

'Very well,' he said with a sly smile. 'It's only right that I look after it from here on in. Remember, you're all coming with me, so no funny business or you'll end up like your headmaster.'

Archie limped forward, reached into his pocket and pulled out a block. He placed it on the ground and withdrew.

Stone, the flamethrower still strapped to his chest, his gun steadied at Archie, moved forward.

Struggling to bend down, Stone fell to his knees, the

casing of the long barrel clacking as it hit the ground. He stared at the stone Archie had deposited.

'It's about this lump of rock, is it,' Stone said, bitterly. 'You're telling me the chaos out there is because of this?' he said spitting on it. 'You really think I'm going to fall for that?' He picked it up and turned it over. 'This is an old house tile from that ruin.'

He tossed it back on the ground.

Archie remained silent.

Stone cocked his head, eying the boy standing in front of him. He raised the gun at Archie, then pointed it at the tablet.

He pulled the trigger.

The first shot crashed into the tile, the noise pinging off.

'NO!' Daisy said, running out.

The second did the same.

Stone stared at the small tablet on the ground. 'Bloody thing! Why doesn't it break?'

Stone fired again. The tablet split in two.

By now, all three of the others stood up behind the fallen bough, watching incredulously.

'You're a damned liar,' Stone seethed. 'All of you! Come out from behind that tree or Archie gets it. Move, now!'

Cautiously they moved forward.

He eyed each one in turn. 'Tell me, what is going on?' Stone said.

Archie struggled to form his words. 'We have been tasked,' he began.

'Tasked? Who by? God?'

Archie shrugged. 'To find three tablets.'

'Bullshit! These are shitty old roof-tiles,' he roared. 'Look.' He pointed at the broken tablet.

'You are not telling me the truth!' Phlegm spat out of his mouth. 'The truth, Archie.'

Archie didn't know what to say.

'Spit it out, boy!'

'Don't tell him,' Isabella yelled.

Stone looked up. 'Tell me everything, de Lowe.'

He pointed the gun at Old Man Wood and with a level of calmness in his voice said, 'I need to know the lot.'

'That is the truth!' Isabella exclaimed.

Stone smiled at her, and then, just as he'd planned, he squeezed the trigger again.

SIXTY-FIVE

DICKINSON ARRIVES

From nowhere, Stone heard a click, and felt the cold imprint of metal on the back of his neck.

'That's enough,' he heard. 'If your magazine wasn't empty, I might have been too late.'

Stone froze. 'Who the hell is it?' he said. 'My name is Commissioner Stone, head of operations for the United Kingdom of the Yorkshire disaster. Remove your weapon.'

'I know exactly who you are,' Dickinson said, coolly.

Stone exhaled. 'Dickinson,' he sighed. 'Well, you took your time. Look who I've found.' He stood up. 'For a moment, I thought you were some ruddy foreigner.'

'Don't move, sir. We're going to escort you back to Swinton Park.'

'What?'

'Enough is enough. Please give yourself over freely. I don't want a scene.'

'What is the meaning of this, Dickinson? You have no authority—'

'I have every authority, especially as you have clearly gone way beyond yours. We heard your antics on the radio, we heard the gunshots and we saw how you gunned down the headmaster. Do you deny it?'

'Move your weapon away, Dickinson!' Stone snarled.

'No.'

'Are you defying me? Right now, my word is basically law. If you do not put that thing away and do as I say, then you will be severely dealt with—'

'We'll see about that,' Dickinson replied. 'Please, put your weapons down.'

'Never,' Stone seethed. You still don't comprehend the situation we're in do you, officer?'

'Wrong. I believe it is you who are now jeopardising the situation. You have three seconds.'

Without warning, Stone pulled the trigger. A whoosh of air splurged and flame blasted into the ground.

Dickinson's gun jerked from the Commissioner's head as a roaring flame blasted out only yards from Archie.

It gave Stone time. He turned and faced them, grinning, his eyes manically moving from Dickinson to the soldier standing next to him and then back to the de Lowes.

'One little squeeze,' Stone said, 'and you are all literally fried human flesh.' Stone fished into his pocket for a fresh magazine. 'Where are these tablets?'

'I'm afraid,' Dickinson said, his voice cold and unwavering, 'that your game is over. You're wrong about them—'

'Me? Never!' The commissioner said. 'You will pay for this, officer.'

'Wrong again,' Dickinson said coolly. 'On either side, I have a gun trained on you, sir. Touch that trigger one more time, and my marksmen will blow you away.'

Stone smirked. 'Is that right?'

'Gates,' Dickinson called out. 'Let the commissioner know you're here?'

A crack rang out followed instantly by a thud.

'Bloody lunatic,' Stone yelled, twisting from the impact.

Gasoline sprayed over the ground.

'Looks like he missed,' Dickinson said. 'I doubt he'll be so careless next time. Probably best to remove that backpack, sir, before it bursts into flames.'

Stone dropped the handgun and gritting his teeth, he

wrenched the sack off his back allowing it to crash to the ground,

Then he bent over, holding himself, his teeth clenched as he fought back the pain.

'You're injured?'

'Kicked by a damn horse.'

Dickinson smiled. 'A white horse by any chance?'

Stone looked up at him quizzically.

'Talbot, do the business, please,' Dickinson said.

'Happily,' the soldier said. Talbot grabbed the commissioner's arms and bound his hands behind his back, with rope.

'This is a bloody outrage,' Stone yelled. 'You will be severely dealt with. All of you. Where are you taking me?'

Dickinson cocked an eye. 'As far from here and as quickly as is humanly possible.'

SIXTY-SIX
KEMP TELLS HIS MOTHER

S hallow voices echoed around the courtyard below. Kemp
slipped over to the window.

'God! They're back!' he said, his face a picture of amaze-
ment. He watched as they limped through the door and, for a
brief moment, his heart soared as Daisy glanced up at the
window.

'Blimey, mother, they're in one hell of a state. Solomon's
being carried in. Don't think he's right.'

Mrs Pye joined him and tutted. 'I'd best get down and
help patch them up,' she said.

Kemp moved away from the window. 'In a minute,
mother. Please, there's one more thing I've got to tell you first,'
he said. 'It might be my only chance.'

'What are you talking about?' she said, lowering herself
into the chair once more.

'I'm afraid it's not easy, especially for you.'

'What's not?'

Kemp stammered. 'Well, the thing is, you're going to have
to make a choice.'

Mrs Pye rocked in her chair her face a little pinker than
before. 'Me? A choice? What choice?' she said. 'Is it to do
with that one last thing you're saying they won't be able
to do?'

Kemp nodded. 'Yup.'

'Go on, son, spill your beans.'

Kemp took a deep breath. 'First of all, you have to promise me that what I'm about to tell you isn't repeated to anyone. It's our secret, right. If you or I so much as breathe it to anyone, then maybe something terrible will happen.'

She agreed.

Kemp continued. 'Now, I want you, truthfully, to answer me this one thing. OK?'

She nodded back.

'Do you think that any one of Archie, Daisy and Isabella could…'

'Could what?'

Kemp closed his eyes. 'If any of them could … commit…'

'What, son?'

'Physically kill someone,' he spat out.

Mrs Pye stared at him, then burst into a shrill laugh. 'Them … murder, like in cold blood, like… killers, them? Who are you kidding? My lot, never. Not in a million years. They're as soft as my apple sponge cakes.'

Kemp's face remained serious.

Mrs Pye noticed and stopped tittering. 'Is there a problem with that? They're not going to have to—'

'The thing is,' he continued, 'unless they commit a murder, they're going to fail. And along with them, the rest of mankind will fail—everyone on this entire planet is going to die.'

'Never!' Mrs Pye's face told of nothing but disgust. 'That's just not right, that isn't.'

'It's like the grossest thing you've ever heard. I know it's not right, but it's true, it really is. And, like you, I don't think any one of them has the way or the means—or the guts.'

She shook her head and muttered about how lovely they were even if Archie was a bit scruffy and Isabella overly bossy and Daisy all-over strange sometimes.

Kemp listened for a bit and then spoke. 'Mother, they

don't even know they've got to do it yet. They've got to work it out.'

'And who is it they've got to… you know… do this terrible thing to?'

Kemp bowed his head. 'An old woman, apparently.'

Mrs Pye stared at him. 'Well, I never,' she exclaimed. 'They need to know—right this moment,' she said standing up and starting towards the door.

'You can't,' Kemp said, blocking her path. 'Now that you know, mysterious, ancient powers that I don't understand will put you in harm's way. In fact, it would be better if you don't go down there at all, for your safety. Please understand, mother. They're locked into something huge, and there's nothing me or you or the government or the soldiers or anyone else for that matter can do about it.' He held her arm tenderly. 'But, there is another way—a way that I can save you and me.'

She sat down heavily.

'It boils down to those choices I told you about. The first is that we stay here and we pray that somehow, either Arch, Daisy or Isabella manage to do this terrible thing. The second is that if and when they don't succeed we stay here and accept that we're going to die like everyone else. Believe me, I've seen enough to know what this plague does to people, and it won't be easy. The third, mother, is that you come with me. But in so doing, you may have to give yourself over, willingly—without hesitation or regret—to a spirit.'

She stared back at him with her mouth open. 'A spirit?'

'Yes. A kind of ghost.' Kemp rubbed his face. 'Look, I told you it wasn't easy.'

Mrs Pye eyed him for a while. 'And what would happen if I did this with you and then they do manage to do this terrible-awful thing and save everyone?'

'I don't know,' Kemp said, his eyes lighting up. 'But perhaps you might wish to consider this one thing. If they could murder one woman in cold blood, who's to say they wouldn't do it again a little closer to home?'

SIXTY-SEVEN

OLD MAN WOOD EXPLAINS A FEW THINGS

'What's so damn funny?' Isabella said, holding her ribs with one hand and her head with the other. 'So you switched the tablet with a manky piece of tile you found. It's not that funny. You damn nearly got us all killed.'

'No. Look at us,' Archie chuckled. 'Your clothes for starters, Bells. Have you seen the state of us?'

A crust of mud covered each one from head to toe. Only their eyes shone out. Their clothes, without exception, were torn to bits or entirely missing. Isabella's black leather jacket seemed to have vanished.

Old Man Wood's deep guffaws filled the room as they fell about laughing—painful laughter too.

'Mrs Pye's going to go absolutely mental when she sees us,' Daisy said and then did her Mrs Pye impression. ''Ere what you been up to NOW,' she mimicked, 'playing on that ruin, AGAIN!'

Archie howled, holding his sides. 'Bagsy I don't see her first!'

Old Man Wood clapped him playfully on the shoulders making him topple to the floor. They laughed harder. Then Archie showed them a rip that went all the way from his hip to his knee. 'Even my pants are ruined.'

It was impossible to know if the tears springing from Isabella's eyes were from laughter or pain.

'May as well clean ourselves up a little,' Old Man Wood said, 'but before that, I'll be dispensing a little of the old healing potion if anyone's interested.'

Resplendix Mix had never been more welcomed, nor more feared. For several minutes, the four of them sat gnashing their teeth, sweat dripping, as the potent, fiery, healing potion set to work.

But after removing their clothing, briefly washing off the larger chunks and smears of blood and mud from their bodies, they hobbled upstairs to replace their rags with new apparel.

Downstairs, the children ate ravenously and, after a long, hungry silence while they munched and slurped away, Isabella asked 'Why didn't you use your branchwandy stick against the serpent?'

'Oh, I tried,' Old Man Wood protested.

'Yes, but what I meant was, why didn't you use it to destroy the monster,' she said.

'Thing is,' he said, 'branchwands don't really work like that. Two battles were going on out there. The one with you with those brave, brave animals against the beast, and mine with the branchwand. If you ask me, I think the branchwands decided to cancel each other out.'

The children looked confused.

'I reckon they did a deal.'

'A deal?' Isabella said.

'Yes. Branchwands works in the same way as now, what were they called, genes... gentiles.'

Everyone looked perplexed.

'Genies?' Daisy guessed.

'That's the one,' he said, clapping his large hands together. 'Genies. They'll obey your commands but only if you ask in the right way and if you mean it from your heart. Our ones were having the most almighty battle until they decided it probably wasn't worth it.'

'I never saw anything,' Archie said.

'That's because what they were up to happened out of sight, littlun. How do you think the flowers died and the sheets of paper that you turned into darts, along with the postcard managed to stay up in the air for so long? Genies don't go round murdering and destroying, willy-nilly,' he said, stretching his arms out wide. 'They help in subtle ways, a bit like the genie from that old story… now, what was it called. Something you lot used to read. Sounds like, now then,' he stroked his chin. "The lad and the bin".'

The confused look on their faces said it all until Daisy clicked. 'You mean, Aladdin!'

'Aha! Right-o. That'll be the one.'

'I didn't know you knew the story of Aladdin,' Archie said.

Old Man Wood chortled. 'The story is an ancient one, based on real events years ago. The original story happened in a place called Cush.'

'Cush?' Archie said. 'In China?'

'No, no! Remember when I read that passage in the Bible – the one that made me laugh and bash my head—it mentions the countries of Havilah, Cush and Assyria…'

'Which are surrounded by the rivers of Gihon and Pishon,' Isabella added.

'Indeed. Now, these places were named *after* the planets of Havilah, Cush, Assyria and, of course, Eden, which you know today as The Garden of Eden.'

'Planets?'

'For sure,' Old Man Wood said, chomping into an apple. 'Planets.'

Daisy and Archie gave him blank looks.

'Planets like Earth, but a great deal more interesting.'

Isabella stamped her foot down. 'They don't exist,' she blurted out. 'If they did, scientists would have come across them.'

'These do exist,' Old Man Wood said firmly. 'Or *existed* in Assyria and Cush's case. The original Havilah, Assyria and

Cush were hidden away in far-away places out there in the deep reaches of what you call, space.'

'Then they must be outside of our solar system, outside of our universe even.'

'That's quite right. I do believe they are.'

'Multiverses?' Isabella said.

Daisy felt a bit overwhelmed. She could hardly point to Paris on a map. 'What's a multiverse?'

'I think I can explain,' Isabella said. 'Imagine England is a galaxy, with London as its sun and the other major cities, like Birmingham and Liverpool and Edinburgh and Norwich and Bristol as planets.' The other two nodded.

'Then imagine that the USA is one whole other galaxy (which it kind of is anyway), with New York as a sun and all the other cities around it as planets, some bigger, some smaller. Some further away, like Phoenix, or Los Angeles or Seattle and some closer, like Boston, Chicago, or Washington DC. Then imagine that every country on Earth represents one whole galaxy out there in never-ending space. Now, if you imagine that the moon and other planets, like Saturn and Mars and Mercury had an almost identical network of galaxies or cities as Earth, then these would be multiverses. Universes in space which we cannot see all kind-of knitted together, indefinitely going on and on into infinity.'

Daisy rolled her eyes. 'And this Havilah place, or planet, is it nice?'

Old Man Wood smiled. 'Oh yes, it is absolutely beautiful,' he said. 'Full of coloured stones and gold; heaps of delights, there's even a waterfall like your Niagara Falls made entirely of crystal and diamonds. Think of that. But all that kind of thing attracts bad, greedy types.'

To Archie, the name of Havilah rang a bell so loud it was like an alarm. 'Is Havilah evil?' he quizzed.

'It depends, I suppose,' Old Man Wood said, rubbing his chin. 'In what you wish to believe, and how you wish to live.'

Isabella shuffled closer to the old man, sensing he was

talking about something of real importance. 'Why? What did they believe, in Havilah?'

'They didn't believe that life should be made,' he said. 'They wanted life to go on alone to see what happened if life continued as it was.'

Isabella frowned.

Noticing the confusion on her face, Old Man Wood continued. 'You see, every living thing was, at some point, created in the Garden of Eden. Creation is the most powerful gift of nature.'

'Like being God,' Daisy piped.

Old Man Wood inclined his head thoughtfully. 'The Garden gave the worlds the opportunity for newer, better, more up-to-date species.'

'Are you suggesting, Old Man Wood,' Daisy said, 'that the Earth hasn't had anything new for a seriously long time?'

'Now you're getting it,' he said, grinning, his wrinkles curving up like strands of thick spaghetti. 'Your success, to borrow one of your expressions, Isabella, will "reboot" the system.'

'I'm still not sure I get it.' Isabella said. 'We've evolved, right? Hasn't humanity proved that we don't require upgrades?'

'If you unlock the key, Isabella, you will have proved that, for now, mankind has done enough to remain as it is,' he said. 'But the power of creation is all-encompassing. It cannot be denied if it is reborn once more.'

Isabella fidgeted. 'I'm not sure I like the sound of this,' she said quietly. 'Essentially, are you saying that we're doing all this to ruin ourselves anyway?'

'No, not 'ruin', littlun,' he laughed. 'New species will be introduced—that's all. Goodness knows how many thousands of species have vanished from this place already. Too many in recent times. A planet needs the right balance of living species. What's that word I'm hearing, dextink...'

'Extinct,' Archie helped.

'Aha, yes! Extinct. That's the one,' the old man said. 'We

used to say, "if it doesn't contribute, there's no use for it—make something better". On Earth, the time has come to freshen up the life-stock. But this change certainly beats the destruction of Earth's current life-stock by starting again—which is what will happen if you fail.'

Old Man Wood helped himself to a swig of apple juice. 'As I said, the power of creation is greater than you can possibly imagine. To protect it, those from the Garden of Eden and some from Earth and even Havilah vowed to safeguard its secrets,' he drained his glass. 'This led to a war of wars.'

'Who won?' Archie asked.

'Well, strangely, everyone lost,' he replied, shaking his head. 'The energies of the universe are a more powerful force than anyone imagined. When blood, sap and scales spilt into its waters, and over the rocks and soil, there was a warning of forty days and forty nights to leave Eden. It was known as the Great Closing. At the end of this time, the Garden razed itself to the ground,' he raised his eyebrows. 'That is what you saw when the first two tablets joined together. No one knows what is there now—more than likely it is a barren, dusty planet, devoid of life.'

'And, all the while, Earth and Havilah survived,' Isabella said, trying to wrap her head around the old man's words. 'So, how do we fit in?'

'Earth was considered a little bit dull,' the old man said. 'Earth's limitations were appreciated, but not considered particularly special—'

'Unlike Havilah?'

'There is much to tell about Havilah which you will learn in the fullness of time,' he said, sharply. 'Most of it leaves a bitter taste—even the thought of it,' he said. 'I will tell you one thing though.' His voice went lower, and he bent forward. 'In a final, desperate protest, the Master of Havilah destroyed its entire human population with a final act of true barbarism.'

The children edged forward.

'He killed every human being on Havilah.'

'Everyone?' Archie asked.

'That's what they said. No one really knows. Rumour had it that those humans inhabit watery puddles on the ground.'

Archie didn't like the sound of this. He needed to change the subject.

'Why, Old Man Wood, of all the people out there in the world, are we the Heirs? There must be tons of more suitable people.'

Old Man Wood smiled. 'A simple explanation is that you are protected by me, following a chain that has continued for many thousands and thousands of years.'

'So, Mum and Dad know about all this?'

'Yes, Archie, I believe your Mother and Father do know a little bit. Knowledge of the tablets has been passed down from generation to generation. And now that I'm sharpening-up on what has happened, I do believe they have made a study of the matter— '

'And the Ancient Woman,' Isabella asked, 'you know, the woman we dreamed about, is she, like, Mother Nature, or something?'

'No!' he said. 'Mother Nature is another way of explaining the forces of life that nurtures us and looks after us. Mother Nature is an energy that flows and weaves through everything in the universe—'

Isabella cut him off. 'Then, who is she? Why did this woman come to us in our dreams, night after night?'

The old man stared at the floor a while then moved his gaze to the children's with his soft nutty-brown eyes. 'The Ancient Woman offered herself as a sacrifice. She gave herself up to Mother Nature to be the gatekeeper of the Garden of Eden. She volunteered to live through time until the Garden of Eden might rise again if indeed that time would ever come. And so, after the Great Closing, she remained on the inside—locked inside the Atrium of the Garden of Eden—while another remained outside to guide and help when the time was right.'

Old Man Wood tilted his head up into the sky, his eyes moist, the whites of his eyes blanched red.

Silence filled the room.

Archie broke it, though his voice wobbled and his eyes glistened. 'That's... that's you, isn't it, Old Man Wood? You're the one on the outside, aren't you, standing here—with us—now.'

Old Man Wood's voice choked with emotion. 'Yes,' he croaked. 'Yes, you're quite right, my littlun.'

After a time, Isabella spoke. 'And the Ancient Woman...' she said, softly, 'she's stuck in the Garden of Eden, right, because she... she's... Eve, isn't she?'

Old Man Wood buried his face in his hands.

'Like Adam... and Eve?'

Old Man Wood looked up and nodded. Tears rolled out of his dark eyes, which he didn't bother to brush away. Now, his voice was almost unrecognisable. 'Beautiful, brave Eve,' he said, trying to force a smile. 'She was my love... my life. I tried to forget... but my dreams would not let me.'

Old Man Wood sobbed as the memories flooded back, and Daisy and Isabella found tears streaking down their cheeks as they tried to comfort him, sharing the burden of his grief.

SIXTY-EIGHT

CAIN MEETS MRS PYE

K emp thought he detected a brief outline, something not entirely right. Then, he realised Cain was back and, as he popped his head around the door, Cain's overcoat and hat hung on the stand next to the staircase. It reminded him of when he'd saved Daisy from slipping into it, and his heart lurched.

He felt a whoosh of air in his ear. 'Hello, boy.'

'Don't do that,' he said, flapping his arm. 'It's really annoying.'

'Time to go,' the voice came back. 'Time to say hello to your future.'

Kemp reddened. 'What about my mother,' he said. 'She knows … about you, about everything.'

'Excellent, boy. You might wish to introduce us.'

Kemp hesitated. 'Could be tricky, but I'll ask,' he said. He turned the handle of the door and re-entered the room. 'Mother?'

Mrs Pye turned.

'I'd like you to meet someone.' Kemp bowed his head while trying to think of a suitable way to bring in Cain. 'You know how I was saying about the spirit, about how it could save us. Well, he's here, and he'd like to say, um, "Hi".' Kemp cringed. Then he smirked, a smile slipping out of the corner of his mouth as he realised that the only person he'd ever brought home to his mother wasn't even a real person.

Mrs Pye looked at him, her face expressionless. 'Well,' she uttered at length, 'where is he?'

'He's looking at you,' Kemp said.

'Looking at me? I can't see him.'

'Because, mother, it's a ghost,' he said, thickly. 'You know, like a spirit from... the spirit world.' He wondered if she'd taken in any of their previous conversations. 'I'll ask him to put on his long overcoat. Would that help?'

Shortly, an overcoat hovered in the doorway.

Mrs Pye covered her hand in her mouth and then began to sob.

'Lord. You alright, mother?' Kemp said. 'Honestly, he's not that bad.'

She grabbed his hand as a lone tear ran down her pink cheek. 'It's not that,' she said.

'What is it? You think I'm crazy?'

'No. The opposite,' she said, snivelling. 'You told me about the ghost, and I wondered if you were, you know, nutty-flakes or that-like. Now I knows you was speaking the truth, what you were saying must be real and not bunkum.'

Kemp beamed. 'Then you'll come with me?'

'You're a strange one, now isn't you? Of course, I will. But on one condition.'

'OK. What is it?'

'I'd like to say a final farewell to my lot. Archie and the girls. That's all—and I won't say a word of what you told me, I promise.'

Cain coughed, making Mrs Pye's head twitch.

'Young lady,' he said.

'Me?' she shrilled.

'Yes. Tell me, what do you know?'

'I told her about the key,' Kemp said. 'I thought she should know.'

They could almost hear Cain thinking. 'My dear,' the ghost said at length, his voice smooth like molten chocolate, 'your knowledge puts you in the direct path of terrible danger. Those who know the final part of the prophecy must not go near the Heirs of Eden.'

'What is he talking about?' Mrs Pye asked.

'Like I told you, you cannot go to them, mother. You'll run into harm's way.'

Mrs Pye harrumphed. 'I'm going. They're my lot, and I'm not going nowhere without a hug from all of 'em, whether you like it or not. And that goes for your see-through friend too. Understand?'

'Well, don't say I haven't warned you,' Cain said, bluntly. 'Do not breathe a word of what you have learned and, with luck, you will be spared.'

Kemp turned to his mother. 'Why not give them half an hour,' he said. 'By the look of them, they're probably changing and having a clean up. They looked a right bloody old mess when they came back.'

'Good idea,' Cain said, his hat tilting towards Kemp. 'Now, boy, I think it is time we had a little catch-up. Why don't we pop off and return when this wonderful lady has said her fond farewells. In my experience, this kind of 'good-bye' is best done alone.'

Kemp grinned. 'Is that all right, mother?' he said. 'Back in less than forty minutes, gives you a little time. But remember, not a single word, right?'

'Yes, my son,' she replied, squeezing him till his breath tightened. 'Not even a little apple pip, I promise.'

Mrs Pye smiled her biggest smile, or grimace, and watched as Kemp slipped his arms into the coat, his body morphing into a curious ashen creature.

Then, calling out the words, 'dreamspinner, dreamspinner, dreamspinner,' with a dive, the ashen body disappeared into a ring of bright, neon-blue light.

SIXTY-NINE
SOLOMON ENTERS

I sabella reached into Old Man Wood's overcoat pocket and pulled out the tablet. She held it, twisting it slowly around her fingers. The others leaned in, mesmerised, examining the familiar circular tree-like patterns as it rotated.

'Woah!' she said, as the stone lurched. She placed it carefully on the table, double checking it. 'Did you see that?'

'What happened?'

'It's as if it has a magnetic force,' Isabella said. 'As if it demands to join up with the others.'

Daisy cuffed her on the shoulder. 'Yeah, well of course it does,' she said, yawning. 'That's what it's here for, dur brains.'

'Thanks, Einstein,' Isabella muttered. 'Most helpful. Where are the other joined tablets?'

'I locked it in my special cellar,' Old Man Wood said. 'I'll bring it out when the time is right.'

Almost immediately, Daisy's frame stiffened. She raised her eyebrows and pointed at the door.

Archie suddenly found his hair spikes erect on his head. He sidled up to the side of the thick oak-framed door.

'What is it now?' Isabella muttered. 'Really? Haven't we had enough excitement?' She examined Daisy. 'You know who it is, don't you?'

'Might do,' she replied, grinning.

The door inched open.

'Hullooo,' came a familiar voice.

'Mr Solomon,' Archie said, relaxing, his hair softening. 'Good to see you again, sir. How is the leg?'

'A little sore, if I'm honest,' he said. 'And to be frank, I'm utterly exhausted,' he shuffled further in, leaning on a stick. 'I am a classic example of a deeply unfit schoolmaster, I'm afraid. I'm not cut out for this kind of drama.'

Isabella went over to him and helped him into a chair.

'Dickinson's been hunting around for Sue but, mysteriously, they haven't located her,' Solomon continued. 'I do hope nothing untoward has happened especially after all she's put up with. And, on that note, you'll be pleased to hear that Stone is being escorted away as we speak, leaving you a clear run for whatever it is that you have to do next.' He eyed the tablet. 'Gosh, look at that. It is rather beautiful in its way, isn't it.' He suddenly had a great urge to touch it. He moved his hand across the table. 'May I?' He looked from one to the other.

'Go on,' Isabella said. 'But not for long. It seems to have a force field around it. I'm not sure I totally trust what it might do,' she said.

Solomon pushed his hand close but then retracted it quickly.

'What is it?'

'I'm not sure,' he said. 'But I'm probably quite close enough.' He smiled, his round face pink from the exertion, his eyes sparkling in the dim light. He pushed his small metal-rimmed glasses along his nose and took a deep breath. 'You'll be cracking on to the next bit now, I suppose—whatever it is? I must say, you do look a good deal better than when I first found you. How are the wounds?'

'Much better,' Old Man Wood said, speaking on everyone's behalf. 'How about I fix you up with a nice cup of tea, or would you care for something a little stronger. I have a dram of rum somewhere. Or did you finish the bottle when you put some in my tea, Archie?'

'Tea for me,' Solomon said. 'But no rum. Thank you.'

Isabella knelt down by the headmaster's chair. 'I'm going to do something about your bullet wound if you'll let me.'

'Dickinson tells me I was rather lucky,' he said, smiling up at her. 'The bullet passed straight through my thigh, missing the bone. Apparently, it's not uncommon to pass out when such a thing happens.' His expression changed. 'Will it hurt?'

'I don't think so,' she said. 'Soon, you'll be as good as new.'

Isabella laid her hands on the leg and shut her eyes. Moments later, pink, swirling energy flowed around the limb, spiralling around the thigh.

'Done,' she said at length, removing her hands.

The headmaster looked on transfixed. He flexed his joint. 'Astonishing. Absolutely astonishing.' He shook his head. 'Thank you, my dear girl.'

'My pleasure! It's the least I can do in return for your help turning Dickinson and for trying to find Sue.'

'Well, I have a duty, not least to dear Gus Williams, to find out what has become of your friend. And I have no intention of getting in your way; I'm probably the very last person you wish to see right now. By the way, has anyone seen Kemp? He seems to appear and then disappear with remarkable regularity. He's becoming rather hard to keep track of; I'm quite sure I heard his voice drifting in the air as I lay in wait for the soldiers.'

Daisy leaned forward a little. 'I think I saw him with Mrs Pye as we came in. But I wasn't concentrating.'

Solomon beamed back. 'Then I'll try Mrs Pye's apartment before I venture out to look for her again—now that I can.' He smiled once more at Isabella and drained his mug.

A rap at the door.

'That will be Dickinson, I suspect,' Solomon said. 'We decided to make some arrangements.'

Dickinson's head appeared at the door. He smiled warmly at the fresh-looking children. 'My, you're all looking a great deal better,' he said. 'Now, if you'd like to follow me, there's one thing I think we should do.'

Archie, Daisy and Isabella shot nervous glances at one another.

Dickinson laughed. 'No, it's nothing scary. We located Gus' body and have brought it down. I think we should lay it to rest, appropriately, don't you think?' He took on board their relieved faces. 'I found a lovely spot halfway down the track. Why don't you follow me? I promise it won't keep you from whatever you have to do.'

AS DICKINSON SAID, GUS' body lay in a hole where a large oak tree had once stood. A bright sky beamed overhead, the sun beginning its slow descent across the vale.

They held hands and bowed their heads.

Solomon began.

'I do not know what creed or belief system Gus followed, so I will be brief and without bias.' He coughed and pushed his glasses up his nose.

'In this spot lies Gus Williams, a boy who will be remembered by all as a man, a great man, who lived and loved life. Like a staunch tree that finds each season by the regular movement of our sun, we will remember Gus for his strength, his resilience, his fortitude in the face of turbulence, his majesty in taking on the uncertainty of the seas, his creativity, his good sense and the graciousness he displayed to all. He offered hope, where there was none. He showed bravery in the face of true darkness, he showed love to all those who knew him, and his smile will forever drift over these lands, as a quiet reminder of our enduring human spirit.

'For whatever happens upon this noble sphere of ours, in good times and in bad, Gus was a hero. And I, for one, am honoured to have known him.'

Daisy leaned into Archie who rubbed her back.

'Dear Gus—mate,' Archie began, addressing the body. 'I

can honestly say, on behalf of us all that we have nothing but the hugest love and respect for you. You are a god, my friend. Braver, funnier, kinder than all of us. Rest in peace, dear friend,' he croaked. 'May your spirit come again, in better times. No one ever did a bolder thing than you. Dust to dust and ashes to ashes my friend.' And he added, softly. 'I will do you bidding, mate, as long as there is breath remaining in my body.'

Isabella squeezed his shoulder.

Solomon turned away, tears in his eyes, grabbed a handful of soil while saying a private prayer, and sprinkled the earth over Gus' body.

With that, each one of them followed Solomon's example before making their way arm in arm back down the track to the cottage.

SEVENTY

CAIN'S PLAN

U nbeknown to the small ensemble, Cain watched as a ghost from the side of the grave.

So, here they were, he thought, these Heirs of Eden who had defeated his beast, his beast who would remain uncelebrated, the beast whose remains would be stuck in the chamber of the labyrinth forever more. The memory of Gorialla Yingarna erased, except in legend. A bitter end to a magnificent life that had spanned aeons.

Cain thought of the future. If these children shed tears at this boy's demise, moisture dropping out of their eyes like small streams, the task that lay ahead of them would never happen. Death was hard to fathom for the young.

He needed a plan, a strategy to bring life back to Havilah, and fast. This dead child in front of him, his spirit now flying around in the sky, was the girl's love. More importantly, this spirit was the one who had defeated Gorialla Yingarna.

A notion sprang into his mind.

Could he save the boy's spirit, as that confounded boy, Archie had said? Not here on this pithy planet, of course. That would never do. The vanquisher of the greatest beast ever known probably deserved another chance. And, furthermore, saving the boy gave him options.

He had an idea and called out into the universe.

. . .

'SPIRITS AWAKEN, spirits come near.
Spirits come close; you have nothing to fear.
I call out to the one whose spirit lies here.'

IN A FLASH, the boy floated next to him.

'You?' Gus said.

'Me,' Cain replied.

'You're the one who got me into this fine mess. Look, I'm dead, alright. Leave me alone.'

'Well, perhaps, dear boy, I can get you out of it.'

'Yeah, right?' Gus replied. 'Fat chance. I'm dead.'

'Is there one thing you truly desire?' Cain asked. 'One thing that your spirit would want that is above all else?'

'Seriously, Cain, I'm a goner. I'm air, like you, just a piece of energy.'

'I am serious,' Cain implored. 'There is one thing that can give you life once again. But it must come from a force within you.'

Gus flew off.

'Drat,' Cain said. How can I do this so that he trusts me?

Moments later Gus reappeared.

'What I meant,' Cain said, 'was—is there something you wish you could do just one more time?'

'Well, if you really must know, I'd like, more than anything else, just to be with Sue again. Just for a bit. I'd like to see her again, say goodbye properly. '

'Why?'

'You wouldn't understand. And besides, as you can see, it's all a little too late.'

'If you tell me. I might be able to help you.'

'Why should I tell you anything? I've got better things to do—'

'Sue is in Havilah, with me. She made up her mind.'

'You captured her?' Gus' ghost said, in disbelief.

'No. She is there *willingly*. She waits,' he paused, 'for a new time.' Cain dangled the carrot right in front of his face. 'She is there with the other boy.'

'Kemp!'

'Yes. There with the boy, you call Kemp. The boy with whom you got into this muddle, the boy you couldn't finish off.'

'But Kemp doesn't love her.'

'Then you're saying you do?'

'Of course. I love Sue with every fragment of energy that I currently don't possess a great deal of.'

Cain smiled. 'Then come with me, Gus. It will not be easy, but if you truly love her, with all your soul, then, believe me, there is another way. And this time,' he said, treacle in his voice, 'I will not let you down.'

SEVENTY-ONE
THE ANCIENT WOMAN'S NEW DILEMMA

E xcitement grew as news filtered back: the Heirs of Eden had defeated Gorialla Yingarna.

Tucked out of harm's way in her corner, away from the fast-moving dreamspinners, the Ancient Woman's arms and legs clattered as if she were invisibly knitting like crazy. Her internal organs were pumping harder than they had for millennia making her bones rattle, the sound like rickety ivories on a piano.

The Heirs of Eden have the third tablet. They had defeated Gorialla Yingarna.

She had imagined this moment more times than she could count. And now, even though she'd run through every possible situation imaginable, the more she thought about it, the more a different kind of worry nibbled away at her. A concern that she had not foreseen:

What would they make of her?

She knew that Genesis would have given the Heirs of Eden dreams that portrayed her as an ancient woman but, in reality, her skin was withered and worn, like dried leather. Bones jutted out here and there, and her heart pumped noticeably in the tiny cavity of her chest.

Her hair and her outer ears, like her eyes, had gone long ago. Bone had replaced the flesh on her toes and, at the ends of her fingers, the nails curled out like small tusks. Her teeth were decayed stumps in a skeletal head, blackened by dirt and grime. As she probed her face and body, she fancied she looked more like a vast, decimated spider than a human being.

Would the Heirs be strong young men perhaps two-hundred in years, full of vigour and magic and energy? Or, older, wiser men, hundreds of years old, with long, grey beards and wizened, powerful eyes?

Whoever appeared, finding and opening the key to unlocking the Garden of Eden would take courage. She placed a hand over her beating heart. Perhaps, collectively, they might find the strength. Maybe, they had already worked out what they had to do.

She sighed. With luck, the process would be quick and painless.

She shuffled these thoughts uneasily in her head and wondered about the next stage; the coming of the Heirs of Eden. She sensed the dreamspinners excitement; she could feel their heightened vibrations. And, unless a travesty occurred, there would be no strangers dropping in on her this time.

This time, the coming of the Heirs of Eden would be for real.

SEVENTY-TWO
SOLOMON LEAVES

S olomon heaved himself up.

'Time for me to take my leave. Time for you lot to do what you've got to do next.'

'You're right,' Archie said. 'We've got to put the three tablets together and finish this off—once and for all.'

'Jolly good,' Solomon replied. 'Well, I'm going to grab a lift with Dickinson and the troops once we've had another look for Sue. They're taking Stone down now, I believe, so he won't be any more trouble.'

'Mr Solomon,' Archie said his voice wobbling, 'you must find Sue. We owe it to Gus. Please don't give up on her.' His tone lightened. 'And please ask Mrs Pye if she'll come over. Tell her that we need a hug!'

'Of course, young man,' the headmaster replied. 'Consider both done. I'll pop in to see her on my way out.'

With that, Solomon walked smartly towards the door. As he let himself out, he turned and examined each one in turn. 'For what it's worth, I am deeply proud of you and I'm sure your parents would be, too,' he said. 'May the task of putting these tablets together and whatever you do thereafter prove easier than the ones preceding it. And, no more deaths, please. Come back in one piece for all our sakes.' He winked. 'Good luck.'

With that, the headmaster smiled and shut the door and the children listened to the sound of his footsteps tip-tapping across the smooth, stone-slabbed courtyard.

TO BE CONTINUED...

(BOOK FIVE, The Eyes of Cain, is due out early in 2019)

A LITTLE HELP...

Dear Reader,

Please tell others what you may (or may not) have liked about THE DRAGON'S GAME by posting a review.

I'm working on several new projects right now. By leaving a review it will spur me on to finish the series.

Thanks.

JKE

The EDEN CHRONICLES series:

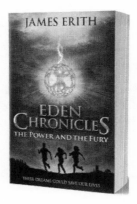

The Power and The Fury—Eden Chronicles, Book One

Spider Web Powder—Eden Chronicles, Book Two

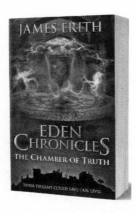

The Chamber of Truth—Eden Chronicles, Book Three

ABOUT THE AUTHOR

James was born in Suffolk in the UK. He travelled the world extensively, worked as a journalist in the 1990's and then turned to his passion for the great outdoors, designing and building gardens for several years before returning to writing.

James moved to North Yorkshire where he lived between the Yorkshire Dales and the Yorkshire Moors. It inspired him to use these beautiful areas as the location for the EDEN CHRONICLES series.

In 2013 James rowed across the English Channel and the length of the Thames to raise money for MND and Breakthrough Breast Cancer.

www.jameserith.com
james@jericopress.com

facebook.com/JamesErithAuthor

twitter.com/jameserith

instagram.com/edenchronicles

goodreads.com/jameserith

pinterest.com/jameserith

amazon.com/author/jameserith

EDEN TEAM

If you'd like to be a part of my exclusive **EDEN TEAM** Facebook group, where I offer each new release to members prior to its official release in exchange for feedback and reviews, go to Facebook and search for **EDEN TEAM**.

(Please note: you must have reviewed one of the Eden Chronicles series as a condition of joining!)

If this isn't for you, drop by my Author Facebook page and give it a like!

My website is: www.jameserith.com